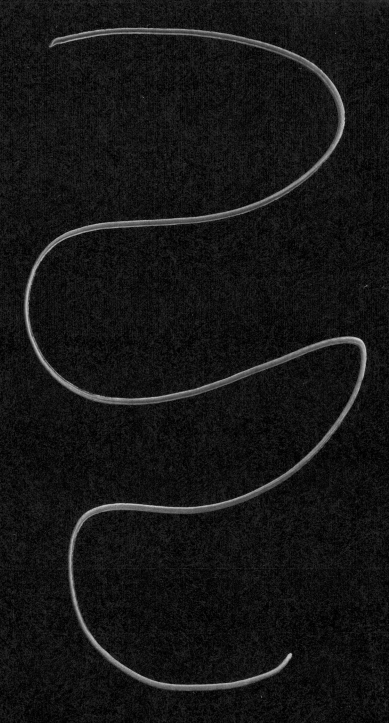

THE BEST OF SHADOWS

1990

Lisa Tuttle 1996

THE BEST

—— OF ——

SHADOWS

Edited by
Charles L. Grant

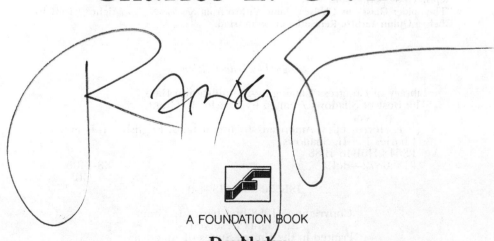

A FOUNDATION BOOK

Doubleday

NEW YORK   LONDON   TORONTO   SYDNEY   AUCKLAND

A Foundation Book
Published by Doubleday,
a division of Bantam Doubleday Dell Publishing Group, Inc.
666 Fifth Avenue, New York, New York 10103

Foundation, Doubleday, and the portrayal of the letter F are trademarks of Doubleday,
a division of Bantam Doubleday Dell Publishing Group, Inc.

"Naples" by Avram Davidson from *Shadows*. Copyright © 1978 by Avram Davidson.
Reprinted by permission.
"The Gorgon" by Tanith Lee from *Shadows 5*. Copyright © 1982 by Tanith Lee.
Reprinted by permission.
"Moving Night" by Nancy Holder from *Shadows 9*. Copyright © 1986 by Nancy Holder.
Reprinted by permission.
"Jamie's Grave" by Lisa Tuttle from *Shadows 10*. Copyright © 1987 by Lisa Tuttle.
Reprinted by permission.
"Sneakers" by Marc Laidlaw from *Shadows 6*. Copyright © 1983 by Marc Laidlaw.
Reprinted by permission.
"The Man Who Would Not Shake Hands" by Stephen King from *Shadows 4*. Copyright ©
1981 by Stephen King. Reprinted by permission.
"At the Bureau" by Steve Rasnic Tem from *Shadows 3*. Copyright © 1980 by Steve
Rasnic Tem. Reprinted by permission.
"Macintosh Willy" by Ramsey Campbell from *Shadows 2*. Copyright © 1979 by Ramsey
Campbell. Reprinted by permission.
"Following the Way" by Alan Ryan from *Shadows 5*. Copyright © 1982 by Alan Ryan.
Reprinted by permission.
"The Storm" by David Morrell from *Shadows 7*. Copyright © 1984 by David Morrell.
Reprinted by permission.
"The Silent Cradle" by Leigh Kennedy from *Shadows 6*. Copyright © 1983 by Leigh
Kennedy. Reprinted by permission.
"Wish" by Al Sarrantonio from *Shadows 8*. Copyright © 1985 by Al Sarrantonio.
Reprinted by permission.
"The Spider Glass" by Chelsea Quinn Yarbro from *Shadows 4*. Copyright © 1981 by
Chelsea Quinn Yarbro. Reprinted by permission.

Designed by Wilma Robin

Library of Congress Cataloging-in-Publication Data
The Best of Shadows / edited by Charles L. Grant.
       p. cm.
    1. Horror tales, American. 2. Horror tales, English.   I. Grant,
Charles L.   II. Shadows.
PS648.H6B46 1988
813'.0872—dc19   88-14960
                                                                CIP

ISBN 0-385-23894-0

Copyright © 1988 by Charles L. Grant
All Rights Reserved
Printed in the United States of America
October 1988
First Edition
BG

This anthology is respectfully dedicated to:

Joseph Payne Brennan

Without him, and his colleagues,
where would any of us be now?

CONTENTS

INTRODUCTION

IN THE DECADE since *Shadows* began, the field of horror has undergone a great number of internal and external changes, not all of them for the better, not all of them all that bad.

About the time the first volume of this series appeared, much of what has evolved into the contemporary horror genre was concerned with the basics of religion—demonology, theology, possession, repossession, exorcism, and the like. It was fairly safe in those days to break into the field—pick a demon no one ever heard of and write a book or make a film about it, include a child or innocent (generally virginal) woman possessed or threatened to be possessed by that demon, find a kindly old man/priest/scholar to banish the creature, and leave a supposedly tantalizing question at the end as to whether the task at hand had been successfully completed. The Antichrist was big then, too. As were gods from a dozen religions which were, not infrequently, created expressly for the purpose. Not to mention, in a close, somewhat related tangent, reincarnation and all its confusing subdivisions.

By the time theology had been mined to and through the core, however, and the public had wearied of yet another confrontation with unspeakable creatures with unpronounceable names, horror began splitting itself into other camps, each with its own ardent supporters, each with its own mythologies, each with its own determination of what, exactly, frightened its read-ers/watchers.

Nesting still quite comfortably in one of the most popular camps is the perversion of the original zombie. Instead of steal-ing a soul and creating a slave through magic, there are mysteri-ous, unexplained (read "we really don't know how, but if we're vague enough people will buy it without too many questions") events which created *things* that, for want of a better word, are called zombies. These creatures, unlike the true zombie, have simple motivations—sustenance for their continuance. They eat people. Or brains. Or drink blood. Or whatever. None of them, you will notice, ever survives by eating lettuce.

Another camp holds the realm of the psycho killer(s). On screen this has evolved (to be kind) into the slasher film; in fiction it has evolved (to be kind) into the slasher book. The most blatant and worst examples of both are less horror stories than they are lazy exercises in cheap or expensive special effects—how many different ways can you kill someone, on screen, with as much blood, shrieking, glistening innards, and machine noise as possible; or, in print, how many different ways can you kill someone as word-graphically as possible. There is, in fact, save the medium, no difference.

The third camp brings horror closer to home by exploiting the fears of ordinary people living ordinary (as opposed to ex-traordinary) lives. Not the supernatural fears that many of us have and don't always (hardly ever) admit to, but the more tangible and accessible fears of everyday living: economic disas-ter, disintegration of society or family, relationships that are far removed from Victorian Romanticism, the exploitation of the innocent and helpless, especially children.

There are a number of smaller camps as well (e.g., the alien-is-among-us-and-it's-really-angry/hungry camp), but the first three are the founts from which most of today's commercial horror springs. Or dribbles.

In and of themselves, they are not necessarily bad. Handled well, with a certain amount of taste, intelligence, and respect for the reader, any one of them can scare your hair white, and give you a good time, too.

But what has happened over the past five years or so is not necessarily good either. It's especially not good for the future of the genre. Loud is fine when loud is needed; but when something is loud all the time, all it does is make you deaf, or, at the least, hard of hearing. It's a desensitizing process which eventually defeats the very reaction the writer hopes to produce in his reader's mind. Instead of a shiver, or a good healthy scare, what you eventually get is a turn of the page, a skip to the next paragraph, a grimace of disgust which has nothing whatsoever to do with being frightened.

A fair number of new writers, for distressing example, appear by their work to be heavily influenced primarily by the stunted (i.e., unimaginative and derivative) crop of slasher films, not by what has gone before in the literature of the field they've chosen to work in. Instead of reading, they watch, and the results of that watching are clearly evident in the way their stories are told.

It is a given to a good writer that once you have found your own voice, your own style, through hard work and determination, you nurture it, prod it, give it room to grow as far as your talent will allow. A mediocre or simply bad writer, on the other hand, cares less about talent and substance than he does about the marketplace. Who gives a damn about good writing, good characters, good plots when the public (whoever that is) demands slice-and-dice, in enough detail and sufficient quantity to overcome that desensitization? Who cares if the scare in horror has been replaced by shock? Why bother paying attention to what has gone before when *this* is what sells now, the hell with integrity, talent, and respect for the reader? Make a buck and get out, and tell your neighbors you sell insurance.

While it is true that writing is a business, and all writers are, in the end, business people who must adapt in order to survive, it is also true that adaptation is not the same as capitulation. A good writer studies the market, watches the trends, takes stock of himself, and does what he thinks is best, *for him.* When one sees that long books sell better than short books, writing long books only makes economic sense; when one sees that a host of characters is more interesting to the reader than two or three, creating that host is a natural and logical step.

But only, *only,* if the book will support the length, or the host, or both.

Only, *only*, if the story you're trying to tell is told better longer, or with more characters than it would be otherwise.

Only, *only*, if you have the talent to do both. Some simply cannot work with long stories, and some simply cannot tell their stories at shorter lengths.

But they do adapt, because they know that in the infield, in order to survive and *grow*, they must change. Adapt. Without compromise. To do it for any other reason is capitulation. Abandoning imagination for the safer realm of mirror image.

And boasting that you're crying all the way to the bank isn't a valid defense. Stephen King, I daresay, weeps copiously all the way to his vault in Maine, but by god, neither he, nor Dean Koontz, nor Peter Straub, or a dozen others have forgotten that nothing, but nothing, replaces a good story. Nothing—not all the bloodletting, intestine-spilling, heart-gouging, brain-eating in the world—is better than the well-crafted scene that forces the reader to face something he'd rather not come to terms with; that produces the scare, the chill, the shiver, the fright; that may be loud or graphic because the moment demands it, but is loud or graphic only because what has gone before hasn't been.

Screaming for ninety minutes isn't nearly as effective as screaming for five seconds—and those five seconds need not be consecutive.

A good writer knows this.

A bad writer either knows it and doesn't care, or doesn't know it at all. And if, after all this time, he doesn't know it or doesn't give a damn, he ought to be selling shoes or counting crates at the Acme, because he has no business despoiling and defiling the work of those who do know and do care and want to do it all better.

The people who write for *Shadows*, and for all the other single and series anthologies that have sprung up over this decade, want to do it better.

They don't always succeed.

But they know damned well the difference between adaptation and capitulation, between simple constructs and real characters, between fear and shock, between scare and revulsion.

They know that the so-called real world can be as terrifying as a world invaded by the supernatural.

They understand that no story survives for very long unless

it contains the foundation for all good writing—a love and concern for the language.

And they also understand and embrace the undeniable fact that their most important ally is a reader's imagination.

Only by engaging that imagination, luring it into the story, forcing it (however gently) to *work*, will the story be effective. Appealing to, and thereby reinforcing, the TV generation's lamentably short attention span is criminally cynical; assuming, consciously or not, that a reader must be spoon-fed rather than led is insulting; denying the reader a partnership in the adventure of reading is tantamount to surrender.

The best in this field, in *any* field, do not surrender.

The rules I set down for this series are simple: I do not want blood and gore in graphic (and ultimately boring) detail; I do not want traditional monsters or styles (unless there is a twist that happens to hit me right); no humor, no science fiction, no "had I but known" stories. Those who ask for what I like are told that I want contemporary horror, with an emphasis on *people* and their problems.

I want quiet horror.

The kind that sneaks up on you, makes you check the windows, the open closet door, the noise in the hallway, the rapping on the porch. Shadows. I want shadows.

Quite naturally, since I make the rules, I also break them now and again when a story strikes me as being too good to pass up. To be honest, I don't always know precisely why I pick the ones I do. They either work for me or they don't, and I know that it's been frustrating to would-be contributors when I send back a manuscript that essentially praises the writing but damns with faint praise the reaction it causes in me.

It's frustrating for me, too, believe me.

Equally as frustrating has been the task of picking the "best" of the stories that have appeared in the first ten volumes. It is, ultimately, a thankless job. Pick this one, and that writer over there gets annoyed; pick that one, and I get hate mail from these folks lighting the torches over here. Critics will lump me for picking X when I should have picked Y—how could I have been so shortsighted? Friends will wonder if my brain has finally atrophied after all these years of reading.

I am, frankly, in a bind.

So I admit to some copping out.

First I reread every story in every volume, amazed that after all this time I was still able to remember them so well (this, after realizing that I had to read well over 2,800 submissions just to find the ones I did choose). Then, being no better off than I was before I started, I immediately picked those which had been nominated for, or had won, various awards. That was the easy part. The copping out.

The rest? All I can say is, what can I say? I like them. I like them a lot. Just as I still like all the others that are listed at the back of this book.

I suppose the best way I can describe them as a group is: They are the essence of *Shadows*, no more or less than any of the others. They define more clearly, I think, than any guidelines I could create what I look for when I read a manuscript.

So instead of calling them the "best," I would rather call them the distinguished representatives of what I hope are distinguished examples of another of the genre's camps.

Individually, and as a group, they define what I think horror ought to be—a little of this, a little of that, and all of it based on respect, love of language, and love of storytelling.

No brain-eating zombies need apply.

These are the shadows that are born without light.

Charles L. Grant
Newton, New Jersey
January 1988

THE BEST OF SHADOWS

NAPLES

By
Avram Davidson

This story opened the first Shadows. *I almost didn't buy it. When I received it from Avram's agent, I dithered because at the time I still wasn't sure exactly what I wanted—although I thought I'd know it when I saw it. Finally I said, "the hell with it," sent out the contract, and . . . Avram Davidson won the World Fantasy Award for Best Short Story. Since then, I don't dither very much at all. This is the perfect example of instinct overruling whatever "editorial requirements" means.*

It is also quintessential Avram Davidson, and you just cannot get any better than that.

IT IS A curious thing, the reason of it being not certainly known to me—though I conjecture it might be poverty—why, when all the other monarchs of Europe were still building palaces in marble and granite, the kings of that anomalous and ill-fated kingdom called Of Naples and the Two Sicilies chose to build theirs in red brick. However, choose it they did: These last of the Italian Bourbons have long since lost their last thrones, no *castrato* singers sing for them from behind screens to lighten their well-deserved melancholy anymore, and their descendants now earn their livings in such occupations as gentlemen-sales-clerks in fashionable jewelry stores—not, perhaps, entirely removed from all memory of the glory that once (such as it was) was theirs. But the red-brick *palazzi* are still there, they still line a part of the waterfront of Naples, and—some of them, at least—are still doing duty as seats of governance. (Elsewhere, for reasons equally a mystery to me, unless there is indeed some connection between red bricks and poverty, buildings in the same style and of the same material usually indicate that within them the Little Sisters of the Poor, or some similar religious group, perform their selfless duties on behalf of the sick, the aged, and the otherwise bereft and afflicted; and which is the nobler function and whose the greater reward are questions that will not long detain us.)

Some twenty years ago or so, a man neither young nor old nor ugly nor comely, neither obviously rich nor equally poor, made his way from the docks past the red-brick *palazzi* and into the lower town of ancient and teeming Naples. He observed incuriously that the streets, instead of swarming with the short and swarthy, as foreign legend implies, swarmed instead with the tall and pale. But the expectations of tradition were served in other ways: by multitudes of donkey carts, by women dressed and draped in black, by many many beggars, and by other signs of deep and evident poverty. Almost at once a young man approached him with a murmured offer of service; the young man clutched the upturned collar of his jacket round about his throat, and, as the day was not even cool, let alone cold, it might have been assumed that the reason for the young man's gesture was that he probably did not wish to reveal the absence of a shirt. It was not altogether certain that the young man had no shirt at all, probably he had a shirt and probably this was its day to be washed and probably it was even now hanging from a line stretched across an alley where the sun did not enter in sufficient strength to dry it quickly.

There were many such alleys and many such lines, and, it is to be feared, many such shirts. There were also many such men, not all of them young; and if a count had been made, it might have been found that there were not enough shirts to go around.

Naples.

The traveler continued, with frequent pauses and considerings, to make his way slowly from the port area and slowly up the steep hill. Now and then he frowned slightly and now and then he slightly smiled. Long ago some humble hero or heroine discovered that if the hard wheat of the peninsula, subject to mold and rust and rot if stored in the ear, be ground into flour and mixed with water into a paste and extruded under pressure in the form of long strips, and dried, it would never rot at all and would keep as near forever as the hunger of the people would allow it. And when boiled it formed a food nutritious as bread and far more durable, and, when combined with such elements as oil or tomato or meat or cheese and perhaps the leaves of the bay and the basil, be good food indeed. However, the passage of time failed to bring these added ingredients within the means and reach of all. So, to vary in some measure at least the monotony of the plain pasta, it was made in the widest conceivable variety of shapes: thin strips and thick strips, ribbons broad and narrow, hollow tubes long and hollow tubes bent like elbows, bows and shells and stars and wheels and rosettes and what-have-you. And, if you have nothing, it is anyway some relief to eat your plain pasta in a different design . . . when you have, of course, pasta to eat.

At least every other doorway in the narrow streets and the narrower alleys kept a shop, and many of the shops sold pasta:

for the further sake of variety the pasta was not merely stacked up in packages, it was also—the straight kinds—splayed about as though the stalks held flowers at their upper ends. And when the traveler saw these he faintly smiled. The young man who paced him step for step also looked at these modest displays. But he never smiled at them. In fact, although he continued his soft murmurs, he never smiled at all.

Most of these ways seemed hardly wide enough for outside displays, but such there were; there were second-hand clothes and fewer by far displays of some few new clothes; there were whole cheeses, although none hereabouts were seen to buy them whole, and perhaps not very many very often bought them by the slice or crumbling piece. And there were small fish, alive, alive-o, and larger fish in dim slabs that had not been alive in a long time, dry and hard and strong-smelling and salty, redolent of distant and storm-tossed seas. Tomatoes and peppers lay about in baskets. Oil was poured in careful drops into tiny bottles. There were also olives in many colors. Pictures of saints were sold, and the same shops sold, too, odd little emblematic images in coral and silver and—this was surely strange in such a scene of poverty—even gold: behind the narrow windows of narrow shops, crosses, too, yes, and beads: the universal signia of that religion. . . . But what were these horns? What were these tiny hands, fingers tucked into a fist with the thumb protruding between first and second fingers?

Best not to ask, you would empty the street in a trice. Everybody in Naples knows, no one in Naples would speak of it above a whisper . . . to a stranger, not at all. Speak not the word, lest it come to pass. Look not overlong at anyone in these streets, particularly not at the children they produce in such numbers of abundance. Who knows if your eye be not evil?

The eye of the traveler passed over the swarming and ragged *bambini* without stopping, and in the same manner he glanced at the scrannel cats and the charcoal braziers fanned by the toiling housewives: When one's home is but one room, one may well prefer the street as a kitchen.

When one has that which to cook, and fuel with whicn to cook it.

At length the passageway widened into a sort of a *piazza*. At one end was a church, on either side were the blank walls of some *palazzio* a good deal more antique than the brick ones down below: perhaps from the days of Spanish viceroys, perhaps from the days of King Robert. Who knows. There were anyway no more shops, no stalls, no wide-open-to-the-street one-room "houses" . . . and, for once, no masses of people . . . no beggars, even . . . there was even a sort of alley that seemingly went nowhere and that, surprisingly, held no one. And the traveler, who had so far only from time to time looked out from the corners of his eyes at the young man cleaving close to him as a shadow does, and who had made no reply at all to the soft murmurs with which the young man (ever clutching his jacket round about his naked throat) continually offered his services as "guide"; now for the first time, the traveler stopped, gave a direct look fleeting-swift, jerked his head toward the tiny passageway, and stepped inside.

The shirtless one's head went up and he looked at the heavens; his head went down and he looked at the filthy worn stones beneath. His shoulders moved in something too slight for a shrug and his unclothed throat uttered something too soft for a sigh.

He followed.

The traveler turned, without looking into the other's eyes, whispered a few short words into the other's ears.

The face of the young man, which had been stiff, expressionless, now went limp. Surprise showed most briefly. His brows moved once or twice.

—But yes—he said.—Surely—he said.

And he said, with a half bow and a small movement of his arm—I pray, follow. Very near—he said.

Neither one paused at the church.

And now the streets became, all of them, alleys. The alleys became mere slits. The shops grew infrequent, their store ever more meager. The lines of clothes dripping and drying overhead seemed to bear little relation to what human beings wore. What actually dangled and flapped in the occasional gusts of flat, warm, and stinking air may once have been clothing. Might once more, with infinite diligence and infinite skill, with scissors and needle and thread, be reconstituted into clothing once again. But for the present, one must either deny the rags that name, or else assume that behind the walls, the scabby walls, peeling walls, broken walls, filthy damp and dripping-ichorous walls, there dwelled some race of goblins whose limbs required garb of different drape.

The traveler began to lag somewhat behind.

How often, now, how carefully, almost how fearfully, the youngman guide turned his head to make sure the other was still with him. Had not stepped upon some ancient obscenely greasy flagstone fixed upon a pivot and gone silently screaming down into God knows what. Had not been slip-noosed, perhaps, as some giant hare, hoisted swiftly up above the flapping rags . . . Rags? Signal flags? What strange fleet might have its brass-bound spyglasses focused hither? Or perhaps it was fear and caution lest the other's fear and caution might simply cause him to turn and flee. In which case the youngman guide would flee after him, though from no greater fear than loss of the fee.

When one has no shirt, what greater fear?

Turned and into a courtyard entered through a worm-eaten door whose worms had last dined centuries ago, perhaps, and left the rest of the wood as inedible. A courtyard as dim, as dank as the antechamber to an Etruscan Hell. Courtyard as it might be the outer lobby of some tumulus, some tomb, not yet quite filled although long awaiting its last occupant. Shadow. Stench. The tatters hung up here could never be clothing again, should they in this foul damp ever indeed dry. At best they might serve to mop some ugly doorstep, did anyone within the yard have yet pride enough for such. And yet, if not, why were they hanging, wet from washing? Perhaps some last unstifled gesture of respectability. Who knows.

Naples.

Around a corner in the courtyard a door, and through the door a passageway and at the end of that a flight of stairs and the end of the flight of stairs a doorway that no longer framed a door. A thing, something that was less than a blanket, was hung. The youngman paused and rapped and murmured. Something made a sound within. Something dragged itself across the floor within. Something seemed simultaneously to pull the hanging aside and to wrap itself behind the hanging.

At the opposite side to the door a man sat upon a bed. The man would seemingly have been the better for having been in the bed and not merely on it. On the cracked and riven and

flaking, sodden walls some pictures, cut from magazines. Two
American Presidents. Two Popes. And one Russian leader. And
two saints. Comparisons are odious. Of those whose likenesses
were on that filthy fearful wall it might be said they had in
common anyway that all were dead.

—Good day—the youngman guide said.

—Good day—the man on the bed said. After a moment. He
might, though, have been excused for not having said it at all.

—This gentleman is a foreigner—

The man on the bed said nothing. His sunken eyes merely
looked.

—And he would like, ahem, ha, he would like to buy—

—But I have nothing to sell—

How dry, how faint, his voice.

—Some little something. Some certain article. An item—

—But nothing. I have nothing. We have nothing here—

His hand made a brief gesture, fell still.

A very small degree of impatience seemed to come over the
face of the older visitor. The younger visitor, observing this, as
he observed everything, took another step closer to the bed.—
The gentleman is a foreigner—he repeated, as one who speaks
to a rather stupid child.

The man on the bed looked around. His stooped shoulders,
all dirty bones, shrugged, stooped more.—He may be a foreigner twice over, and what is it to me—he said, low-voiced,
seemingly indifferent.

—He is a foreigner. He has, fool, son of a jackal, son of a
strumpet, he has money—the youngman turned, abruptly, to
the traveler. Said—Show him—

The traveler hesitated, looked all about. His mouth moved.
So, too, his nose. His hands, no.

—You will have to show, you know. Can you pay without
showing—

The traveler suddenly took a wallet from an inner pocket of
his coat, abruptly opened it, and abruptly thrust it in again,
placed his back not quite against the noisome wall, crossed his
arms over his chest.

Slowly, slowly, the man on the bed slid his feet to the floor.

—Wait outside—he said.—Halfway down—he added.

On the half landing they waited. Listened. Heard.

Dragging, dragging footsteps. A voice they had not heard before.—*No*NO—A voice as it might be from behind the curtain or the blanket or the what-was-it in place of the door. The faint sounds of some faint and grisly struggle. Voices but no further words. Gasps, only.

Something began to wail, in a horrid broken voice. Then, outside the doorframe, at the head of the stairs, the man, tottering against the wall. Extending toward them his hands, together, as though enclosing something within.

—Be quick—he said. Panting.

And, all the while, the dreadful wail went on from behind him.

The youngman sprang up the stairs, his left hand reaching forward. Behind his back his right hand formed a fist with its thumb thrust out between first and second fingers; then both his hands swept up and met both hands of the other. The youngman, face twisted, twisting, darted down the steps to the half landing.

—The money—

Again, hands met. The traveler thrust his deep into his bosom, kept one there, withdrew the other. Withdrew his wallet, fumbled.

—Not here, not here, you know—the youngman warned.— The police, you know—

One look the older man flung about him.—Oh no. Oh God, not here—he said.—On the ship—

The youngman nodded. Roughly divided the money, tossed half of it up and behind without looking back. He did not come close to the older man as they hurried down the stairs.

Above, the wailing ceased. That other voice spoke, in a manner not to be described, voice changing register on every other word, almost.

—Curse the day my daughter's daughter gave you birth. May you burn, son of a strega and son of a strumpet, burn one hundred thousand years in Purgatory without remission—

The voice broke, crocked wordlessly a moment. Resumed.

—One dozen times I have been ready to die, and you, witch's bastard, you have stolen my death away and you have sold my death to strangers, may you burst, may you burn—

Again the voice broke, again began to wail.

The two men reached the bottom of the stained stairs, and parted, the younger one outdistancing the other and this time never looking back.

Above, faintly, in a tone very faintly surprised, the man who had been on the bed spoke.

—Die? Why should you die when I must eat?—

Naples.

THE GORGON

By
Tanith Lee

Tanith Lee has been, from the beginning of her remarkable career, one of the best, most sensitive purveyors of Dark Fantasy —that is, someone who understands that a story does not have to be thunderous and explicit throughout in order to succeed on the primary, horror, level. Her people are people, *and her settings, fantastical or not, are* real. *She also is about the best in layering her stories; none are exactly what they seem. This, perhaps more than anything, is what gives Ms. Lee's material that marvelous depth peculiar to her. Not necessarily a philosophical depth, but the kind you find in a black-water lake— deceptive; but it's just as terrifying down there as it is up here, and there isn't a damn thing you can do about it once you go under.*

"The Gorgon" is yet another example of what a shadow can do; it also won the World Fantasy Award for Best Short Story.

THE SMALL ISLAND, which lay off the larger island of Daphaeu, obviously contained a secret of some sort, and, day by day, and particularly night by night, began to exert an influence on me, so that I must find it out.

Daphaeu itself (or more correctly herself, for she was a female country, voluptuous and cruel by turns in the true antique fashion of the Goddess) was hardly enormous. A couple of roads, a tangle of sheep tracks, a precarious, escalating village, rocks and hillsides thatched by blistered grass. All of which overhung an extraordinary sea, unlike any sea which I have encountered elsewhere in Greece. Water which might be mistaken for blueness from a distance, but which, from the harbor or the multitude of caves and coves that undermined the island, revealed itself a clear and succulent green, like milky limes or the bottle glass of certain spirits.

On my first morning, having come on to the natural terrace (the only recommendation of the hovel-like accommodation) to look over this strange green ocean, I saw the smaller island, lying like a little boat of land moored just wide of Daphaeu's three hills. The day was clear, the water frilled with white where it hit the fangs in the interstices below the terrace. About the smaller island, barely a ruffle showed. It seemed to glide up from the sea, smooth as mirror. The little island was verdant, also. Unlike Daphaeu's limited stands of stone pine, cypress, and cedar, the smaller sister was clouded by a still, lambent haze of foliage that looked to be woods. Visions of groves, springs, a ruined temple, a statue of Pan playing the panpipes forever in some glade—where only yesterday, it might seem, a thin column of aromatic smoke had gone up—these images were enough, fancifully, to draw me into inquiries about how the small island might be reached. And when my inquiries met first with a polite bevy of excuses, next with a refusal, last with a blank wall of silence, as if whoever I mentioned the little island to had gone temporarily deaf or mad, I became, of course, insatiable to get to it, to find out what odd superstitious thing kept these people away. Naturally, the Daphaeui were not friendly to me at any time beyond the false friendship one anticipates extended to a man of another nationality and clime, who can be relied on to pay his bills, perhaps allow himself to be overcharged, even made a downright monkey of in order to preserve goodwill. In the normal run of things, I could have had anything I wanted in exchange for a pack of local lies, a broad local smile, and a broader local price. That I could not get to the little island puzzled me. I tried money and I tried barter. I even, in a reckless moment, probably knowing I would not succeed, offered Pitos, one of the younger fishermen, the gold and onyx ring he coveted. My sister had made it for me, the faithful copy of an intaglio belonging to the House of Borgia, no less. Generally, Pitos could not pass the time of day with me without mentioning the ring, adding something in the nature of: "If ever you want a great service, any great service, I will do it for that ring." I half believe he would have stolen or murdered for it, certainly shared the bed with me. But he would not, apparently, even for the Borgia ring, take me to the little island.

"You think too much of foolish things," he said to me. "For a big writer, that is not good."

I ignored the humorous aspect of "big," equally inappropriate in the sense of height, girth, or fame. Pitos's English was fine, and when he slipped into mild inaccuracies, it was likely to be a decoy.

"You're wrong, Pitos. That island has a story in it somewhere. I'd take a bet on it."

"No fish today," said Pitos. "Why you think that is?"

I refrained from inventively telling him I had seen giant swordfish leaping from the shallows by the smaller island.

I found I was prowling Daphaeu, but only on the one side, the side where I would get a view—or views—of her sister. I would climb down into the welter of coves and smashed emerald water to look across at her. I would climb up and stand, leaning on the sunblasted walls of a crumbling church, and look at the small island. At night, crouched over a bottle of wine, a scatter of manuscript, moths falling like rain in the oil lamp, my stare stayed fixed on the small island, which, as the moon came up, would seem turned to silver or to some older metal, Nemean metal perhaps, sloughed from the moon herself.

Curiosity accounts for much of this, and contrasuggestiveness. But the influence I presently began to feel, that I cannot account for exactly. Maybe it was only the writer's desire to fantasize rather than to work. But each time I reached for the manuscript I would experience a sort of distraction, a sort of calling—uncanny, poignant, like nostalgia, though for a place I had never visited.

I am very bad at recollecting my dreams, but one or twice, just before sunrise, I had a suspicion I had dreamed of the island. Of walking there, hearing its inner waters, the leaves brushing my hands and face.

Two weeks went by, and precious little had been done in the line of work. And I had come to Daphaeu with the sole intention of working. The year before, I had accomplished so much in a month of similar islands—or had they been similar?—that I had looked for results of some magnitude. In all of fourteen days I must have squeezed out two thousand words, and most of those dreary enough that the only covers they would ever get between would be those of the trash can. And yet it was not that I could not produce work, it was that I knew, with blind and damnable certainty, that the work I needed to be doing sprang from that spoonful of island.

The first day of the third week I had been swimming in the calm stretch of sea west of the harbor and had emerged to sun myself and smoke on the parched hot shore. Presently Pitos appeared, having scented my cigarettes. Surgical and government health warnings have not yet penetrated to spots like Daphaeu, where filtered tobacco continues to symbolize Hollywood or some other amorphous, anacronistic surrealism still hankered after and long vanished from the real world beyond. Once Pitos had acquired his cigarette, he sprawled down on the dry grass, grinned, indicated the Borgia ring, and mentioned a beautiful cousin of his, whether male or female I cannot be sure. After this had been cleared out of the way, I said to him, "You know how the currents run. I was thinking of a slightly more adventurous swim. But I'd like your advice."

Pitos glanced at me warily. I had had the plan as I lazed in the velvet water. Pitos was already starting to guess it.

"Currents are very dangerous. Not to be trusted, except by harbor."

"How about between Daphaeu and the other island? It can't be more than a quarter mile. The sea looks smooth enough, once you break away from the shoreline here."

"No," said Pitos. I waited for him to say there were no fish, or a lot of fish, or that his brother had gotten a broken thumb, or something of the sort. But Pitos did not resort to this. Troubled and angry, he stabbed my cigarette, half-smoked, into the turf. "Why do you want to go to the island so much?"

"Why does nobody else want me to go there?"

He looked up then, and into my eyes. His own were very black, sensuous, carnal earthbound eyes, full of orthodox sins, and extremely young in a sense that had nothing to do with physical age, but with race, I suppose, the youngness of ancient things, like Pan himself, quite possibly.

"Well," I said at last, "are you going to tell me or not? Because believe me, I intend to swim over there today or tomorrow."

"No," he said again. And then: "You should not go. On the island there is a . . ." and he said a word in some tongue neither Greek nor Turkish, not even the corrupt Spanish that sometimes peregrinates from Malta.

"A *what?*"

Pitos shrugged helplessly. He gazed out to sea, a safe sea without islands. He seemed to be putting something together in his mind and I let him do it, very curious now, pleasantly unnerved by this waft of the occult I had already suspected to be the root cause of the ban.

Eventually he turned back to me, treated me once more to the primordial innocence of his stare, and announced:

"The cunning one."

"Ah," I said. Both irked and amused, I found myself smiling. At this, Pitos's face grew savage with pure rage, an expression I had never witnessed before—the façade kept for foreigners had well and truly come down.

"Pitos," I said, "I don't understand."

"*Meda,*" he said then, the Greek word, old Greek.

"Wait," I said. I caught at the name, which was wrong, trying to fit it to a memory. Then the list came back to me, actually from Graves, the names which meant "the cunning": Meda, Medea, Medusa.

"Oh," I said. I hardly wanted to offend him further by bursting into loud mirth. At the same time, even while I was trying not to laugh, I was aware of the hair standing up on my scalp and neck. "You're telling me there is a gorgon on the island."

Pitos grumbled unintelligibly, stabbing the dead cigarette over and over into the ground.

"I'm sorry, Pitos, but it can't be Medusa. Someone cut her head off quite a few years ago. A guy called Perseus."

His face erupted into that awful expression again, mouth in a rictus, tongue starting to protrude, eyes flaring at me—quite abruptly I realized he wasn't raging, but imitating the visual panic-contortions of a man turning inexorably to stone. Since that is what the gorgon is credited with, literally petrifying men by the sheer horror of her countenance, it now seemed almost pragmatic of Pitos to be demonstrating. It was, too, a creditable facsimile of the sculpted gorgon's face sometimes used to seal ovens and jars. I wondered where he had seen one to copy it so well.

"All right," I said. "OK, Pitos, fine." I fished in my shirt, which was lying on the ground, and took out some money to give him, but he recoiled. "I'm sorry," I said, "I don't think it merits the ring. Unless you'd care to row me over there after all."

The boy rose. He looked at me with utter contempt, and without another word, before striding off up the shore. The mashed cigarette protruded from the grass and I lay and watched it, the tiny strands of tobacco slowly crisping in the heat of the sun, as I plotted my route from Daphaeu.

Dawn seemed an amiable hour. No one in particular about on that side of the island, the water chill but flushing quickly with warmth as the sun reached over it. And the tide in the right place to navigate the rocks. . . .

Yes, dawn would be an excellent time to swim out to the gorgon's island.

The gods were on my side, I concluded as I eased myself into the open sea the following morning. Getting clear of the rocks was no problem, their channels only half filled by the returning tide. While just beyond Daphaeu's coast I picked up one of those contrary currents that lace the island's edges and which, tide or no, would funnel me away from shore.

The swim was ideal, the sea limpid and no longer any more than cool. Sunlight filled in the waves and touched Daphaeu's retreating face with gold. Barely altered in thousands of years, either rock or sea or sun. And yet one knew that against all the claims of romantic fiction, this place did not look now as once it had. Some element in the air or in time itself changes things. A young man of the Bronze Age, falling asleep at sunset in his own era, waking at sunrise in mine, looking about him, would not have known where he was. I would swear to that.

Such thoughts I had leisure for in my facile swim across to the wooded island moored off Daphaeu.

As I had detected, the approach was smooth, virtually inviting. I cruised in as if sliding along butter. A rowboat would have had no more difficulty. The shallows were clear, empty of rocks, and, if anything, greener than the water off Daphaeu.

I had not looked much at Medusa's Island (I had begun jokingly to call it this) as I crossed, knowing I would have all the space on my arrival. So I found myself wading in on a seamless beach of rare glycerine sand and, looking up, saw the mass of trees spilling from the sky.

The effect was incredibly lush—so much heavy green, and seemingly quite impenetrable, while the sun struck in glistening shafts, lodging like arrows in the foliage, which reminded me very intensely of huge clusters of grapes on a vine. Anything might lie behind such a barricade.

It was already beginning to get hot. Dry, I put on the loose cotton shirt and ate breakfast packed in the same waterproof wrapper, standing on the beach impatient to get on.

As I moved forward, a bird shrilled somewhere in its cage of boughs, sounding an alarm of invasion. But surely the birds, too, would be stone on Medusa's Island, if the legends were correct. And when I stumbled across the remarkable stone carving of a man in the forest, I would pause in shocked amazement at its verisimilitude to life. . . .

Five minutes into the thickets of the wood, I did indeed stumble on a carving, but it was of a moss-grown little faun. My pleasure in the discovery was considerably lessened, however, when investigation told me it was scarcely classical in origin. Circa 1920 would be nearer the mark.

A further minute and I had put the faun from my mind. The riot of waterfalling plants through which I had been picking my way broke open suddenly on an inner vista much wider than I had anticipated. While the focal point of the vista threw me completely, I cannot say what I had really been expecting. The grey-white stalks of pillars, some temple shrine, the spring with its votary of greenish rotted bronze, none of these would have surprised me. On the other hand, to find a house before me took me completely by surprise. I stood and looked at it in abject dismay, cursing its wretched normality until I gradually began to see the house was not normal in the accepted sense.

It had been erected probably at the turn of the century, when such things were done. An eccentric two-storied building, intransigently European—that is, the Europe of the north—with its dark walls and arched roofing. Long windows, smothered by the proximity of the wood, received and refracted no light. The one unique and startling feature—startling because of its beauty —was the parade of columns that ran along the terrace, in form and choreography for all the world like the columns of Knossos, differing only in color. For these stems of the gloomy house were of a luminous sea-green marble, and shone as the windows did not.

Before the house was a stretch of rough-cut lawn, tamarisk, and one lost dying olive tree. As I was staring, an apparition seemed to manifest out of the center of the tree. For a second we peered at each other before he came from the bushes with a clashing of gnarled brown forearms. He might have been an elderly satyr; I, patently, was only a swimmer, with my pale foreigner's tan, my bathing trunks, the loose shirt. It occurred to me at last that I was conceivably trespassing. I wished my Greek were better.

He planted himself before me and shouted intolerantly, and anyone's Greek was good enough to get his drift. "Go! Go!" He was ranting, and he began to wave a knife with which, presumably, he had been pruning or mutilating something. "Go. You go!"

I said I had been unaware anybody lived on the island. He took no notice. He went on waving the knife and his attitude provoked me. I told him sternly to put the knife down, that I would leave when I was ready, that I had seen no notice to the effect that the island was private property. Generally I would never take a chance like this with someone so obviously qualified to be a lunatic, but my position was so vulnerable, so ludicrous, so entirely indefensible, that I felt bound to act firmly. Besides which, having reached the magic grotto and found it was not as I had visualized, I was still very reluctant to abscond with only a memory of dark windows and sea-green columns to brood upon.

The maniac was by now quite literally foaming, due most likely to a shortage of teeth, but the effect was alarming, not to mention unaesthetic. As I was deciding which fresh course to take and if there might be one, a woman's figure came out on to the terrace. I had the impression of a white frock, before an odd, muffled voice called out a rapid—too rapid for my translation—stream of peculiarly accented Greek. The old man swung around, gazed at the figure, raised his arms, and bawled another foaming torrent to the effect that I was a bandit or some other kind of malcontent. While he did so, agitated as I was becoming, I nevertheless took in what I could of the woman standing between the columns. She was mostly in shadow, just the faded white dress with a white scarf at the neck marking her position. And then there was an abrupt flash of warmer pallor that was her hair. A blond Greek, or maybe just a peroxided Greek. At any rate, no snakes.

The drama went on, from his side, from hers. I finally got tired of it, went by him, and walked toward the terrace, pondering, rather too late, if I might not be awarded the knife in my back. But almost as soon as I started to move, she leaned forward a little and she called another phrase to him, which this time I made out, telling him to let me come on.

When I reached the foot of the steps, I halted, really involuntarily, struck by something strange about her. Just as the strangeness of the house had begun to strike me, not its evident strangeness, the ill-marriage to location, the green pillars, but a strangeness of atmosphere, items the unconscious eye notices, where the physical eye is blind and will not explain. And so with her. What was it? Still in shadow, I had the impression she might be in her early thirties, from her figure, her movements, but she had turned away as I approached, adjusting some papers on a wicker table.

"Excuse me," I said. I stopped and spoke in English. For some reason I guessed she would be familiar with the language, perhaps only since it was current on Daphaeu. "Excuse me. I had no idea the island was private. No one gave me the slightest hint—"

"You are English," she broke in, in the vernacular, proving the guess to be correct.

"Near enough. I find it easier to handle than Greek, I confess."

"Your Greek is very good," she said with the indifferent patronage of one who is multilingual. I stood there under the steps, already fascinated. Her voice was the weirdest I had ever heard, muffled, almost unattractive, and with the most incredible accent, not Greek at all. The nearest approximation I could come up with was Russian, but I could not be sure.

"Well," I said. I glanced over my shoulder and registered that the frothy satyr had retired into his shrubbery; the knife glinted as it slashed tamarisk in lieu of me. "Well, I suppose I should retreat to Daphaeu. Or am I permitted to stay?"

"Go, stay," she said. "I do not care at all."

She turned then, abruptly, and my heart slammed into the base of my throat. A childish silly reaction, yet I was quite unnerved, for now I saw what it was that had seemed vaguely peculiar from a distance. The lady on Medusa's Island was masked.

She remained totally still and let me have my reaction, neither helping nor hindering me.

It was an unusual mask, or usual—I am unfamiliar with the norm of such things. It was made of some matt-light substance that toned well with the skin of her arms and hands, possibly not so well with that of her neck, where the scarf provided camouflage. Besides which, the chin of the mask—this certainly an extra to any mask I had ever seen—continued under her own. The mask's physiognomy was bland, nondescriptly pretty in a way that was somehow grossly insulting to her. Before confronting the mask, if I had tried to judge the sort of face she would have, I would have suspected a coarse, rather heavy beauty, probably redeemed by one chiseled feature—a small slender nose, perhaps. The mask, however, was vacuous. It did not suit her, was not true to her. Even after three minutes I could tell as much, or thought I could, which amounts to the same thing.

The blond hair, seeming natural as the mask was not, cascaded down, lush as the foliage of the island. A blond Greek, then, like the golden Greeks of Homer's time, when gods walked the earth in disguise.

In the end, without any help or hindrance from her, as I have said, I pulled myself together. As she had mentioned no aspect of her state, neither did I. I simply repeated what I had said before: "Am I permitted to stay?"

The mask went on looking at me. The astonishing voice said: "You wish to stay so much. What do you mean to do here?"

Talk to you, oblique lady, and wonder what lies behind the painted veil.

"Look at the island, if you'll let me. I found the statue of a faun near the beach." Elaboration implied I should lie: "Someone told me there was an old shrine here."

"Ah!" She barked. It was apparently a laugh. "No one," she said, "*told* you anything about this place."

I was at a loss. Did she know what was said? "Frankly, then, I romantically hoped there might be."

"Unromantically, there is not. No shrine. No temple. My father bought the faun in a shop in Athens. A tourist shop. He had vulgar tastes but he knew it, and that has a certain charm, does it not?"

"Yes, I suppose it does. Your father—"

She cut me short again.

"The woods cover all the island. Except for an area behind the house. We grow things there, and we keep goats and chickens. We are very domesticated. Very sufficient for ourselves. There is a spring of fresh water, but no votary. No *genius loci*. I am *so* sorry to dash your dreams to pieces."

It suggested itself to me, from her tone of amusement, from little inflections that were coming and going in her shoulders now, that she might be enjoying this, enjoying, if you like, putting me down as an idiot. Presumably visitors were rare. Perhaps it was even fun for her to talk to a man, youngish and unknown, though admittedly never likely to qualify for anyone's centerfold.

"But you have no objections to my being here," I pursued. "And your father?"

"My parents are dead," she informed me. "When I employed the plural, I referred to him," she gestured with a broad sweep of her hand to the monster on the lawn, "and a woman who attends to the house. My servants, my unpaid servants. I have no money anymore. Do you see this dress? It is my mother's dress. How lucky I am the same fitting as my mother, do you not think?"

"Yes. . . ."

I was put in mind, suddenly, of myself as an ambassador at the court of some notorious female potentate, Cleopatra, say, or Catherine de Medici.

"You are very polite," she said as if telepathically privy to my fantasies.

"I have every reason to be."

"What reason?"

"I'm trespassing. You treat me like a guest."

"And how," she said, vainglorious all at once, "do you rate my English?"

"It's wonderful."

"I speak eleven languages fluently," she said with off-handed boastfulness. "Three more I can read very well."

I liked her. This display, touching and magnificent at once, her angular theatrical gesturings, which now came more and more often, her hair, her flat-waisted figure in its 1940s dress, her large well-made hands, and her challenging me with the mask, saying nothing to explain it, all this hypnotized me.

I said something to express admiration and she barked again, throwing back her blond head and irresistibly, though only for a moment, conjuring Garbo's Queen Christina.

Then she walked down the steps straight to me, demonstrating something else I had deduced, that she was only about an inch shorter than I.

"I," she said, "will show you the island. Come."

She showed me the island. Unsurprisingly, it was small. To go directly around it would maybe have taken less than thirty minutes. But we lingered, over a particular tree, a view, and once we sat down on the ground near the gushing milk-white spring. The basin under the spring, she informed me, had been added in 1910. A little bronze nymph presided over the spot, dating from the same year, which you could tell in any case from the way her classical costume and her filleted hair had been adapted to the fashions of hobble skirt and Edwardian coiffeur. Each age imposes its own overlay on the past.

Behind the house was a scatter of the meager white dwellings that make up such places as the village on Daphaeu, now plainly unoccupied and put to other uses. Sheltered from the sun by a colossal cypress, six goats played about in the grass. Chickens and an assortment of other fowl strutted up and down, while a pig—or pigs—grunted somewhere out of sight. Things grew in strips and patches, and fruit trees and vines ended the miniature plantation before the woods resumed. Self-sufficiency of a tolerable kind, I supposed. But there seemed, from what she said, no contact maintained with any other area, as if the world did not exist. Postulate that a blight or harsh weather intervened, what then? And the old satyr, how long would he last to tend the plots? He looked two hundred now, which on the islands probably meant sixty. I did not ask her what contingency plans she had for these emergencies and inevitabilities. What good, after all, are most plans? We could be invaded from Andromeda tomorrow, and what help for us all then? Either it is in your nature to survive—somehow, anyhow—or it is not.

She had well and truly hooked me, of course. If I had met her in Athens, some sun-baked afternoon, I would have felt decidedly out of my depth, taken her for cocktails, and foundered before we had even reached the dinner hour. But here, in this pulsing green bubble of light and leaves straight out of one's most irrational visions of the glades of Arcadia, conversation, however erratic, communication, however eccentric, was happening. The most inexplicable thing of all was that the mask had ceased almost immediately to bother me. I cannot, as I look back, properly account for this, for to spend a morning, a noon, an afternoon, allowing yourself to become fundamentally engaged by a woman whose face you have not seen, whose face you

are actively being prevented from seeing, seems now incongru-
ous to the point of perversity. But there it is. We discussed Ibsen,
Dickens, Euripides, and Jung. I remembered trawling anecdotes
of a grandfather, mentioned my sister's jewelry store in St.
Louis, listened to an astonishing description of wild birds flying
in across a desert from a sea. I assisted her over rocky turf, flirted
with her, felt excited by and familiar with her, all this with her
masked face before me. As if the mask, rather than being a part
of her, meant no more than the frock she had elected to wear or
the narrow-heeled vanilla shoes she had chosen to put on. As if I
knew her face totally and had no need to be shown it, the face of
her movements and her ridiculous voice.

But in fact, I could not even make out her eyes, only the
shine in them when they caught the light, flecks of luminescence
but not color, for the eyeholes of the mask were long-lidded and
rather small. I must have noticed, too, that there was no aper-
ture in the lips, and this may have informed me that the mask
must be removed for purposes of eating or drinking. I really do
not know. I can neither excuse nor quite understand myself,
seen in the distance there with her on her island. Hartley tells us
that the past is another country. Perhaps we also were other
people—strangers—yesterday. But when I think of this, I remember, too, the sense of drawing I had had, of being magne-
tized to that shore, those trees, the nostalgia for a place I had
never been to. For she, it may be true to say, was a figment of
that nostalgia, as if I had known her and come back to her. Some
enchantment, then. Not Medusa's Island, but Circe's.

The afternoon, even through the dapple *L'Après-midi d'un
Faune* effect of the leaves, was a viridian furnace when we
regained the house. I sat in one of the wicker chairs on the
terrace and woke with a start of embarrassment to hear her
laughing at me.

"You are tired and hungry. I must go into the house for a
while. I will send Kleia to you with some wine and food."

It made a bleary sense, and when I woke again it was to find
an old fat woman in the ubiquitous Grecian island black—de-
monstrably Kleia—setting down a tray of pale red wine, amber
cheese, and dark bread.

"Where is—" I realized I did not know the enchantress's
name.

In any event, the woman only shook her head, saying brusquely in Greek: "No English. No English."

And when I attempted to ask again in Greek where my hostess had gone, Kleia waddled away, leaving me unanswered. So I ate the food, which was passable, and drank the wine, which was very good, imagining her faun-buying father putting down an enormous patrician cellar, then fell asleep again, sprawled in the chair.

When I awoke, the sun was setting and the clearing was swimming in red light and rusty violet shadows. The columns burned as if they were internally on fire, holding the core of the sunset, it appeared, some while after the sky had cooled and the stars became visible, a trick of architectural positioning that won my awe and envy. I was making a mental note to ask her who had been responsible for the columns, and jumped when she spoke to me, softly and hoarsely, almost seductively, from just behind my chair—thereby promptly making me forget to ask any such thing.

"Come into the house now. We will dine soon."

I got up, saying something lame about imposing on her, though we were far beyond that stage.

"Always," she said to me, "you apologize. There is no imposition. You will be gone tomorrow."

How do you know? I nearly inquired, but prevented myself. What guarantee? Even if the magic food did not change me into a swine, perhaps my poisoned dead body would be carried from the feast and cast into the sea, gone, well and truly, to Poseidon's fishes. You see, I did not trust her, even though I was somewhat in love with her. The element of her danger—for she *was* dangerous in some obscure way—may well have contributed to her attraction.

We went into the house, which in itself alerted me. I had forgotten the great curiosity I had had to look inside it. There was a shadowy, unlit entrance hall, a sort of Roman atrium of a thing. Then we passed, she leading, into a small salon that took my breath away. It was lined all over—floor, ceiling, walls—with the sea-green marble the columns were made of. Whether in good taste or bad I am not qualified to say, but the effect, instantaneous and utter, was of being beneath the sea. Smoky oil lamps of a very beautiful Art Nouveau design hung from the profundity of the green ceiling, lighting the dreamlike swirls and oceanic variations of the marble so they seemed to breathe, definitely to move, like nothing else but waves. Shoes on that floor would have squeaked or clattered unbearably, but I was barefoot and so now was she.

A mahogany table with a modest placing for eight stood centrally. Only one place was laid.

I looked at it and she said, "I do not dine, but that will not prevent you."

An order. I considered vampires idly, but mainly I was subject to an infantile annoyance. Without quite realizing it, I had looked for the subtraction of the mask when she ate and now this made me very conscious of the mask for the first time since I had originally seen it.

We seated ourselves, she two places away from me. And I began to feel nervous. To eat this meal while she watched me did not appeal. And now the idea of the mask, unconsidered all morning, all afternoon, stole over me like an incoming tide.

Inevitably, I had not dressed for dinner, having no means, but she had changed her clothes and was now wearing a high-collared, long, grey gown, her mother's again, no doubt. It had the fragile look of age, but was very feminine and appealing for all that. Above it, the mask now reared, stuck out like the proverbial sore thumb.

The mask. What on earth was I going to do, leered at by that myopic, soulless face which had suddenly assumed such disastrous importance?

Kleia waddled in with the dishes. I cannot recall the meal, save that it was spicy and mostly vegetable. The wine came too, and I drank it. And as I drank the wine, I began to consider seriously, for the first time (which seems very curious indeed to me now) the reason for the mask. What did it hide? A scar, a birthmark? I drank her wine and I saw myself snatch off the mask, take in the disfigurement, unquelled, and behold the painful gratitude in her eyes as she watched me. I would inform her of the genius of surgeons. She would repeat she had no money. I would promise to pay for the operation.

Suddenly she startled me by saying: "Do you believe that we have lived before?"

I looked in my glass, that fount of wisdom and possibility,

and said, "It seems as sensible a proposition as any of the others I've ever heard."

I fancied she smiled to herself and do not know why I thought that; I know now I was wrong.

Her accent had thickened and distorted further when she said, "I rather hope that I have lived before. I could wish to think I may live again."

"To compensate for this life?" I said brutishly. I had not needed to be so obvious when already I had been given the implication on a salver.

"Yes. To compensate for this."

I downed all the wisdom and possibility left in my glass, swallowed an extra couple of times, and said, "Are you going to tell me why you wear a mask?"

As soon as I had said it, I grasped that I was drunk. Nor was it a pleasant drunkenness. I did not like the demanding tone I had taken with her, but I was angry at having allowed the game to go on for so long. I had no knowledge of the rules, or pretended I had not. And I could not stop myself. When she did not reply, I added on a note of ghastly banter, "Or shall I guess?"

She was still, seeming very composed. Had this scene been enacted before? Finally she said, "I would suppose you do guess it is to conceal something that I wear it."

"Something you imagine worth concealing, which, perhaps, isn't."

That was the stilted fanfare of bravado. I had braced myself, flushed with such stupid confidence.

"Why not," I said, and I grow cold when I remember how I spoke to her, "take the damn thing off. Take off the mask and drink a glass of wine with me."

A pause. Then, "No," she said.

Her voice was level and calm. There was neither eagerness nor fear in it.

"Go on," I said, the drunk not getting his way, aware (oh God) he could get it by the power of his intention alone, "please. You're an astounding woman. You're like this island. A fascinating mystery. But I've seen the island. Let me see you."

"No," she said.

I started to feel, even through the wine, that I had made an indecent suggestion to her, and this, along with the awful clichés I was bringing out, increased my anger and my discomfort.

"For heaven's sake," I said, "do you know what they call you on Daphaeu?"

"Yes."

"This is absurd. You're frightened—"

"No. I am not afraid."

"Afraid. Afraid to let me see. But maybe I can help you."

"No. You cannot help me."

"How can you be sure?"

She turned in her chair, and all the way to face me with the mask. Behind her, everywhere about her, the green marble dazzled.

"If you know," she said, "what I am called on Daphaeu, are you not uneasy as to what you may see?"

"Jesus. Mythology and superstition and ignorance. I assure you, I won't turn to stone."

"It is I," she said quietly, "who have done that."

Something about the phrase, the way in which she said it, chilled me. I put down my glass and, in that instant, her hands went to the sides of the mask and her fingers worked at some complicated strap arrangement which her hair had covered.

"Good," I said, "good. I'm glad—"

But I faltered over it. The cold night sea seemed to fill my veins where the warm red wine had been. I had been heroic and sure and bold, the stuff of celluloid. But now that I had my way, with hardly any preliminary, what *would* I see? And then she drew the plastic away and I saw.

I sat there, and then I stood up. The reflex was violent, and the chair scraped over the marble with an unbearable noise. There are occasions, though rare, when the human mind grows blank of all thought. I had no thought as I looked at her. Even now, I can evoke those long, long, empty seconds, that lapse of time. I recollect only the briefest confusion, when I believed she still played some kind of hideous game, that what I witnessed was a product of her decision and her will, a gesture—

After all, Pitos had done this very thing to illustrate and endorse his argument, produced this very expression, the eyes bursting from the head, the jaw rigidly outthrust, the tendons in the neck straining, the mouth in the grimace of a frozen, agonized scream, the teeth visible, the tongue slightly protruding. The gorgon's face on the jar or the oven. The face so ugly, so demented, so terrible, it could petrify.

The awful mouth writhed.

"You have seen," she said. Somehow the stretched and distorted lips brought out these words. There was even that nuance of humor I had heard before, the smile, although physically a smile would have been out of the question. "You have seen."

She picked up the mask again, gently, and put it on, easing the underpart of the plastic beneath her chin to hide the convulsed tendons in her throat. I stood there, motionless. Childishly I informed myself that now I comprehended the reason for her peculiar accent, which was caused, not by some exotic foreign extraction, but by the atrocious malformation of jaw, tongue, and lips, which somehow must be fought against for every sound she made.

I went on standing there, and now the mask was back in place.

"When I was very young," she said, "I suffered, without warning, from a form of fit or stroke. Various nerve centers were paralyzed. My father took me to the very best of surgeons, you may comfort yourself with that. Unfortunately, any effort to correct the damage entailed a penetration of my brain so uncompromisingly delicate that it was reckoned impossible, for it would surely render me an idiot. Since my senses, faculties, and intelligence were otherwise unaffected, it was decided not to risk this dire surgery, and my doctors resorted instead to alternative therapies, which, patently, were unsuccessful. As the months passed, my body adjusted to the unnatural physical tensions resulting from my facial paralysis. The pain of the rictus faded, or grew acceptable. I learned both how to eat, and how to converse, although the former activity is not attractive and I attend to it in private. The mask was made for me in Athens. I am quite fond of it. The man who designed it had worked a great many years in the theatre and could have made me a face of enormous beauty or character, but this seemed pointless, even wasteful."

There was a silence, and I realized her explanation was finished.

Not once had she stumbled. There was neither hurt nor madness in her inflection. There *was* something . . . at the time I missed it, though it came to me after. Then I knew only that she was far beyond my pity or my anguish, far away indeed from my terror.

"And now," she said, rising gracefully, "I will leave you to eat your meal in peace. Good night."

I wanted, or rather I felt impelled, to stay her with actions or sentences, but I was incapable of either. She walked out of the green marble room and left me there. It is a fact that for a considerable space of time I did not move.

I did not engage the swim back to Daphaeu that night; I judged myself too drunk and slept on the beach at the edge of the trees, where at sunrise the tidal water woke me with a strange low hissing. Green sea, green sunlight through leaves. I swam away and found my course through the warming ocean and fetched up, exhausted and swearing, bruising myself on Daphaeu's fangs that had not harmed me when I left her. I did not see Pitos anywhere about, and that evening I caught the boat which would take me to the mainland.

There is a curious thing which can happen with human beings. It is the ability to perform for days or weeks like balanced and cheerful automata, when some substrata, something upon which our codes or our hopes had firmly rested, has given way. Men who lose their wives or their God are quite capable of behaving in this manner for an indefinite season. After which the collapse is brilliant and total. Something of this sort had happened to me. Yet to fathom what I had lost, what she had deprived me of, is hard to say. I found its symptoms, but not the sickness which it was.

Medusa (I must call her that, she has no other name I know), struck by the extraordinary arrow of her misfortune, condemned to her relentless, uncanny, horrible isolation, her tragedy most deeply rooted in the fact that she was not a myth, not a fabulous and glamorous monster. . . . For it came to me one night in a bar in Corinth, to consider if the first Medusa might have been also such a victim, felled by some awesome fit, not petrifying but petrified, so appalling to the eyes and, more significantly, to the brooding aesthetic spirit that lives in man that she too was shunned and hated and slain by a murderer who would observe her only in a polished surface.

I spent some while in bars that summer. And later, much later, when the cold climate of the year's end closed the prospect of travel and adventure, I became afraid for myself, that dreadful writer's fear which has to do with the death of the idea, with the inertia of hand and heart and mind. Like one of the broken leaves, the summer's withered plants, I had dried. My block was sheer. I had expected a multitude of pages from the island, but instead I saw those unborn pages die on the horizon, where the beach met the sea.

And this, merely a record of marble, water, a plastic shell strapped across a woman's face, this is the last thing, it seems, which I shall commit to paper. Why? Perhaps only because she was to me such a lesson in the futility of things, the waiting fist of chance, the random despair we name the World.

And yet, now and then, I hear that voice of hers, I hear the way she spoke to me. I know now what I heard in her voice, which had neither pain nor shame in it, nor pleading, nor whining, nor even a hint of the tragedy—the Greek tragedy—of her life. And what I heard was not dignity either, or acceptance, or nobleness. It was *contempt.* She despised me. She despised all of us who live without her odds, who struggle with our small struggles, incomparable to hers. "Your Greek is very good," she said to me with the patronage of one who is multilingual. And in that same disdain she says over and over to me: "That you live is very good." Compared to her life, her existence, her multilingual endurance, what are my life or my ambitions worth? Or anything.

It did not occur immediately, but still it occurred. In its way, the myth is perfectly accurate. I see it in myself, scent it, taste it, like the onset of inescapable disease. What they say about the gorgon is true. She has turned me to stone.

MOVING NIGHT

By
Nancy Holder

I really have no idea why this series has lasted so long, but in the process of surviving, it has been able to lure a few new talents to its pages—or rather, talents new to the field. Nancy Holder is one of them. A professional writer with a love of Dark Fantasy, she was finally persuaded (read "bullied") into submitting some stories. She was nervous; I was confident. And "Moving Night," and the other pieces which have appeared in Shadows *and elsewhere, proves another valuable point for those of us who care—love for what you're doing, excitement for the craft as well as the story, always shows through in the finished piece. You can't always see it, but you can definitely feel it. And no amount of faking will save either the story or the writer. Nancy Holder doesn't fake it. She's too damn good for that.*

MOVING NIGHT

By
Nancy Holder

It moved.

Petey lay in his bed, shaking with terror, his eight-year-old eyes bulging so widely they ached. His head throbbed; his grubby fists clenched tight to keep him from screaming, as the moonlight gleamed on the chair that rattled near the closet door.

It had moved, oh, no, oh *no,* it had moved, and no one would ever believe him. All those nights his mom and dad would come in and talk to him in syrupy voices, and tell him, *Why, Petey, nothing moved. Only live things can move. And your stuffed rabbit isn't alive, and that pile of laundry isn't alive, and Mr. Robot isn't alive, and . . .*

And they never believed him. *They never did!*

But the chair had moved. He had seen it. When he'd pretended to look away, then looked quickly back, he knew the chair had inched closer to the bed. He knew it was coming to get him, to eat him all up and spit out his bones, to fling him to the monsters and the bogeymen and witches with rotten teeth and no eyes who lived in the closet . . .

. . . who stuck their heads out at midnight and laughed at him when his mom and dad were asleep; and waited until the last minute for the sleepy *pad pad pad* of slippers, the creak of the bedroom door . . .

Petey? Are you having another nightmare, dear? Don't give yourself one of those headaches!

There, it moved again! Petey wanted to scream but his throat was so dry he couldn't make a sound, not even a hoarse gasp. It moved, he swore it, please, please, someone, it *moved!*

He whimpered like a wounded kitten. Only live things could move. Only things that were alive.

Why didn't they ever believe him? When he whooped with white-hot fever over the dwarf in the toy chest, they just laughed. When he pleaded with them to listen *listen!* about the skeleton in the mattress, they said he had an active imagination. They only believed about the headaches. Headaches were real.

Maybe he needs glasses. Maybe he's allergic to pollen.

Maybe, maybe . . .

It moved again!

Peter bolted upright and pressed his back against the headboard. His head was splitting. They had believed him about *that,* but they had never done anything! They had never helped him! They had never taken away the pain!

"Stop!" Petey begged. "Stop!"

His head always hurt, like a little gremlin lived inside, sticking pins in his brain. And they talked about taking him to the doctor, and talked about taking him for tests, and talked and talked . . .

"Stop!"

. . . but they didn't care about him. They didn't love him, because his mom had had a boyfriend while his dad was on his battleship; and when he came back, she was going to have a baby. Him. Petey . . .

It was still moving!

. . . and he heard them late at night, fighting. His dad (not his read dad, his real dad was a bogeyman) would shout, "Ya shoulda gotten an abortion, Barb! Ya shoulda gotten rid of him!"

And his mother would cry and say, "I know, Jack, I know. I'm sorry."

Then last Sunday, after the kitten, his dad (the fake one) had shouted, "He's a monster! He's not human! We should send him away!" And his mother, sobbing, had replied, "Yes, Jack. I know. We will."

It moved. Tears streamed down Petey's face.

But only things that were alive could move. And the chair was not alive.

And neither was the thing sitting in it.

"I didn't mean to hurt the cat," he whispered. "Or the dog, or Mrs. Garcia's niece . . ." He crammed his fists in his mouth; no one knew about *that.*

It moved again. Much closer.

"I didn't mean to," he cried wildly. "Grown-ups are supposed to help little kids! And nobody . . ."

He thought of Mrs. Martin, the school nurse. She had *tried* to help him. When his head hurt really badly, she would let him lie down on a canvas cot in her office while she knitted. She had a big bag full of yarn and light green needles that flashed between her fingers. She wouldn't call home unless he asked her to. She would let him lie there, not moving, and every once in a while she would smile at him and say, "Feeling better?"

Sometimes he would say no just so he could stay with her. She was older than his mother but she was pretty anyway, and she always smelled like roses. She sang to him sometimes while she knitted, in-and-out, in-and-out

Bye, baby bunting, Daddy's gone a-hunting

like he was just a baby, and she told him he could grow up to be whatever he wanted.

He should be locked up! Did you see what he did to that cat? My God, Barb, he's not normal!

I know, Jack, I know.

Whatever he wanted, even President of the United States. And once he laughed and said, "Not me, Mrs. Martin!" But she shrugged and asked, "Why not? You're a bright boy with your future ahead of you."

Who was that guy you cheated on me with? Who the hell was he?

The headaches! The headaches!

At Halloween she lent him a doctor's bag and a stethoscope and told him maybe he could go to medical school and become a doctor.

"You're a good boy, Petey," she would say. "A fine young man."

He tried to tell her about the skeleton and the dwarf and the witches—oh, the witches, with their laughing, waiting for the *pad, pad, pad* of the slippers before they disappeared! But she didn't believe him either, and that *hurt* him, worse than the headaches. Mrs. Martin cared about him. He knew that. But she didn't believe him, and the pain never got better, never did.

And then she stopped working at the school and he was all alone again.

"Nobody helped me!" Petey screamed as loud as he could. "You should've helped me!"

"I'll help you now," slurred the thing in the chair.

It used to be his mother, but now she was all bloody from where he had stabbed her *wasn't my fault, wasn't, was not!* and the rest of her was white. Her lips were blue and her eyes were full of blood and flies were buzzing in her hair.

She hadn't moved for four days.

"It's not my fault!" he shrieked, scrabbling against the headboard. Maybe if he made a run for the door, he could escape. But she was moving, even though she was just a dead thing, not a live thing, and only live things moved.

Except his pretend dad, who *was* still alive—Petey could hear him moaning in the hallway—had not moved since Tuesday.

Anything he wanted to be . . . a fine young man.

"I'm coming for you, Petey," his mother whispered through broken teeth. He had punched her when she screamed "Monster! Monster!" until she stopped. "I'm going to give you to the skeleton in the mattress and the dwarf in the toy chest. I'm going to fling you to the eyeless witches in the closet."

President of the United States.

"Not me, Mrs. Martin!"

"Why not?"

He heard a mad, gleeful gibbering underneath the bed.

"No!" He buried his face in his hands and sobbed. "Oh, please, no! I'm sorry! Please, someone!"

The gibbering faded. The room was still.

Maybe it was just another headache. A bad dream. There was nothing . . .

Bye, baby bunting

When he raised his head, his mother, all oozy and gory, smelling terribly, was standing beside the bed. She smiled a toothless, gummy smile. "No more headaches."

And the chair skittered up next to her just as the closet door opened.

Anything he wanted . . .

And then *everything* moved.

JAMIE'S GRAVE

By
Lisa Tuttle

Lisa Tuttle does not restrict herself to Dark Fantasy. As a writer (as opposed to an author), she prefers to stretch her considerable talents in as many directions as she can, not always succeeding, but, more importantly, always learning. When she does write fantasy, however, she brings a voice to the field that borrows from no other. "Jamie's Grave," I have said before, is the perfect Shadows *story. Don't ask me why. I just know it, as I did the first time I read it and thanked all my lucky stars that the piece came here first. I didn't dither over this one. I've learned my lesson.*

MARY SAT AT the kitchen table, a cup of tea gone cold by her left hand, and listened to the purring of the electric clock on the wall.

The house was clean and the larder well stocked. She had done the laundry and read her library books and it was too wet for gardening. She had baked a cake yesterday and this wasn't her day for making bread. She had already phoned Clive twice this week and could think of no excuse to phone again. Once she might have popped across the road to visit Jen, but she had been getting the feeling that her visits were no longer so welcome. There had been a time when Jen was grateful for Mary's company, a time when she had been lonely, too, but now Jen had her own baby to care for, and whenever Mary went over there—no matter what Jen said—Mary couldn't help feeling that she was intruding.

She looked at the clock again. In twenty minutes she could start her walk to the school.

Clive said she should get a job. He was right, and not just for the money. Mary knew she would be happier doing something useful. But what sort of job could she get? She had no experience, and in this Wiltshire village there was not much scope for employment. Other mothers already held the school jobs of crossing-guard and dinner-lady, and what other employer would allow her to fit her working hours to those when Jamie was in school? She wouldn't let someone else look after Jamie—no job was worth that. Her son was all she had in the world, all she cared about. If she could have kept him home with her and taught him herself, instead of having to send him to school, Mary knew she would have been perfectly content. She had been so happy when she had her baby, she hadn't even minded losing Clive. But babies grew up, and grew away. Jen was going to find that out in a few years.

Mary rose and walked to the sink, poured away the tea, rinsed and set the cup on the draining-board. She took her jacket from the hook beside the door and put it on, straightening her collar and fluffing her hair without a mirror. The clock gave a dim, clicking buzz, and it was time to leave.

The house where Mary lived with her son was one of six bungalows on the edge of a Wiltshire village, close enough to London, as well as to Reading, to be attractive to commuters. After the grimy, cramped house in Islington, the modern bungalow with its large garden and fresh country air had seemed the perfect place to settle down and raise a family. But while Mary had dreamed of being pregnant again, Clive had been dreaming of escape. The house for him was not a cosy nest, but a gift to Mary and a sop to his conscience as he left.

Five minutes' leisurely walk brought the village school in sight. Mary saw the children tumbling out the door like so many brightly colored toys, and she reached the gate at the same moment as Jamie from the other side.

Jamie was involved with his friends, laughing and leaping around. His eyes flickered over her, taking in her presence but not acknowledging it, and when she hugged him she could feel his reluctance to return to her and leave the exciting, still new world of school.

He pulled away quickly, and wouldn't let her hold his hand as they walked. But he talked to her, needing to share his day's experiences, giving them to her in excited, discontented bursts of speech. She tried to make sense of what he said, but she couldn't always. He used strange words—sometimes in a different accent—picked up from the other children, and the events he described might have been imaginary, or related to schoolyard games rather than to reality. Once they had spent all their time together, in the same world. She had understood him better then, had understood him perfectly before he could even talk.

She looked at the little stranger walking beside her, and caught a sudden resemblance to Clive in one of his gestures. It struck her unpleasantly, that he was well on his way to becoming a man.

"Would you like to help me make some biscuits this afternoon?" she asked.

He shook his head emphatically. "I got to dig," he said.
"Dig? In the garden? Oh, darling, it's so wet!"
He frowned and tilted back his head. "Isn't."
"I know it's stopped raining, but the ground . . ." Mary
sighed, imagining the mess. "Why not wait until tomorrow? It
might be nicer then, the sun might come out, it might be much
nicer to dig in the garden tomorrow."
"I dig tomorrow, too," Jamie said. He began to chant,
swinging his arms stiffly as he marched, "Dig! Dig! Dig!"
During the summer they had taken a trip to the seashore
and Mary had bought him a plastic shovel. He had enjoyed
digging in the soft sand, then, but had not mentioned it since.
Mary wondered what had brought it back to mind—was it a
chance word from his teacher, or an enthusiasm caught from
one of the other children?—and realized she would probably
never know.
He found his shovel in the toy chest, flinging other toys
impatiently across the room. Not even the offer of a piece of cake
could distract him. He suffered himself to be changed into other
clothes, twitching impatiently all the while. When he had rushed
out into the garden, Mary stood by the window and watched.
The plastic shovel, so useful for digging at the beach, was
less efficient in the dense soil of the garden. As Jamie busily
applied himself, the handle suddenly broke off in his hands. He
looked for a moment almost comically shocked; then he began
to howl.
Mary rushed out to comfort him, but he would not be distracted by her promises of other pleasures. All he wanted was to
dig, and he would only be happy if she gave him a new shovel.
Finally, she gave him one of her gardening spades, and left him
to it.
She felt rejected, going into the house and closing the door,
staying away from the windows. He didn't want her to hover,
and she had no reason to fear for his safety in their own garden.
Had she waited all day just for this?
The next day, Saturday, was worse. Mary looked forward to
Saturdays now more fervently than she ever had as a child. On
Saturdays she had Jamie to herself all day. They played games,
she read him stories, they went for walks and had adventures.
But that Saturday all Jamie wanted to do was dig.

She stood in the garden with him, staring at the vulnerable white bumps of his knees, and then at his stubborn, impatient face. "Why, darling? Why do you want to dig?"

He shrugged and looked at the ground, clutching the spade as if she might take it away from him.

"Jamie, please answer me. I asked you a question. Why are you digging?"

"I might find something," he said, after a reluctant pause. Then he looked at her, a slightly shifty, sideways look. "If I find something . . . can I keep it?"

"May I," she corrected automatically. Her spirits lifted as she imagined a treasure hunt, a game she might play with him. Already, her thoughts were going to her old costume jewelry, and coins . . . "Probably," she said. "Almost certainly, anything you find in our garden would be yours to keep. But there are exceptions. If it is something *very* valuable, like gold, it belongs to the Queen by right, so you would have to get her permission."

"Not gold," he said scornfully.

"No?"

"No. Not treasure." He shook his head and then he smiled and looked with obvious pride at his small excavation. "I'm digging a grave," he said. "You know what they do with graves? They put dead people inside. I might find one. I might find a skellington!"

"Skeleton," she said without thinking.

"Skeleton, yeah! Wicked, man! Skellyton!" He flopped down and resumed his digging.

Feeling stunned, Mary went inside.

"And that's what you phoned me about?" said Clive.

"He's your son, too, you know."

"I know he's my son. And I like to hear what he's doing. But you know I like to sleep in . . . you could have picked a better time than early on a Saturday morning to fill me in on his latest game."

"It's not a game."

"Well, what is it, then? A real grave? A real skeleton?"

"It's morbid!"

"It's natural. Look, he probably saw something on television, or heard something at school . . ."

"When I was little, I was afraid of dead things," Mary said.

"You think that's healthier? What do you want me to say, Mary? It'll pass, this craze. He'll forget about it and go on to something else. If you make a big deal about it, he'll keep on, to get a reaction. Don't make him think it's wrong. Want me to come over tomorrow and take him out somewhere? That's the quickest way to get his mind on to other things."

Mary thought of how empty the house was when her son was gone. At least now, although he was preoccupied, she was aware of his presence nearby. And, as usual, she reacted against her ex-husband. She was shaking her head before he had even finished speaking.

"No, not tomorrow. I had plans for tomorrow. I—"

"Next weekend. He could come here, spend the night—"

"Oh, Clive, he's so young!"

"Mary, you can't have it both ways. He's my son, too. You can't complain that I take no interest and leave it all to you, and then refuse to let me see him. I do miss him, you know."

"All right, next weekend. But just one day, not overnight. Please. He's all I have. When he's not here I miss him dreadfully."

Mary stood by the window watching Jamie dig his grave, and she missed him. She could see him, and she knew that if she rapped on the glass he would look up and see her, but that wasn't enough; it would never be enough. Once, she had been the whole world to him. Now, every day took him farther from her.

She thought of Heather, Jen's little baby. She thought of the solid weight of her in her arms, and that delicious, warm, milky smell of new babies. She remembered how it had felt to hold her, and how she had felt when she had to give her back. She remembered watching Jen nurse her child. The envy which had pierced her. The longing. It wasn't Jen's feelings which made Mary reluctant now to visit her but her own jealousy. She wanted a baby.

She went on standing by the window for nearly an hour, holding herself and grieving for the child she didn't have, while Jamie dug a grave.

For lunch Mary made cauliflower soup and toasted cheese sandwiches. Ignoring his protests that he could wash his own hands, she marched Jamie to the bathroom and scrubbed and scrubbed until all the soil beneath his fingernails was gone.

Twenty minutes later, a soup moustache above his upper lip, Jamie said, "I got to go back to my digging."

Inside, she cried a protest, but she remembered Clive's words. Maybe he did want a reaction from her. Maybe he would be less inclined to dig a grave if his mother seemed to favour it. So, with a false, bright smile she cheered him on, helped him back into his filthy pullover and wellies, and waved vigorously from the back door, as if seeing him off on an expedition.

"Come back in when you get cold," she said. "Or if you get hungry . . ."

She turned on Radio Four, got out her knitting and worked on the sweater which was to be a Christmas present for her sister in Scotland. She worked steadily for about an hour. Then the panic took her.

A falling-elevator sensation in her stomach, and then the cold. It was a purely visceral, wordless, objectless fear. Her shaking fingers dropped stitches and then dropped the knitting, and she lurched clumsily to her feet.

If anything happened to Jamie she would never forgive herself. If she was too late, if anything had happened to him—

She knew he was safe in the back garden, where there was nothing to hurt him. She knew she'd had this experience before, and there had never been anything threatening her son. Logic made no impact on the fear.

He was so fragile, he was so young, and the world was so dangerous. How could she have let him out of her sight for even a moment?

She ran to the back door and out, cursing herself.

She saw his bright yellow boots first. He was lying flat on the ground, on his stomach, and she couldn't see his head. It must have been hanging over the edge, into the hole he had dug.

"Jamie!" She didn't want to alarm him, but his name came out as a shriek of terror.

He didn't move.

Mary fell on the ground beside him and caught his body up

in her arms. She was so frightened she couldn't breathe. But he was breathing; he was warm.

Jamie gave a little grunt and his eyelids fluttered. Then he was gazing up at her, dazed and sleepy-looking.

"Are you all right?" she demanded, although it was clear to her, now the panic had subsided, that he was fine.

"What?" he said groggily.

"Oh, you silly child! What do you mean by lying down out here, when the ground's so cold and wet . . . you'll catch your death . . . if you were tired, you should have come in. What a silly, to work so hard you had to lie down and take a nap!" She hugged him to her, and for once he seemed content to be held so, rubbing his dirty face against her sweater and clinging.

They rocked together in the moist grey air and country silence for a time, until Jamie gave a deep, shuddering sigh.

"What is it?"

"Hungry," he said. His voice was puzzled.

"Of course you are, poor darling, after so much hard work. It's not time for tea yet, but come inside and I'll give you a glass of milk and a biscuit. Would you like that?"

He seemed utterly exhausted, and she carried him inside. Although he had claimed to be hungry, he drank only a little milk and seemed without the energy even to nibble a biscuit. Mary settled him on the couch in front of the television, and when she came back a few minutes later she found him asleep.

After she had put Jamie to bed, Mary went back to the garden to look at his excavation.

It was a hole more round than square, no more than a foot across and probably not more than two foot deep. As Mary crouched down to look into it she saw another, smaller hole, within. She didn't think Jamie had made it; it seemed something quite different. She thought it looked like a tunnel, or the entrance to some small animal's burrow. She thought of blind, limbless creatures tunnelling through the soft earth, driven by needs and guided by senses she couldn't know, and she shuddered. She thought of worms, but this tunnel was much too large. She had not been aware of moles in the garden, but possibly Jamie had accidentally uncovered evidence of one.

She picked up the spade which Jamie had abandoned, and used it to scoop earth back into the hole. Although she began

casually, she soon began to work with a purpose, and her heart
pounded as she pushed and shovelled furiously, under a pressure she could not explain to fill it in, cover up the evidence,
make her garden whole again.

Finally she stood and tamped the earth down beneath her
feet. With the grass gone, the marks of digging were obvious.
She had done the best she could, but it wasn't good enough. It
wasn't the same; it couldn't be.

As she walked back into the house, Mary heard a brief, faint
scream, and immediately ran through to Jamie's room.

He was sitting up in bed, staring at her with wide-open yet
unseeing eyes.

"Darling, what's wrong?"

She went to him, meaning to hug him, but her hands were
covered with dirt from the hole; she couldn't touch him.

"What's that?" he asked, voice blurred with sleep, turning
towards the window.

Mary looked and saw with a shock that the window was
open, if only by a few inches. She didn't remember opening it,
and she was sure it was too heavy for Jamie to lift by himself.

"I'll close it," she said, and went to do so. Her hands looked
black against the white-painted sash, and she saw bits of earth
crumble and fall away. She felt as disturbed by that as if it really
had been grave-dirt, and felt she had to sweep it up immediately.

When she returned to the bed Jamie was lying down, apparently asleep. Careful not to touch him with her dirty hands, she
bent down and kissed him, hovering close for a time to feel the
warmth of his peaceful breathing against her face. She loved him
so much she could not move or speak.

In the morning Jamie was subdued, so quiet that Mary
worried he might be getting ill, and kept feeling his face for
some evidence of a fever. His skin was cool, though, and he
showed no other signs of disease. He said nothing more about
wanting to dig, nothing about graves or skeletons—that craze
appeared to have vanished as suddenly and inexplicably as it had
arrived.

It was a wet and windy day, and Mary was glad Jamie didn't
want to play in the garden. He seemed worried about something, though, following her around the house and demanding

her attention. Mary didn't mind. In fact, she cherished this evidence that she was still needed.

When she asked what he wanted for his tea, the answer came promptly. "Two beefburgers. Please."

"Two!"

"Yes. Two, please."

"I think one will be enough, really, Jamie. You never have two. If you are very hungry, I could make extra chips."

He had that stubborn look on his face, the look that reminded her of his father. "Extra chips, too. But please may I have two beefburgers."

She was certain he wouldn't be able to eat them both. "Very well," she said. "After you've eaten your first beefburger, if you still want another one, I'll make it then."

"I want two—I know I want two! I want two now!"

"Calm down, Jamie," she said quietly. "You shall have two. But one at a time. That's the way we'll do it."

He sulked, and he played with his food when she served it, but he did manage to eat all the beefburger, and then immediately demanded a second, forgetting, this time, to say "please."

"You haven't eaten all your chips," she pointed out.

He glared. "You didn't *say* I had to eat all my chips first. You *said* if I ate one burger I could have another—you *said.*"

"I know I said it, lovey, but the chips are part of your dinner, too, and if you're really hungry—"

"You *said!*"

His lower lip trembled, and there were tears in his eyes. How could she deny him? She couldn't bear his unhappiness, even though she was quite certain that he wasn't hungry and wouldn't be able to eat any more meat.

"All right, my darling," she said, and left her own unfinished meal to grow cold while she went back to the cooker. Clive would have been firm with him, she thought, and wondered if she had been wrong to give in. Maybe Jamie had wanted her to say no. The thought wearied her. It was too complicated. He had asked for food, and she would give it to him.

Jamie fidgeted in his chair when she put the food before him, and would not meet her eyes. He asked if he could watch TV while he ate. Curious, she agreed. "Just bring your plate in to me when you've finished."

A suspiciously few minutes later, Jamie returned with his plate. The second beefburger had vanished without a trace. There were only a few smashed peas and stray chips on the plate. Jamie went back to watch television while Mary did the washing-up. Almost immediately, above the noise of the television, she heard the back door open and close quietly. When she rejoined Jamie he seemed happier than he had all day, freed of some burden. They played together happily—if a little more rowdily than Mary liked—until his bedtime.

But after she had tucked him into bed, Mary went out into the dark garden. In the gloom the whiteness of a handkerchief gave off an almost phosphorescent glow, drawing her across the lawn to the site of Jamie's excavation.

Like some sort of offering, the beefburger had been placed on a clean white handkerchief and laid on the ground, on the bare patch. Mary stared at it for a moment, and then went back inside.

Mary usually woke to the sounds of Jamie moving about, but on Monday morning for once she had to wake him. He was pale and groggy, with greenish shadows beneath his eyes. But when she suggested he could stay home and spend the day resting in bed, he rallied and became almost frantic in his determination to go to school. He did seem better, out in the fresh air and away from the house, but she continued to worry about him after she had left him at school. Her thoughts led her to the doctor's. She didn't mind waiting until all the scheduled patients had been seen; she paged through old magazines, with nothing better to do.

Dr. Abden was a brisk, no-nonsense woman who had raised two children to safe and successful adulthood; Mary was able to trust her maternal wisdom enough to tell her the whole story of Jamie's grave.

"Perhaps he found his skeleton and didn't like it so much," said Dr. Abden. "There, don't look so alarmed, my dear! I didn't mean a human skeleton, of course. You mentioned seeing something like a tunnel . . . isn't it possible that your son came across a mole—a dead one? That first encounter with death can be a disturbing one. Perhaps he thought he killed it with his little shovel and so is guiltily trying to revive it . . . Perhaps he

doesn't realize it is dead, and imagines he can make a pet of it. If
you can get him to confide in you, I'm sure you'll be able to set
his mind at rest. Of course, he may have forgotten the whole
thing after a day at school."

Mary hoped that would be the case, but it was obvious as
soon as she saw him that afternoon that his secret still worried
him. He rejected all her coaxing offers of help, pushing her
away, hugging his fear to himself, uneasy in her presence. So
Mary waited, kept the distance he seemed to want, and watched.

He was sneaking food outside. Biscuits, bits of chocolate, an
apple . . . she meant to let him continue, but at the thought of
the mess eggs and baked beans would make in his pockets, she
caught his hand before he could transfer food from his plate to
his lap.

"Darling, you don't have to do that," she said. "I'll give you
a plate, and you can put the food on that and take it out to your
little friend. Just eat your own meal first."

His pale face went paler. "You know?"

Mary hesitated. "I know . . . you're upset about something. And I know you've been leaving food outside. Now, why
don't you tell Mummy what's going on, and I'll help you."

Emotions battled on his face; then, surrender.

"He's hungry," Jamie said plaintively. "He's so hungry, so,
so hungry. I keep giving him food, but it's not right . . . he
won't eat it. I don't know what he . . . I don't want . . . I can't
. . . I'm giving him everything and he won't eat. What does he
eat, Mummy? What *else* does he eat?"

Mary imagined a mole's tiny corpse, Jamie thrusting food
beneath its motionless snout. "Maybe he doesn't eat anything,"
she said.

"No, he has to! If you're alive, you have to eat."

"Well, Jamie, maybe he's dead."

She half expected some outburst, an excited protest against
that idea, but Jamie shook his head, an oddly mature and
thoughtful expression on his face. He had obviously considered
this possibility before. "No, he's not dead. I thought, I thought
when I found him in my grave, I thought he was dead, but then
he wasn't. He isn't dead."

"Who isn't dead? What is this you're talking about, Jamie?
Is it an animal?"

He looked puzzled. "You don't know?"

She shook her head. "Will you show him to me, darling?"

Jamie looked alarmed. He shook his head and began to tremble. Mary knelt beside his chair and put her arms around him, holding him close, safe and tight.

"It's all right," she said. "Mummy's here. It's all right . . . ."

When he had calmed she thought to distract him, but he returned to the subject of feeding this unknown creature.

"Well," said Mary, "if he's not eating the food you give him, maybe he doesn't need to be fed. He might find his own food—animals usually do, you know, except for pets and babies."

"He's like a baby."

"How is he like a baby? What does he look like?"

"I don't know. I don't remember now—I can't. He doesn't look like anything—not like anything except himself."

It was only then that it occurred to Mary that there might be no animal at all, not even a dead mole. This creature Jamie had found was probably completely imaginary—that was why he couldn't show it to her.

"He can probably find his own food," Mary said.

But this idea obviously bothered Jamie, who began to fidget. "He needs me."

"How do you know that? Did he tell you? Can't he tell you what sort of food he wants, then?"

Jamie shrugged, nodded, then shook his head. "I have to get something for him."

"But he must have managed on his own before you found him—"

"He was all right before," Jamie agreed. "But he needs me now. I found him, so now I have to take care of him. But . . . he won't eat. I keep trying and trying, but he won't take the food. And he's hungry. What can I give him, Mummy? What can I give him to eat?"

Mary stopped trying to be reasonable, then, and let herself enter his fantasy.

"Don't worry, darling," she said. "We'll find something for your little friend—we'll try everything in the kitchen if we have to!"

With Jamie's help, Mary prepared a whole trayful of food: a saucer of milk and one of sweetened tea; water-biscuits spread with peanut butter; celery tops and chopped carrots; lettuce leaves; raisins; plain bread, buttered bread, and bread spread with honey. As she carried the tray outside, Mary wondered what sort of pests this would attract, then dismissed it as unimportant. She pretended to catch sight of Jamie's imaginary friend.

"Oh, we've got something he likes here," she said. "Just look at him smacking his lips!"

Jamie gave her a disapproving look. "You don't see him."

"How do you know? Isn't that him over there by the hedge?"

"If you saw him, you'd probably scream. And, anyway, he hasn't *got* lips."

"What does he look like? Is he so frightening?"

"It doesn't matter," Jamie said.

"Shall I put the tray down here?"

He nodded. The playfulness and interest he had shown in the kitchen had vanished, and he was worried again. He sighed. "If he doesn't eat this . . ."

"If he doesn't, there's plenty more in the kitchen we can try," said Mary.

"He's so hungry," Jamie murmured sadly.

He was concerned, when they went back inside, about locking the house. This was not a subject which had ever interested him before, but now he followed Mary around, and she demonstrated that both front and back doors were secure, and all the windows—particularly the window in his room—were shut and locked.

"There are other ways for things to get in, though," he said.

"No, of course not, darling."

"How do my dreams get in, then?"

"Your dreams?" She crouched beside him on the bedroom floor and stroked his hair. "Dreams don't come in from the outside, darling. Dreams are inside, in your head."

"They're already inside?"

"They aren't real, darling. They're imaginary. They aren't real and solid like I am, or like you are . . . they're just . . . like thoughts. Like make-believe. And they go away when you're awake."

"Oh," he said. She couldn't tell what he thought, or if her

words had comforted him. She hugged him close until he wriggled to be free, and then she put him to bed.

She checked on him twice during the night, and both times he appeared to be sleeping soundly. Yet in the morning, again, he had the darkened eyes and grogginess of one who'd had a disturbed night.

She thought about taking him to the doctor instead of to school, but the memory of her conversation with Dr. Abden stopped her. This was something she had to cope with herself. There was nothing physically wrong with Jamie. His sleeplessness was obviously the result of worry, and the doctor had already reminded her that it was her duty, as his mother, to set his mind at rest. If only he would tell her what was wrong!

That afternoon Jamie was again subdued, quiet and good. Mary actually preferred him like this, but because such behavior wasn't normal for him, she worried even while she appreciated his nearness. They sat together playing games and looking through his books, taking turns reading to each other. Later, she left the dishes to soak in the sink and watched her son as he sat with his crayons and his coloring book, wondering what went on in his mind.

"Has your little friend gone away, to find food somewhere else?" she asked.

Jamie shook his head.

"We could put some more food out for him, you know. I don't mind. Anything you like."

Jamie was silent for a while, and then he said, "He doesn't need food."

"Doesn't he? That's very unusual. What does he live on?"

Jamie stopped coloring, the crayon frozen in his hand. Then he drew a deep, shuddering breath. "Love," he said, and began coloring again.

He was no longer worried about the doors and windows, and it was Mary, not Jamie, who prolonged the bedside chat and goodnight kisses, reluctant to leave him alone. He didn't seem afraid, but she was afraid for him, without knowing why.

"Goodnight, my darling," she said for the fifth or sixth last time, and made herself rise and move away from the bed. "Sleep well . . . call me if you need anything . . . I'll be awake . . ." Her voice trailed off. Already, it appeared, he was sleeping. She went out quietly and left his bedroom door ajar. If he made a sound, she would hear it.

She turned the television on low and slumped in a chair before it. She was too tired to think, too distracted to be entertained. She might as well go to bed herself, she thought.

So she turned off the television, tidied up, turned out the lights and checked the doors one last time. On her way to her own bedroom she decided to look in on Jamie, just to reassure herself that all was well.

Pushing the door open let in a swathe of light from the corridor. It fell across the bed, revealing Jamie lying uncovered, half curled on one side, and not alone.

There was something nestled close to him, in the crook of his arm; something grey and wet-looking, a featureless lump about the size of a loaf of bread; something like a gigantic slug pressed against his pyjama-covered chest and bare neck.

Horror might have frozen her—she couldn't have imagined coping with something like that in the garden or on the kitchen floor—but fear for her son propelled her forward. As she moved, the soft grey body rippled, turning, and it looked at Mary. For a face there was only a slightly flattened area with two round, black eyes and no mouth.

In her haste and terror Mary almost fell onto the bed. She caught hold of the thing and pulled it off her son, sobbing with revulsion.

She had expected it to be as cold and slimy as it looked, perhaps even insubstantial enough that the harsh touch of her hands could destroy it. In fact, it was warm and solid and surprisingly heavy. And it smelled like Jamie. Not like Jamie now, but like Jamie as a baby—that sweet, milky scent which made her melt inside. Like Jen's baby. Like every helpless, harmless newborn. She closed her eyes, remembering.

Mary pressed her face against the soft flesh and inhaled. No skin had ever been so deliciously, silkenly smooth. Her lips moved against it. She could never have enough of touching and kissing it; she wished she was a cat and could lick her baby clean a hundred times a day.

Responding, it nuzzled back, head butting at her blindly, and she unbuttoned her blouse. Her breasts felt sore and heavy with milk, and she longed for the relief of nursing.

Somewhere nearby a child was crying, a sound that rasped at her nerves and distracted her. Someone was tugging at her clothes, at her arm, and crying, "Mummy," until she had, finally, to open her eyes.

A little boy with a pale, tear-stained face gazed up at her. "Don't," he said. "Don't, Mummy."

She knew who he was—he was her son. But he seemed somehow threatening, and she wrapped her arms more tightly around the creature that she held.

"Go to bed," she said firmly.

He began to weep, loudly and helplessly.

But that irritated her more, because he wasn't helpless; she knew he wasn't helpless.

"Stop crying," she said. "Go to bed. You're all right." She pushed him away from her with her hip, not daring to let go. But as she looked down she glimpsed something grey and formless lying pressed between her breasts. For just a moment she had a brief, distracting vision of a face without a mouth, always hungry, never satisfied. She thought of an open grave, and she closed her eyes.

"He needs me," she said.

At last she felt complete. She would never be alone again.

Within the protective circle of her arms, the creature had begun to feed.

SNEAKERS

By
Marc Laidlaw

It's easy to exploit the fears of the young. Easier still because those fears never entirely leave us. We think we've outgrown them; we believe that maturity has taught us better; we hope that all those fears weren't presentments of the future. And when someone like Marc Laidlaw comes along and gives us a piece like "Sneakers," we know—even though we don't want to know—that maturity and experience and sophistication count for nothing when the sun goes down and there are sounds out there we cannot identify. And they don't mean a thing when a shadow climbs the wall without a light to cast it.

WHAT ARE YOU dreaming, kid?

Oh, don't squeeze your eyes, you can't shut me out. Rolling over won't help—not that blanket either. It might protect you from monsters but not from me.

Let me show you something. Got it right here. . . .

Well look at that. Is it your mom? Can't you see her plain as day? Yeah, well try moonlight. Cold and white, not like the sun, all washed out; a five-hundred-thousandth of daylight. It can't protect you.

She doesn't look healthy, kid. Her eyes are yellow, soft as cobwebs—touch them and they'll tear. Her skin is like that too, isn't it? No, Mom's not doing so good. Hair all falling out. Her teeth are swollen, black, and charred.

Yeah, something's wrong.

You don't look so good yourself, kiddo—

"Mom . . . ?"

What if she doesn't answer?

Louder this time: "Mom!"

Brent sat up, wide-awake now, sensing the shadows on the walls taking off like owls in flight. And that voice. He could still hear it. Were those rubber footsteps running away down the alley, a nightmare in tennis shoes taking off before it was caught? He could still see his mother's face, peeling, rotten, dead.

Why wouldn't she answer?

He knew it was only a dream, she just hadn't heard him calling, tied up in her own dreams. A dream like any other. Like last night, when he had seen his father burning up in an auto wreck, broken bones coming through the ends of his chopped-off arms; and the night before that, an old memory of torturing a puppy, leaving it in the street where it got hit and squashed and spilled. And the night before? Something bad, he knew, though he couldn't quite capture it.

Every night he had come awake at the worst moments. Alone, frightened of the dream's reality, of the hold it had on the dark corners of his waking world. If that voice had whispered when he was awake, he knew the walls might melt and bulge, breathing, as the blankets crawled up his face and snaked down his throat, suffocating him. That voice knew all his secrets, it whispered from a mouth filled with maggots, fanged with steel pins, a slashed and twisting tongue.

How did it know him?

Brent lay back and watched the dark ceiling until it began to spin, and he felt himself drifting back to sleep. Everything would be safe now, the voice had run away, he would have okay dreams. At least until tomorrow night.

It was not fear, the next night, that kept him from sleeping. Curiosity. He stuffed pillows beneath his covers to create an elongated shape, then he sat on the floor inside his closet with a flashlight. He had drunk a cup of instant coffee after dinner, to help him stay awake.

He heard the clock downstairs chiming eleven; sometime later the television went off and the shower splashed briefly in his parents' bathroom. Midnight passed. A car went through the alley, though its headlights could not reach him in the closet.

At one o'clock, a cat's meow.

The sneakers came at two. Footsteps in the alley.

Brent nudged the door ajar and looked out at the pane of his window. He could see windows in the opposite house, a drooping net of telephone wires, the eye of a distant streetlight.

Footsteps coming closer. It could be just anyone. He thought he heard the squeak of rubber; it was such a real sound. This couldn't be the whisperer.

Then they stopped outside, just below his window. Not a sound did they make, for five minutes, ten, until he knew that he had fallen asleep and dreamed their approach, was dreaming even now, listening to his heart beating and a dog barking far away, and then the voice said, You're awake.

Brent pressed back into the closet, holding his flashlight as if it were a crucifix or a stake in a vampire movie. He didn't have a hammer, though.

Why don't you come out of there?

He shook his head, wishing that he were sound asleep now, where these whispers could only touch his dreams, could only make him see things. Not awake, like this, where if he took that talk too seriously, he knew the walls could melt.

I'm still here, kiddo. What did you wait up for?

Holding his flashlight clenched.

A walk, maybe?

He opened the closet door and crept out, first toward the bed, then toward the door of his room. Into the hall.

That's right.

Was he really doing this? No. It was a dream after all, because the hall was different, it wasn't the hall in his house: the paintings were of places that didn't exist, changing color, blobs of grey and blue shifting as if worms had been mashed on the canvases, were still alive. That wasn't his parents' door swinging wide, with something coming to look out. He mustn't look. There was a cage across the door so he was safe, but he mustn't look.

Downstairs, though, it was his living room. Dreams were like that. Completely real one minute, nonsense the next.

Like Alice in Wonderland. Like the Brothers Grimm or *Time Bandits*.

Who's real, kid? Not me. Not you. I promise.

Don't wake the White King.

Don't pinch yourself unless you want to know who's dreaming.

Don't open the back door and look into the alley, because here I am.

He turned on his flashlight.

Right behind you.

The black bag—if it was a bag—came down fast over Brent's eyes and whipped shut around his neck, smothering. He got lifted up and thrown across a bony shoulder. The sneakers started squeaking as he heard the alley gravel scatter.

Say bye-bye to Mommy and Daddy.

He was dreaming, this wasn't real.

There, that's what I meant, whispered the voice.

THE MAN WHO WOULD NOT SHAKE HANDS

By

Stephen King

Stephen King shares with many of his fellow fantasists a love for the "club story." It's a grand tradition in the field, and just when we think it's been done to death, that no one among us has the nerve to try yet another one, someone does. It is, almost as much as his storytelling, a hallmark of King's that he's not afraid to try his hand at something old. He does it, not because it's quick or easy, but because there are some stories that simply cannot be told any other way, no matter which way you slice them. And there is, he knows, value in tradition. Stories like this have not survived this long because they're quaint; it's because they can, in a few pages, illuminate more than simply the tale. And what better place than a clubroom with a fireplace to cast a few not always friendly shadows?

WHEN DINNER WAS over, those of us who made up the club's winter attendance—old bachelors all—retired to the large second-floor lounge to drink brandy and swap tales.

It was a bitter, snowy night outside, and a huge blaze had been laid in the hearth. Havelock switched off the overhead light, bathing the old, high-vaulted room in maroon, leaping shadows. Conversation lagged, and we looked into the flames with varying degrees of introspection—I imagine we saw our respective pasts played out in the leaping flames. We were certainly all too old to have any romantic, daring plans for the future, and it was thoughts of romance that the night engendered—perhaps the dark romance of the doomed.

I suppose we all jumped a little when Tremain's scratchy, almost querulous voice broke the silence; I know that I did. Tremain was usually the most close-mouthed of men, offering little yet absorbing everything as he constantly lit and relit his briar pipe with his weathered and gnarled old hands. Yet, on the few occasions I had heard him recount a story I had gone home with plenty of food for thought—and the feeling that the man must have seen some passing queer things in his time, things that would cause more frequent speakers to fall silent and consider.

"I once saw a man murdered right in this room," said Tremain now, "although no juror would have convicted the killer. Yet, at the end of the business, he convicted himself—and served as his own executioner!"

There was a pause while he lit his pipe, a tall man whom time had overloaded with invisible sacks of age. Smoke drifted around his seamed face in a blue raft, and he shook the wooden match out with the slow, declamatory gestures of a man whose joints have been clotted with arthritis. He threw the stick over the fire screen and watched the flames char the wood. His sharp blue eyes brooded beneath their bushy salt-and-pepper brows. His nose was large and hooked, his lips thin and firm, his shoulders hunched almost to the back of his skull. In the dim and shifting light, I could almost fancy that it was not a man at all that sat there, but a fierce and introspective eagle.

"Don't tease us, Clint!" growled Fred Varney. "Bring it on!"

"No fear. Be patient, Freddy." And we all waited until Tremain had his pipe fired to his complete satisfaction. When a fine bed of coals had been laid in the large briar bowl, Tremain folded his large, slightly palsied hands over one knee and said:

"Very well, then. I'm seventy-nine and what I'm going to tell you occurred when I was twenty-five or thereabouts. It was 1919, at any rate, and I was just back from the Great War. My fiancée had died only five months earlier, of influenza. She was only twenty-two, and I fear I drank and played cards a great deal more than I should. She had been waiting for three years, you understand, and during that period I received a letter faithfully each week. Perhaps you may understand why I indulged myself so heavily. I had no religious beliefs, finding the general tenets and theories of Christianity rather comic in the trenches, and no family. And so I can say with truth that the good friends who saw me through my time of trial rarely left me. There were fifty-three of them—more than most people have!—fifty-two cards and a bottle of Cutty Sark whiskey. I had taken up residence in the very rooms I inhabit now, on Brennan Street. But they were much cheaper then, and there were considerably fewer medicine bottles and pills and nostrums cluttering the shelves. Yet I spent most of my time here, for there was almost always a poker game to be found.

"I was in the game room playing patience the first and only time I met Henry Brower. There were four of us who were ready to sit down and play; we only wanted a fifth to make the evening go. When Jason Davidson told me that George Oxley, our usual fifth, had broken his leg and was laid up in bed with his cast at the end of a damned pulley contraption, it seemed that we should have no game that night. I was contemplating the prospect of finishing the evening with nothing to take my mind off my own thoughts but patience and a mind-blotting quantity of whiskey when the fellow across the room said in a calm and pleasant voice, 'If you gentlemen have been speaking of poker, I would very much enjoy picking up a hand, if you have no particular objections.'

"He had been buried behind a copy of the *Times* until now, so that when I looked over I was seeing him for the first time. He was a young man with an old face, if you take my meaning. Some of the marks I saw on his face I had begun to see stamped on my own since the death of Rosalie. Some—but not all. Although the fellow could have been no older than twenty-eight from his hair and hands and manner of walking, his face seemed marked with experience and his eyes, which were very dark, seemed more than sad; they seemed almost haunted. He was quite good-looking, with a short, clipped moustache and darkish blond hair. He wore a good-looking brown suit and his top collar button had been loosened. 'My name is Henry Brower,' he said.

"Davidson immediately rushed across the room to shake hands; in fact, he acted as though he might actually snatch it out of Brower's lap. And an odd thing happened: Brower dropped his paper and held both hands up and out of reach. The expression on his face was one of horror.

"Davidson halted, quite confused, more bewildered than angry. He was only twenty-two himself—God, how young we all were in those days—and a bit of a puppy.

" 'Excuse me,' Brower said with complete gravity, 'but I never shake hands!'

"Davidson blinked. 'Never?' he said. 'How very peculiar. Why in the world not?' Well, I've told you that he was a bit of a puppy. Brower took it in the best possible way, with an open (yet rather troubled) smile.

" 'I've just come back from Bombay,' he said. 'It's a strange, crowded, filthy place, full of disease and pestilence. The vultures strut and preen on the very city walls by the thousands. I was there on a trade mission for two years, and I seem to have picked up a horror of our Western custom of handshaking. I know I'm foolish and impolite, and yet I cannot seem to bring myself to it. So if you would excuse me . . .'

" 'Only on one condition,' Davidson said with a smile.

" 'And that is?'

" 'That you draw up to the table and share a tumbler of

Clint's whiskey while I go for Baker and French and Jack Willden.'

"Brower smiled at him, nodded, and put his paper away. Davidson made a brash circled thumb-and-finger, and chased away to get the others. Brower and I drew up to the green-felted table, and when I offered him a drink he declined with thanks and ordered his own bottle. I suspected it might have something to do with his odd fetish and said nothing.

" 'It's good to be here,' Brower said reflectively. 'I've shunned any kind of companionship since I returned from my post. It's not good for a man to be alone, you know. I think that, even for the most self-sufficient of men, being isolated from the flow of humanity must be the worst form of torture!' He said this with a queer kind of emphasis, and I nodded. I had experienced a form of the loneliness of which he spoke, in the trenches and again after learning of Rosalie's death. I found myself warming to him in spite of his self-professed eccentricity.

" 'Bombay must have been a fascinating place,' I said.

" 'Fascinating . . . and terrible! There are things over there which are undreamed of in our philosophy. Their reaction to the motorcar is amusing: the children shrink from them, yet follow them for blocks. They find the airplane terrifying and incomprehensible. Of course, we Americans view these contraptions with complete equanimity—even complacency!—but I assure you that my reaction was exactly the same as theirs when I first observed a street-corner beggar swallow an entire packet of steel needles and then pull them, one by one, from the open sores at the end of his fingers. Yet here is something that natives of that part of the world take utterly for granted.

" 'Perhaps,' he added somberly, 'the two cultures were never intended to mix, but to keep their separate wonders to themselves. For an American such as you or I to swallow a packet of needles would result in a slow, horrible death. And as for the motorcar . . .' He trailed off, and a bleak, shadowed expression came to his face.

"I was about to speak when the boy appeared with Brower's bottle of scotch, and directly following him, Davidson with the others.

"Davidson prefaced the introductions by saying, 'I've told them all of your little fetish, Henry, so you needn't fear for a thing. This is Darrell Baker, the fearsome-looking fellow with the beard is Andrew French, and last but not least, Jack Willden. Clint you already know.'

"Brower smiled and nodded at all of them in lieu of shaking hands. Poker chips and three fresh decks of cards were produced, money was changed for markers, and the game began.

"We played for better than six hours, and I won perhaps two hundred dollars. Darrell Baker, who was not a particularly good player, lost about eight hundred (not that *he* would ever feel the pinch; his father owned three of the largest shoe factories in the state), and the rest had split Baker's losses with me about evenly. Davidson was a few dollars up and Brower a few down; yet for Brower to be near even was no mean feat, for he had had astoundingly bad cards for most of the evening. He was adroit at both the traditional five-card draw and the newer seven-card-stud variety of the game, and I thought that several times he had won money on cool bluffs that I myself would have hesitated to try.

"I did notice one thing: although he drank quite heavily—by the time French prepared to deal the last hand, he had polished off almost an entire bottle of scotch—his speech did not slur at all, his card-playing skill never faltered, and his odd fixation about the touching of hands never flagged. When he won a pot, he never touched it if someone had markers to change or if someone had 'gone light' and still had chips to contribute. Once, when Davidson placed his glass rather close to his elbow, Brower flinched back abruptly, almost spilling his own drink. Baker looked surprised, but Davidson passed it off with a remark.

"Jack Willden had commented a few moments earlier that he had a drive to Albany staring him in the face later that morning, and once more around the table would do for him. So the deal came to French, and he called seven-card stud.

"I can remember that final hand as clearly as my own name, although I should be pressed to describe what I had for lunch yesterday or whom I ate it with. The mysteries of age, I suppose, and yet I think that if any of you other fellows had been there, you might remember it as well.

"I was dealt two hearts down and one up. I can't speak for Willden or French, but young Davidson had the ace of hearts and Brower the ten of spades. Davidson bet two dollars—five was our limit—and the cards went round again. I drew a heart to make four, Brower drew a jack of spades to go with his ten. Davidson had caught a trey which did not seem to improve his hand, yet he threw three dollars into the pot. 'Last hand,' he said merrily. 'Drop it in, boys! There's a lady who would like to go out on the town with me tomorrow night!''

"I don't suppose I would have believed a fortune-teller if he had told me how often that remark, with its later ironic overtones, would come back to haunt me at odd moments, right down to this day.

"French dealt our third round of up cards. I got no help with my flush, but Baker, who was the big loser, paired up something—kings, I think. Brower had gotten a deuce of diamonds that did not seem to help anything. Baker bet the limit on his pair, and Davidson promptly raised him five. Everyone stayed in the game, and our last up card came round the table. I drew the king of hearts to fill up my flush, Baker drew a third to his pair, and Davidson got a second ace that fairly made his eyes sparkle. Brower got a queen of clubs, and for the life of me I couldn't see why he remained in. His cards looked as bad as any he had folded that night.

"The betting began to get a little steep. Baker bet five, Davidson raised five, Brower called. Jack Willden said, 'Somehow I don't think my pair is quite good enough,' and threw in his hand. I called the ten and raised another five. Baker called and raised again.

"Well, I needn't bore you with a raise-by-raise description. I'll only say that there was a three-raise limit per man, and Baker, Davidson, and I each took three raises of five dollars. Brower merely called each bet and raise, being careful to wait until all hands were clear of the pot before throwing his money in. And there was a lot of money—slightly better than two hundred dollars as French dealt us our last card face down.

"There was a pause as we all looked, although it meant nothing to me; I had my hand, and from what I could see on the table it was good. Baker threw in five, Davidson raised, and we waited to see what Brower would do. His face was slightly flushed with alcohol, he had removed his tie and unbuttoned a second shirt button, but he seemed quite calm. 'I call . . . and raise five,' he said.

"I blinked a little, for I had fully expected him to fold. Still, the cards I held told me I must play to win, and so I raised five. We played with no limit to the number of raises a player could make on the last card, and so the pot grew marvelously. I stopped first, being content simply to call in view of the full house I had become more and more sure someone must be holding. Baker stopped next, blinking warily from Davidson's pair of aces to Brower's mystifying junk hand. Baker was not the best of card players, but he was good enough to sense something in the wind.

"Between them, Davidson and Brower raised at least ten more times, perhaps more. Baker and I were carried along, unwilling to cast away our large investments. The four of us had run out of chips, and greenbacks now lay in a drift over the huge sprawl of markers.

" 'Well,' Davidson said, following Brower's latest raise, 'I believe I'll simply call. If you've been running a bluff, Henry, it's been a fine one. But I have you beaten and Jack's got a long trip ahead of him tomorrow.' And with that he put a five-dollar bill on top of the pile and said, 'I call.'

"I don't know about the others, but I felt a distinct sense of relief that had little to do with the large sum of money I had put into the pot. The game had been becoming cutthroat, and while Baker and I could afford to lose, if it came to that, Jase Davidson could not. He was currently at loose ends, living on a trust fund —not a large one—left him by his aunt. And Brower—how well could he stand the loss? Remember, gentlemen, that by this time there was better than a thousand dollars on the table."

Tremain paused here. His pipe had gone out.

"Well, what happened?" Varney leaned forward. "Don't tease us, Clint. You've got us all on the edge of our chairs. Push us off or settle us back in."

"Be patient," Tremain said, unperturbed. He produced another match, scratched it on the sole of his shoe, and puffed at his pipe. We waited intently, without speaking. Outside, the wind screeched and hooted around the eaves.

When the pipe was aglow and things seemed set to rights, Tremain continued:

"As you know, the rules of poker state that the man who has been called should show first. But Baker was too anxious to end the tension; he pulled out one of his three down cards and turned it over to show four kings.

" 'That does me,' I said. 'A flush.'

" 'I have you,' Davidson said to Baker, and showed two of his down cards. Two aces, to make four. 'Damn well played.' And he began to pull in the huge pot.

" 'Wait!' Brower said. He did not reach out and touch Davidson's hand, as most would have done, but his voice was enough. Davidson paused to look, and his mouth fell—actually *fell* open as if all the muscles there had turned to water. Brower had turned over *all three* of his down cards, to reveal a straight flush, from the eight to the queen. 'I believe this beats your aces?' Brower said politely.

"Davidson went red, then white. 'Yes,' he said slowly, as if discovering the fact for the first time. 'Yes, it does.'

"I would give a great deal to know Davidson's motivation for what came next. He knew of Brower's extreme aversion to being touched; the man had showed it in a hundred different ways that night. It may be that Davidson simply forgot it in his desire to show Brower (and all of us) that he could cut his losses and take even such a grave reversal in a sportsmanlike way. I've told you that he was something of a puppy, and such a gesture would probably be in his character. But puppies can also nip, when they are provoked. They aren't killers—a puppy won't go for the throat; but many a man has had his fingers stitched to pay for teasing a little dog too long with a slipper or a rubber bone. That would also be a part of Davidson's character, as I remember him.

"I would, as I say, give a great deal to know . . . but the results are all that matter, I suppose.

"When Davidson took his hands away from the pot, Brower reached over to rake it in. At that instant, Davidson's face lit up with a kind of ruddy good fellowship, and he plucked Brower's hand from the table and wrung it firmly. 'Brilliant playing, Henry, simply brilliant. I don't believe I've ever—'

"Brower cut him off with a high, womanish scream that was frightful in the deserted silence of the game room, and jerked away. Chips and currency cascaded every which way as the table tottered and nearly fell over.

"We were all immobilized with the sudden turn of events, and quite unable to move. Brower staggered away from the table, holding his hand out in front of him like a masculine Lady Macbeth. He was as white as a corpse, and the stark terror on his face is beyond my powers of description. I felt a bolt of horror go through me such as I had never experienced before or since, not even when they brought me the telegram with the news of Rosalie's death.

"Then he began to moan. It was a hollow, awful sound, cryptlike. I remember thinking, *Why, the man's quite insane;* and then he said the queerest thing: 'The switch . . . I've left the switch on in the motorcar . . . O God, I'm *sorry!*' And he fled up the stairs toward the main lobby.

"I was the first to come out of it. I lurched out of my chair and chased after him, leaving Baker and Willden and Davidson sitting around the huge pot of money Brower had won like graven Inca statues guarding a tribal treasure.

"The front door was still swinging to and fro, and when I dashed out into the street I saw Brower at once, standing on the edge of the sidewalk and looking vainly for a taxi. When he saw me he cringed so miserably that I could not help feeling pity intermixed with wonder.

" 'Here,' I said, 'wait! I'm sorry for what Davidson did and I'm sure he didn't mean it; and if you must go, you must. But you've left a great deal of money behind and it belongs to you and you shall have it.'

" 'I should never have come,' he groaned. 'But I was so desperate for any kind of human fellowship that I . . . I . . .' Without thinking, I reached out to touch him—the most elemental gesture of one human being to another when he is grief-stricken, but Brower shrank away from me and cried, 'Don't touch me! Isn't one enough? O God, why don't I just die?'

"His eye suddenly lit feverishly on a stray dog with slat-thin sides and mangy, chewed fur that was making its way up the other side of the deserted, early morning street. The cur's tongue hung out and it walked with a wary, three-legged limp. It was looking, I suppose, for garbage cans to tip over and forage in.

" 'That could be me over there,' he said reflectively, as if to himself. 'Shunned by everyone, forced to walk alone and venture out only after every other living thing is safe behind locked doors. Pariah dog!'

" 'Come now,' I said, a little sternly, for such talk smacked more than a little of the melodramatic. 'You've had some kind of nasty shock and obviously something has happened to put your nerves in an awful state, but nothing is quite as bad as that. Now if you will only come back inside and—'

" 'You don't believe me?' He cried, and his eyes were wild enough to make me acutely uneasy. There was no light of sanity left in them, and he reminded me of nothing so much as the battle-fatigued psychotics I had seen carried away in carts from the front lines: husks of men with awful, blank eyes like portholes to hell, mumbling and gibbering. 'Would you care to see how one outcast responds to another?' he asked me with a strange, twitching smile. 'Watch, then, and see what I've learned in strange ports of call!'

"And he suddenly raised his voice and said imperiously, 'Dog!'

"The dog raised its head, looked at him with wary, rolling eyes (one glittered with rabid wildness; the other was filmed by a cataract), and suddenly changed direction and came limpingly, reluctantly, across the street to where Brower stood.

"It did not want to come; that much was obvious. It whined and growled and tucked its mangy rope of a tail between its legs; but it came—a dog that surely would have shied from any living thing upon two legs and most upon four. It came right up to Brower's feet and then lay upon its belly, whining and crouching and shuddering. Its emaciated sides went in and out like bellows, and its good eye rolled horribly in its socket.

"Brower uttered a hideous, despairing laugh that I still hear in my dreams, and squatted by it. 'There,' he said. 'You see? It knows me as one of its kind . . . and knows what I bring it!' He reached for the dog's paw and the cur uttered a snarling, lugubrious howl and bared its teeth.

" 'Don't!' I cried sharply. 'He'll bite!'

"Brower took no notice. In the glow of the streetlight his face was livid, hideous, the eyes black holes burnt in parchment. 'Nonsense,' he crooned. 'Nonsense. I only want to shake hands with him . . . as your friend shook with me!' And suddenly he seized the dog's paw and shook it. The dog made a horrible howling noise, but made no move to bite him.

"Suddenly Brower stood up. His eyes seemed to have cleared somewhat, and except for his excessive pallor, he might have again been the man who had offered courteously to pick up a hand with us earlier the night before.

" 'I'm leaving now,' he said quietly. 'Please apologize to your friends and tell them I'm sorry to have acted the fool. Perhaps I'll have a chance to . . . redeem myself another time.'

" 'It's we who owe you the apology,' I said. 'And have you forgotten the money? It's better than a thousand dollars.'

" 'O yes! The money!' And his mouth curved in one of the bitterest smiles I have ever seen.

" 'If you will promise to wait right here, I'll bring it,' I said. 'Will you do that?'

" 'Yes,' he said. 'If you wish, I'll do that.' And he looked reflectively down at the dog whining at his feet. 'Perhaps he would like to come to my lodgings with me and have a square meal for once in his miserable life.' And the bitter smile reappeared.

"I left him then, before he could reconsider, and went downstairs. Someone—probably Jack Willden; he always had an orderly mind—had changed all the markers for greenbacks and had stacked the money neatly in the center of the green felt. None of them spoke to me as I gathered it up. Baker and Jack Willden were smoking wordlessly; Jason Davidson was hanging his head and looking at his feet. His face was a picture of misery and shame. I touched him on the shoulder as I went back to the stairs and he looked at me gratefully.

"And when I reached the street again, it was utterly deserted. Brower had gone. I stood there with a handful of greenbacks in each hand, looking vainly either way, but nothing moved. I called once, tentatively, in case he should be standing in the shadows someplace near, but there was no response. Then I happened to look down. The stray dog was still there, and he would never tip over another trash can. He was quite dead. The fleas and ticks were leaving his body in marching columns across the cement. I stepped back, revolted and yet also filled with an odd, dreamy terror. I had a premonition that I was not yet through with Henry Brower, and so I wasn't; but I never saw him again."

The fire in the grate had died to guttering flames and cold had begun to creep out of the shadows, but no one moved or spoke while Tremain lit his pipe again. He sighed and recrossed his legs, making the old joints crackle, and resumed.

"Needless to say, the others who had taken part in the game were unanimous in opinion: we must find Brower and give him his money. I suppose some would think we were insane to feel so, but that was a more honorable age. Davidson was in an awful funk when he left; I tried to draw him aside and offer him a good word or two, but he only shook his head and shuffled out. I let him go. Things would look different to him after a night's sleep, and we could go looking for Brower together, I thought. Willden was going out of town, and Baker had "social rounds" to make. It would be a good way for him to gain back a little self-respect, I thought.

"But when I went round to his apartment the next morning, I found him not yet up. I might have wakened him, but he was a young fellow and I decided to let him sleep the morning away while I spaded up a few elementary facts.

"I called here first, and talked to Kelley Earnshaw, who was on the door in those days. He said that Raymond Greer, a fellow I knew slightly, had spoken for Brower. Greer was with the city trade commission, and I immediately went to his office in the Trade Center Building that used to stand over on Market Street. I found him in, and he spoke to me immediately.

"When I told him what had happened the night before, his face became filled with a confusion of pity, gloom, and fear.

" 'Poor old Henry!' he exclaimed. 'I knew it was coming to this, but I never suspected it would arrive so quickly.'

" 'What?' I asked.

" 'His breakdown,' Greer said. 'It stems from his year in Bombay, and I suppose no one but Henry will ever know the whole story. But I'll tell you what I can.'

"The story that Greer unfolded to me in his office that day increased both my sympathy and understanding. Henry Brower, it appeared, had been unluckily involved in an authentic rarity of our times: a real tragedy. And, like all tragedy, it had stemmed from a fatal flaw—in Brower's case, forgetfulness.

"As a member of the trade commission group in Bombay, he had enjoyed the use of a motorcar, a relative rarity there. Greer said that Brower took an almost childish pleasure in driving it through the narrow streets and byways of the city, scaring up chickens in great, gabbling flocks and making the women and men fall on their knees to their heathen gods. He drove it everywhere, attracting great attention and huge followings of ragged children that followed him about but always hung back when he offered them a ride in the marvelous device, which he constantly did. The auto was a Model-A Ford with a truck body, and one of the earliest cars able to start not only by crank but by the touch of a button. I ask you to remember that.

"One day Brower took the auto far across the city to visit one of the high poobahs of that place concerning possible consignments of jute rope. He attracted his usual notice as the Ford machine growled and backfired through the streets, sounding like an artillery barrage in progress—and, of course, the children followed.

"Brower was to take dinner with the jute manufacturer, an affair of great ceremony and formality, and they were only halfway through the second course, seated on an open-air terrace above the teeming street below, when the familiar racketing, coughing roar of the car began below them, accompanied by screams and shrieks.

"One of the more adventurous boys—and the son of an obscure holy man—had crept into the cab of the auto, convinced that whatever dragon there was under the iron hood could not be roused without the white man behind the wheel. And Brower had left the switch on and the spark retarded.

"One can imagine the boy growing more daring before the eyes of his peers as he touched the mirror, waggled the wheel, and made mock tooting noises. Each time he thumbed his nose at the dragon under the hood, the awe in the faces of the others must have grown.

"His foot must have been pressed down on the clutch, perhaps for support, when he pushed the starter button. The engine was hot; it caught fire immediately. The boy, in his extreme terror, would have reacted by removing his foot from the clutch immediately, preparatory to jumping out. Had the car been older or in poorer condition, it would have stalled. But

Brower cared for it scrupulously, and it leaped forward in a series of bucking, roaring jerks. Brower was just in time to see this as he rushed from the jute manufacturer's house.

"The boy's fatal mistake must have been little more than an accident. Perhaps, in his flailings to get out, an elbow accidentally struck the throttle. Perhaps he pulled it with the panicky hope that this was how the white man choked the dragon. But it was his last mistake. The auto gained suicidal speed and charged down the crowded, roiling street, bumping over bundles and bales, crushing the wicker cages of the animal vendors, smashing a flower cart to splinters. It roared straight downhill toward the street's turning, leaped over the stone gutter of the house at the bottom, crashed into a stone wall and exploded in a ball of flame."

Tremain switched his briar from one side of his mouth to the other.

"This was all Greer could tell me, because it was all Brower had told him that made any sense. The rest was a kind of deranged harangue on the folly of two such disparate cultures ever mixing. The dead boy's father evidently confronted Brower before he was recalled and flung a slaughtered chicken at him. There was a curse. At this point, Greer gave me a smile which said that we were both men of the world, lit a cigarette, and remarked, 'There's always a curse when a thing of this sort happens. The miserable heathens must keep up appearances at all costs. It's their bread and butter.'

" 'What was the curse?' I wondered.

" 'I should have thought you would have guessed,' said Greer. 'The wallah told him that his black magic would answer Brower's, or some such drivel. Told him that a man who would practice sorcery on a small child should become a pariah, an outcast. Then he told Brower that any living thing he touched with his hands would die.'

" 'Brower believed it?'

"Greer sighed. 'Apparently he did. You must remember that the man had suffered a dreadful shock. And now, from what you tell me, his obsession is worsening rather than curing itself.'

" 'Can you tell me his address?'

"Greer hunted through his files, and finally came up with a listing. 'I don't guarantee that you'll find him there,' he said.

'People have been naturally reluctant to hire him, and I understand he hasn't a great deal of money.'

"I felt a pang of guilt at this, but said nothing. Greer struck
me as a little too pompous, a little too smug, to deserve what
little information I had on the miserable Henry Brower. But as I
rose, something prompted me to say, 'I saw Brower shake hands
with a mangy street cur last night. Fifteen minutes later the dog
was dead.'

" 'Really? How interesting.' He raised his eyebrows as if the
remark had no bearing on anything we had been discussing.

"I rose to take my leave and was about to shake Greer's
hand when the secretary opened his office door. 'Pardon me, but
are you Mr. Tremain?'

"I told her I was.

" 'A man named Baker has just called. He's asked you to
come to four seventeen Westfall Street immediately.'

"It gave me quite a nasty start, because that was Jason
Davidson's address. When I left Greer's office, he was just settling back with his pipe and *The Wall Street Journal.* I never saw
him again either, and don't count it any great loss. I was filled
with a very specific dread—the kind that will not quite crystallize
into an actual fear with a fixed object, because it is too awful, too
unbelievable to actually be considered."

Here Havelock interrupted Tremain's narrative: "Good
God, Clint! You're not going to tell us he was dead?"

"Quite dead," Tremain said. "I arrived almost simultaneously with the coroner. His death was listed as a coronary throm-
bosis. He was short of his twenty-third birthday by sixteen days.

"In the days that followed, I tried to tell myself that it was all
a nasty coincidence, best forgotten. I did not sleep well, even
with the help of my good friend Mr. Cutty Sark. I told myself
over and over that the thing to do was divide that night's last pot
between the three of us and forget that Henry Brower had ever
stepped into our lives. But I could not. I drew a cashier's check
for the sum instead, and went to the address that Greer had
given me, which was in the Seventies—a fashionable district in
those days.

"He was not there, quite as Greer had prophesied. His
forwarding address was in the Sixties, a slightly less well-off
neighborhood of respectable brownstones. He had left those

lodgings a full month before the poker game, and the new address was on Dock Street, an area of ramshackle tenements.

"The building superintendent, a scrawny man with a huge
black mastiff snarling at his knee, told me that Brower had
moved out on April third—the day after our game. I asked for a
forwarding address and he threw back his head and emitted a
screaming gobble that apparently served him in the place of
laughter.

" 'The only forradin' address they gives when they leave
here is Hell, boss. But sometimes they stops in the Mission
Districk on their way there.'

"The Mission District is the same now as it was then: the
home of the homeless, the last stop for the faceless men who
only care for another bottle of cheap wine or another shot of the
white powder that brings long dreams. I went there. It's near the
docks, and there are dozens of flophouses, a few benevolent
missions that take drunks in for the night, and hundreds of alleys
where a man might hide an old, louse-ridden mattress. The salt
stench was always in the air, and the screaming gulls whirled
endlessly over the gray and peeling warehouses that clustered at
land's end. I saw scores of men, all of them little more than
shells, eaten by drink and drugs. No names were known or used.
When a man has sunk to a final basement level, his liver rotted
by wood alcohol, his nose an open, festering sore from the
constant sniffing of cocaine and potash, his fingers destroyed by
frostbite, his teeth rotted to black stubs—a man no longer has a
use for a name. But I described Henry Brower to every man I
saw, with no response. Bartenders shook their heads and
shrugged. The others just looked at the ground and kept walking.

"I didn't find him that day, or the next, or the next. Two
weeks went by, and then I talked to a man who said a fellow like
that had been in Devarney's Rooms three nights before.

"I walked there; it was only two blocks from the area I had
been covering. The man at the desk was a scabrous ancient with
a peeling bald skull and rheumy, glittering eyes. Rooms were
advertised in the flyspecked window facing the piers at a dime a
night. I went through my description of Brower, and the old
fellow nodded all the way through it. When I had finished, he
said:

" 'I know him, young Mister. Know him well. But I can't quite recall . . . I think ever s'much better with a dollar in front of me.'

"I produced the dollar, and he made it disappear neat as a button, arthritis notwithstanding.

" 'He was here, young Mister, but he's gone.'

" 'Do you know where?'

" 'I can't quite recall,' the desk clerk said. 'I might, howsomever, with a dollar in front of me.'

"I produced a second bill, which he made disappear as neatly as he had the first. At this, something seemed to strike him as being deliciously funny, and a rasping, tubercular cough came out of his chest.

" 'You've had your amusement,' I said, 'and been well paid for it as well. Now, do you know where this man is?'

"The old man laughed gleefully again. 'Yes—Potter's Field is his new residence; eternity's the length of his lease; and he's got the Devil for a roommate. He must've died sometime yesterday morning, for when I found him at noon he was still warm and toasty. Sitting bolt upright by the winder, he was. I'd gone up to either have his dime or show him the door. As it turned out, the city showed him six feet of earth.' This caused another unpleasant outburst of senile glee.

" 'Was there anything unusual?' I asked, not quite daring to examine the import of my own question. 'Anything out of the ordinary?'

" 'I seem to recall somethin' . . . Let me see . . .'

"I produced a dollar to aid his memory, but this time it did not produce laughter, although it disappeared with the same speed.

" 'Yes, there was somethin' passin' odd about it,' the old man said. 'I've called the city hack for enough of them to know. Bleedin' Jesus, ain't I! I've found 'em hangin' from the hook on the door, found 'em dead in bed, found 'em out on the fire escape in January with a bottle between their knees frozen just as blue as the Atlantic. I even found one fella that drowned in the washstand, although that was over thirty years ago. But this fella —sittin' bolt-upright in his brown suit, just like some swell from uptown, with his hair all combed. Had hold of his right wrist with his left hand, he did. I've seen all kinds, but he's the only one I ever seen that died shakin' his own hand.'

"I left and walked down to the docks, and the old man's last words seemed to play over and over again in my brain like a phonograph record that has gotten stuck in one groove. *He's the only one I ever seen that died shakin' his own hand.*

"I walked out to the end of one of the piers, out to where the dirty gray water lapped the encrusted pilings. And then I ripped that cashier's check into a thousand pieces and threw it into the water." Tremain shifted and cleared his throat. The fire had burned down to reluctant embers, and cold was creeping into the deserted game room. The tables and chairs seemed spectral and unreal, like furnishings glimpsed in a dream where past and present merge.

"I only saw him once," Tremain said, "but once was wholly enough; I've never forgotten it. But it did serve to bring me out of my own time of mourning, for any man who can walk among his fellows is not wholly alone."

AT THE BUREAU

By
Steve Rasnic Tem

Steve Rasnic Tem has a poet's-eye view of the world and his love for precision of language. When he first began writing prose, his stories reflected his background by their length; when he grew more confident, so did his stories grow. But, although his stories have gotten longer, he has not abandoned his trademark—concise characterization and a view of the ordinary that forces his readers to realize that ordinary need not mean safe. Anything but. Especially when the ordinary comprises experiences virtually all of us have had at one time or another. Reading a Tem story means, simply, that you'll never stand in line, or see a hobo, or buy a box of Cheerios without wondering what the catch is, and if you're the one who's going to be caught.

I'VE BEEN THE administrator of these offices for twenty-five years now. I wish my employees were as steady. Most of them last only six months or so before they start complaining of boredom. It's next to impossible to find good help. But I've always been content here.

My wife doesn't understand how I could remain with the job this long. She says it's a dead end; I'm at the top of my pay scale, there'll be no further promotions, or increase in responsibilities. I've no place to go but down, she says. Her complaints about my job always lead to complaints about the marriage itself, of course. No children. Few friends. All the magic's gone, she says. But I've always been content.

When I started in the office we handled building permits. After a few years we were switched to peddling, parade, demolition licenses. Two years ago it was dog licenses. Last year they switched us to nothing but fishing permits.

Not too many people fish these days; the streams are too polluted. Last month I sold one permit. None the two months before. They plan to change our function again, I'm told, but a final decision apparently hasn't been made. I really don't care, as long as my offices continue to run smoothly.

A photograph of my wife taken the day of our marriage has sat on my desk the full twenty-five years, watching over me. At least she doesn't visit the office. I'm grateful for that.

Last week they reopened the offices next door. About time, I thought; the space had been vacant for five years. Ours was the last office still occupied in the old City Building. I was afraid maybe we too would be moved.

But I haven't been able as yet to determine just what it is exactly they do next door. They've a small staff, just one lone man at a telephone, I think. No one comes in or out of the office all day, until five, when he goes home.

I feel it's my business to find out what he does over there, and what it is he wants from me. A few days ago I looked up from my newspaper and saw a shadow on the frosted glass of our front door. Imagine my irritation when I rushed out into the hallway only to see his door just closing. I walked over there, intending to knock, and ask him what it was he wanted, but I saw his shadow within the office, bent over his desk. For some reason this stopped me, and I returned to my own office.

The next day the same thing happened. Then the day after that. I then refused to leave my desk. I wouldn't chase a shadow; he would not use me in such a fashion. I soon discovered that when I didn't go to the door, the shadow remained in my frosted glass all day long. He was standing outside my door all day long, every day.

Once there were two shadows. That brought me to my feet immediately. But when I jerked the door open I discovered two city janitors, sent to scrape off the words "Fish Permits" from my sign, "Bureau of Fish Permits." When I asked them what the sign was to be changed to, they told me they hadn't received those instructions yet. Typical, I thought; nor had I been told.

Of course, after the two janitors had left, the single shadow was back again. It was there until five.

The next morning I walked over to his office door. The lights were out; I was early. I had hoped that the sign painters had labeled his activity for me, but his sign had not yet been filled in. "Bureau Of . . ." There were a few black streaks where the paint had been scraped away years ago, bare fragments of the letters that I couldn't decipher.

I'm not a man given to emotion. But the next day I lost my temper. I saw the shadow before the office door and I exploded. I ordered him away from my door at the top of my voice. When three hours had passed and he still hadn't left, I began to weep. I pleaded with him. But he was still there.

The next day I moaned. I shouted obscenities. But he was always there.

Perhaps my wife is right; I'm not very decisive, I don't like to make waves. But it's been days. He is always there.

Today I discovered the key to another empty office adjacent to mine. It fits a door between the two offices. I can go from my office to this vacant office without being seen from the hallway. At last, I can catch this crazy man in the act.

I sit quietly at my desk, pretending to read the newspaper. He hasn't moved for hours, except to occasionally peer closer at the frosted glass in my door, simulating binoculars with his two hands to his eyes.

I take off my coat and put it on the back of my chair. A strategically placed flower pot will give the impression of my head. I crawl over to the door to the vacant office, open it as quietly as possible, and slip through.

Cobwebs trace the outlines of the furniture. Files are scattered everywhere, some of the papers beginning to mold. The remains of someone's lunch are drying on one desk. I have to wonder at the city's janitorial division.

Unaccountably, I worry over the grocery list my wife gave me, now lying on my desk. I wonder if I should go back after it. Why? It bothers me terribly, the list unattended, unguarded on my desk. But I must push on. I step over a scattered pile of newspapers by the main desk, and reach the doorway leading into the hall.

I leap through the doorway with one mighty swing, prepared to shout the rude man down, in the middle of his act.

The hall is empty.

I am suddenly tired. I walk slowly to the man's office door, the door to the other bureau. I stand waiting.

I can see his shadow through the office door. He sits at his desk, apparently reading a newspaper. I step closer, forming my hands into imaginary binoculars. I press against the glass, right below the phrase, "Bureau Of," lettered in bold, black characters.

He orders me away from his door. He weeps. He pleads. Now he is shouting obscenities.

I've been here for days.

MACKINTOSH WILLY

By
Ramsey Campbell

Ramsey Campbell is a laughing man with a grim pen and story. And as he grows, so grows the field. There isn't anything you can say about him, in fact, that hasn't been said already, and better—the true measure of a writer who is, indeed, a master of his talent. "Macintosh Willy," of all the stories he has had in Shadows, *is probably the most illustrative of what he can do—it's more than a shadow, more than a story that makes you wonder, makes you pause; it is in many ways a poignant piece as well, and proof that Campbell knows better than most that a story that's all gloss and polish has little chance of being more than . . . gloss and polish. The English teacher demands, "What does it mean?" The writer says, "You've got a brain and imagination. Use them."*

MACKINTOSH WILLY

By

Ramsey Campbell

TO START WITH, he wasn't called Mackintosh Willy. I never knew who gave him that name. Was it one of those nick-names that seem to proceed from a group subconscious, names recognized by every member of the group yet apparently origi-nated by none? One has to call one's fears something, if only to gain the illusion of control. Still, sometimes I wonder how much of his monstrousness we created. Wondering helps me not to ponder my responsibility for what happened at the end.

When I was ten I thought his name was written inside the shelter in the park. I saw it only from a distance; I wasn't one of those who made a game of braving the shelter. At ten I wasn't afraid to be timid—that came later, with adolescence.

Yet if you had walked past Newsham Park you might have wondered what there was to fear: why were children advancing, bold but wary, on the red-brick shelter by the twilit pool? Surely there could be no danger in the shallow shed, which might have held a couple of dozen bicycles. By now the fishermen and the model boats would have left the pool alone and still; lamps on the park road would have begun to dangle luminous tails in the water. The only sounds would be the whispering of children, the murmur of trees around the pool, perhaps a savage incompre-hensible muttering whose source you would be unable to locate. Only a game, you might reassure yourself.

And of course it was: a game to conquer fear. If you had waited long enough you might have heard shapeless movement in the shelter, and a snarling. You might have glimpsed him as he came scuttling lopsidedly out of the shelter, like an injured spider from its lair. In the gathering darkness, how much of your glimpse would you believe? The unnerving swiftness of the obese limping shape? The head which seemed to belong to another, far smaller, body, and which was almost invisible within a gray Balaclava cap, except for the small eyes which glared through the loose hole?

All of that made us hate him. We were too young for toler-
ance—and besides, he was intolerant of us. Ever since we could
remember he had been there, guarding his territory and his
bottle of red biddy. If anyone ventured too close he would start
muttering. Sometimes you could hear some of the words:
"Damn bastard prying interfering snooper . . . thieving bastard layabout . . . think you're clever, eh? . . . I'll give you
something clever . . ."

We never saw him until it was growing dark: that was what
made him into a monster. Perhaps during the day he joined his
cronies elsewhere—on the steps of ruined churches in the center of Liverpool, or lying on the grass in St. John's Gardens, or
crowding the benches opposite Edge Hill Public Library, whose
stopped clock no doubt helped their draining of time. But if
anything of this occurred to us, we dismissed it as irrelevant. He
was a creature of the dark.

Shouldn't this have meant that the first time I saw him in
daylight was the end? In fact, it was only the beginning.

It was a blazing day at the height of summer, my tenth. It
was too hot to think of games to while away my school holidays.
All I could do was walk errands for my parents, grumbling a
little.

They owned a small newsagent's on West Derby Road. That
day they were expecting promised copies of the *Tuebrook Bugle*.
Even when he disagreed with them, my father always supported
the independent newspapers—the *Bugle*, the *Liverpool Free Press*:
at least they hadn't been swallowed or destroyed by a monopoly.
The lateness of the *Bugle* worried him; had the paper given in?
He sent me to find out.

I ran across West Derby Road just as the traffic lights at the
top of the hill released a flood of cars. Only girls used the
pedestrian subway so far as I was concerned; besides, it was
flooded again. I strolled past the concrete police station into the
park, to take the long way round. It was too hot to go anywhere
quickly or even directly.

The park was crowded with games of football, parked
prams, sunbathers draped over the greens. Patients sat outside
the hospital on Orphan Drive beside the park. Around the lake,
fishermen sat by transistor radios and whipped the air with
hooks. Beyond the lake, model boats snarled across the shallow

circular pool. I stopped to watch their patterns on the water, and caught sight of an object in the shelter.

At first I thought it was an old gray sack that someone had dumped on the bench. Perhaps it held rubbish—sticks which gave parts of it an angular look. Then I saw that the sack was an indeterminate stained garment, which might have been a mackintosh or raincoat of some kind. What I had vaguely assumed to be an ancient shopping bag, resting next to the sack, displayed a ragged patch of flesh and the dull gleam of an eye.

Exposed to daylight, he looked even more dismaying: so huge and still, less stupefied than dormant. The presence of the boatmen with their remote-control boxes reassured me. I ambled past the allotments to Pringle Street, where a terraced house was the editorial office of the *Bugle*.

Our copies were on the way, said Chrissie Maher the editor, and insisted on making me a cup of tea. She seemed a little upset when, having gulped the tea, I hurried out into the sudden rain. Perhaps it was rude of me not to wait until the rain had stopped —but on this parched day I wanted to make the most of it, to bathe my face and my bare arms in the onslaught, gasping almost hysterically.

By the time I had passed the allotments, where cabbages rattled like toy machine-guns; the downpour was too heavy even for me. The park provided little cover; the trees let fall their own belated storms, miniature but drenching. The nearest shelter was by the pool, which had been abandoned to its web of ripples. I ran down the slippery tarmac hill, splashing through puddles, trying to blink away rain, hoping there would be room in the shelter.

There was plenty of room, both because the rain reached easily into the depths of the brick shed and because the shelter was not entirely empty. He lay as I had seen him, face upturned within the sodden Balaclava. Had the boatmen avoided looking closely at him? Raindrops struck his unblinking eyes and trickled over the patch of flesh.

I hadn't seen death before. I stood shivering and fascinated in the rain. I needn't be scared of him now. He'd stuffed himself into the gray coat until it split in several places; through the rents I glimpsed what might have been dark cloth or discolored hairy flesh. Above him, on the shelter, where graffiti which at last

I saw were not his name at all, but the names of three boys:
MACK TOSH WILLY. They were partly erased, which no doubt
was why one's mind tended to fill the gap.

I had to keep glancing at him. He grew more and more
difficult to ignore; his presence was intensifying. His shapeless-
ness, the rents in his coat, made me think of an old bag of
washing, decayed and moldy. His hand lurked in his sleeve;
beside it, amid a scattering of Coca-Cola caps, lay fragments of
the bottle whose contents had perhaps killed him. Rain roared
on the dull green roof of the shelter; his staring eyes glistened
and dripped. Suddenly I was frightened. I ran blindly home.

"There's someone dead in the park," I gasped. "The man
who chases everyone."

"Look at you!" my mother cried. "Do you want pneumonia? Just you get out of those wet things this instant!"

Eventually I had a chance to repeat my news. By this time
the rain had stopped. "Well, don't be telling us," my father said.
"Tell the police. They're just across the road."

Did he think I had exaggerated a drunk into a corpse? He
looked surprised when I hurried to the police station. But I
couldn't miss the chance to venture in there—I believed that
elder brothers of some of my schoolmates had been taken into
the station and hadn't come out for years.

Beside a window which might have belonged to a ticket
office was a bell which you rang to make the window's partition
slide back and display a policeman. He frowned down at me.
What was my name? What had I been doing in the park? Who
had I been with? When a second head appeared beside him he
said reluctantly, "He thinks someone's passed out in the park."

A blue-and-white Mini called for me at the police station,
like a taxi; on the roof a red sign said POLICE. People glanced in
at me as though I were on the way to prison. Perhaps I was:
suppose Mackintosh Willy had woken up and gone? How long a
sentence did you get for lying? False diamonds sparkled on the
grass and in the trees. I wished I'd persuaded my father to tell
the police.

As the car halted, I saw the gray bulk in the shelter. The
driver strode, stiff with dignity, to peer at it. "My God," I heard
him say in disgust.

Did he know Mackintosh Willy? Perhaps, but that wasn't the

point. "Look at this," he said to his colleague. "Ever see a corpse with pennies on the eyes? Just look at this, then. See what someone thought was a joke."

He looked shocked, sickened. He was blocking my view as he demanded, "Did you do this?"

His white-faced anger, and my incomprehension, made me speechless. But his colleague said, "It wouldn't be him. He wouldn't come and tell us afterwards, would he?"

As I tried to peer past them he said, "Go on home, now. Go on." His gentleness seemed threatening. Suddenly frightened, I ran home through the park.

For a while I avoided the shelter. I had no reason to go near, except on the way home from school. Sometimes I'd used to see schoolmates tormenting Mackintosh Willy; sometimes, at a distance, I had joined them. Now the shelter yawned emptily, baring its dim bench. The dark pool stirred, disturbing the green beards of the stone margin. My main reason for avoiding the park was that there was nobody with whom to go.

Living on a main road was the trouble. I belonged to none of the side streets, where they played football among parked cars or chased through the back alleys. I was never invited to street parties. I felt like an outsider, particularly when I had to pass the groups of teen-agers who sat on the railings above the pedestrian subway, lazily swinging their legs, waiting to pounce. I stayed at home, in the flat above the newsagent's, when I could, and read everything in the shop. But I grew frustrated: I did enough reading at school. All this was why I welcomed Mark. He could save me from my isolation.

Not that we became friends immediately. He was my parents' latest paper boy. For several days we examined each other warily. He was taller than me, which was intimidating, but seemed unsure how to arrange his lankiness. Eventually he said, "What're you reading?"

He sounded as though reading was a waste of time. "A book," I retorted.

At last, when I'd let him see that it was Mickey Spillane, he said, "Can I read it after you?"

"It isn't mine. It's the shop's."

"All right, so I'll buy it." He did so at once, paying my father. He was certainly wealthier than me. When my resentment of his gesture had cooled somewhat, I realized that he was letting me finish what was now his book. I dawdled over it to make him complain, but he never did. Perhaps he might be worth knowing.

My instinct was accurate: he proved to be generous—not only with money, though his father made plenty of that in home improvements, but also in introducing me to his friends. Quite soon I had my place in the tribe at the top of the pedestrian subway, though secretly I was glad that we never exchanged more than ritual insults with the other gangs. Perhaps the police station, looming in the background, restrained hostilities.

Mark was generous too with his ideas. Although Ben, a burly lad, was nominal leader of the gang, it was Mark who suggested most of our activities. Had he taken to delivering papers to save himself from boredom—or, as I wondered afterward, to distract himself from his thoughts? It was Mark who brought his skates so that we could brave the slope of the pedestrian subway, who let us ride his bicycle around the side streets, who found ways into derelict houses, who brought his transistor radio so that we could hear the first Beatles records as the traffic passed unheeding on West Derby Road. But was all this a means of distracting us from the park?

No doubt it was inevitable that Ben resented his supremacy. Perhaps he deduced, in his slow and stolid way, that Mark disliked the park. Certainly he hit upon the ideal method to challenge him.

It was a hot summer evening. By then I was thirteen. Dust and fumes drifted in the wakes of cars; wagons clattered repetitively across the railway bridge. We lolled about the pavement, kicking Coca-Cola caps. Suddenly Ben said, "I know something we can do."

We trooped after him, dodging an aggressive gang of taxis, toward the police station. He might have meant us to play some trick there; when he swaggered past, I'm sure everyone was relieved—everyone except Mark, for Ben was leading us onto Orphan Drive.

Heat shivered above the tarmac. Beside us in the park, twilight gathered beneath the trees, which stirred stealthily. The island in the lake creaked with ducks; swollen litter drifted sluggishly, or tried to climb the bank. I could sense Mark's nervousness. He had turned his radio louder; a misshapen Elvis Presley blundered out of the static, then sank back into incoherence as a neighboring wave band seeped into his voice. Why was Mark on edge? I could see only the dimming sky, trees on the far side of the lake diluted by haze, the gleam of bottle caps like eyes atop a floating mound of litter, the glittering of broken bottles in the lawns.

We passed the locked ice-cream kiosk. Ben was heading for the circular pool, whose margin was surrounded by a fluorescent orange tape tied between iron poles, a makeshift fence. I felt Mark's hesitation, as though he were a scared dog dragged by a lead. The lead was pride: he couldn't show fear, especially when none of us knew Ben's plan.

A new concrete path had been laid around the pool. "We'll write our names in that," Ben said.

The dark pool swayed, as though trying to douse reflected lights. Black clouds spread over the sky and loomed in the pool; the threat of a storm lurked behind us. The brick shelter was very dim, and looked cavernous. I strode to the orange fence, not wanting to be last, and poked the concrete with my toe. "We can't," I said; for some reason, I felt relieved. "It's set."

Someone had been there before us, before the concrete had hardened. Footprints led from the dark shelter toward us. As they advanced, they faded, no doubt because the concrete had been setting. They looked as though the man had suffered from a limp.

When I pointed them out, Mark flinched, for we heard the radio swing wide of comprehensibility. "What's up with you?" Ben demanded.

"Nothing."

"It's getting dark," I said, not as an answer but to coax everyone back toward the main road. But my remark inspired Ben; contempt grew in his eyes. "I know what it is," he said, gesturing at Mark. "This is where he used to be scared."

"Who was scared? I wasn't bloody scared."

"Not much you weren't. You didn't look it," Ben scoffed, and told us, "Old Willy used to chase him all round the pool. He used to hate him, did old Willy. Mark used to run away from him. I never. I wasn't scared."

"You watch who you're calling scared. If you'd seen what I did to that old bastard—"

Perhaps the movements around us silenced him. Our surroundings were crowded with dark shifting: the sky unfurled darkness, muddy shapes rushed at us in the pool, a shadow huddled restlessly in one corner of the shelter. But Ben wasn't impressed by the drooping boast. "Go on," he sneered. "You're scared now. Bet you wouldn't dare go in his shelter."

"Who wouldn't? You watch it, you!"

"Go on, then. Let's see you do it."

We must all have been aware of Mark's fear. His whole body was stiff as a puppet's. I was ready to intervene—to say, lying, that I thought the police were near—when he gave a shrug of despair and stepped forward. Climbing gingerly over the tape as though it were electrified, he advanced onto the concrete.

He strode toward the shelter. He had turned the radio full on; I could hear nothing else, only watch the shifting of dim shapes deep in the reflected sky, watch Mark stepping in the footprints for bravado. They swallowed his feet. He was nearly at the shelter when I saw him glance at the radio.

The song had slipped awry again; another wave band seeped in, a blurred muttering. I thought it must be Mark's infectious nervousness which made me hear it forming into words. "Come on, son. Let's have a look at you." But why shouldn't the words have been real, fragments of a radio play?

Mark was still walking, his gaze held by the radio. He seemed almost hypnotized; otherwise he would surely have flinched back from the huddled shadow which surged forward from the corner by the bench, even though it must have been the shadow of a cloud.

As his foot touched the shelter I called nervously, "Come on, Mark. Let's go and skate." I felt as though I'd saved him. But when he came hurrying back, he refused to look at me or at anyone else.

For the next few days he hardly spoke to me. Perhaps he thought of avoiding my parents' shop. Certainly he stayed away from the gang—which turned out to be all to the good, for Ben, robbed of Mark's ideas, could think only of shoplifting. They were soon caught, for they weren't very skillful. After that my father had doubts about Mark, but Mark had always been scrupulously honest in deliveries; after some reflection, my father kept him on. Eventually Mark began to talk to me again, though not about the park.

That was frustrating: I wanted to tell him how the shelter looked now. I still passed it on my way home, though from a different school. Someone had been scrawling on the shelter. That was hardly unusual—graffiti filled the pedestrian subway, and even claimed the ends of streets—but the words were odd, to say the least: like the scribbles on the walls of a psychotic's cell, or the gibberish of an invocation. DO THE BASTARD. BOTTLE UP HIS EYES. HOOK THEM OUT. PUSH HIS HEAD IN. Tangled amid them, like chewed bones, gleamed the eroded slashes of MACK TOSH WILLY.

I wasn't as frustrated by the conversational taboo as I might have been, for I'd met my first girl friend. Kim was her name; she lived in a flat on my block, and because of her parents' trade, seemed always to smell of fish and chips. She obviously looked up to me—for one thing, I'd begun to read for pleasure again, which few of her friends could be bothered attempting. She told me her secrets, which was a new experience for me, strange and rather exciting—as was being seen on West Derby Road with a girl on my arm, any girl. I was happy to ignore the jeers of Ben and cronies.

She loved the park. Often we strolled through, scattering charitable crumbs to ducks. Most of all she loved to watch the model yachts, when the snarling model motorboats left them alone to glide over the pool. I enjoyed watching too, while holding her warm, if rather clammy, hand. The breeze carried away her culinary scent. But I couldn't help noticing that the shelter now displayed screaming faces with red bursts for eyes. I have never seen drawings of violence on walls elsewhere.

My relationship with Kim was short-lived. Like most such teenage experiences, our parting was not romantic and poignant, if partings ever are, but harsh and hysterical. It happened one evening as we made our way to the fair which visited Newsham Park each summer.

Across the lake we could hear shrieks that mingled panic and delight as cars on metal poles swung girls into the air, and the blurred roaring of an ancient pop song, like the voice of an enormous radio. On the Ferris Wheel, colored lights sailed up, painting airborne faces. The twilight shone like a Christmas tree; the lights swam in the pool. That was why Kim said, "Let's sit and look first."

The only bench was in the shelter. Tangles of letters dripped trails of dried paint, like blood; mutilated faces shrieked soundlessly. Still, I thought I could bear the shelter. Sitting with Kim gave me the chance to touch her breasts, such as they were, through the collapsing deceptively large cups of her bra. To-night she smelled of newspapers, as though she had been wrapped in them for me to take out; she must have been serving at the counter. Nevertheless I kissed her, and ignored the fact that one corner of the shelter was dark as a spider's crevice.

But she had noticed; I felt her shrink away from the corner. Had she noticed more than I? Or was it her infectious wariness which made the dark beside us look more solid, about to shuffle toward us along the bench? I was uneasy, but the din and the lights of the fairground were reassuring. I determined to make the most of Kim's need for protection, but she pushed my hand away. "Don't," she said irritably, and made to stand up.

At that moment I heard a blurred voice. "Popeye," it mut-tered as if to itself; it sounded gleeful. "Popeye." Was it part of the fair? It might have been a stallholder's voice, distorted by the uproar, for it said, "I've got something for you."

The struggles of Kim's hand in mine excited me. "Let me go," she was wailing. Because I managed not to be afraid, I was more pleased than dismayed by her fear—and I was eager to let my imagination flourish, for it was better than reading a ghost story. I peered into the dark corner to see what horrors I could imagine.

Then Kim wrenched herself free and ran around the pool. Disappointed and angry, I pursued her. "Go away," she cried. "You're horrible. I never want to speak to you again." For a while I chased her along the dim paths, but once I began to plead I grew furious with myself. She wasn't worth the embar-rassment. I let her go, and returned to the fair, to wander desul-torily for a while. When I'd stayed long enough to prevent my parents from wondering why I was home early, I walked home.

I meant to sit in the shelter for a while, to see if anything happened, but someone was already there. I couldn't make out much about him, and didn't like to go closer. He must have been

wearing spectacles, for his eyes seemed perfectly circular and
gleamed like metal, not like eyes at all.

I quickly forgot that glimpse, for I discovered Kim hadn't
been exaggerating: she refused to speak to me. I stalked off to
buy fish and chips elsewhere. I decided that I hadn't liked her
anyway. My one lingering disappointment, I found glumly, was
that I had nobody with whom to go to the fairground. Eventually, when the fair and the school holidays were approaching
their end, I said to Mark, "Shall we go to the fair tonight?"

He hesitated, but didn't seem especially wary. "All right,"
he said with the indifference we were beginning to affect about
everything.

At sunset the horizon looked like a furnace, and that was
how the park felt. Couples rambled sluggishly along the paths;
panting dogs splashed in the lake. Between the trees the lights of
the fairground shimmered and twinkled, cheap multicolored
stars. As we passed the pool, I noticed that the air was quivering
above the footprints in the concrete, and looked darkened, perhaps by dust. Impulsively I said, "What did you do to old Willy?"

"Shut up." I'd never heard Mark so savage or withdrawn. "I
wish I hadn't done it."

I might have retorted to his rudeness, but instead I let
myself be captured by the fairground, by the glade of light amid
the balding rutted green. Couples and gangs roamed, ha-
rangued a shade halfheartedly by stallholders. Young children
hid their faces in pink candy floss. A siren thin as a Christmas
party hooter set the Dodgems running. Mark and I rode a tilting
bucket above the fuzzy clamor of music, the splashes of glaring
light, the cramped crowd. Secretly I felt a little sick, but the ride
seemed to help Mark regain his confidence. Shortly, as we were
playing a pinball machine with senile flippers, he said, "Look,
there's Lorna and what's-her-name."

It took me a while to be sure where he was pointing: at a tall,
bosomy girl, who probably looked several years older than she
was, and a girl of about my height and age, her small bright face
sketched with makeup. By this time I was following him eagerly.

The tall girl was Lorna; her friend's name was Carol. We
strolled for a while, picking our way over power cables, and
Carol and I began to like each other; her scent was sweet, if
rather overpowering. As the fair began to close, Mark easily won

trinkets at a shooting gallery and presented them to the girls, which helped us persuade them to meet us on Saturday night. By now Mark never looked toward the shelter—I think not from wariness but because it had ceased to worry him, at least for the moment. I glanced across, and could just distinguish someone pacing unevenly round the pool, as if impatient for a delayed meeting.

If Mark had noticed, would it have made any difference? Not in the long run, I try to believe. But however I rationalize, I know that some of the blame was mine.

We were to meet Lorna and Carol on our side of the park in order to take them to the Carlton cinema, nearby. We arrived late, having taken our time over sprucing ourselves; we didn't want to seem too eager to meet them. Beside the police station, at the entrance to the park, a triangular island of pavement, large enough to contain a spinney of trees, divided the road. The girls were meant to be waiting at the nearest point of the triangle. But the island was deserted except for the caged darkness beneath the trees.

We waited. Shop windows on West Derby Road glared fluorescent green. Behind us trees whispered, creaking. We kept glancing into the park, but the only figure I could distinguish on the dark paths was alone. Eventually, for something to do, we strolled desultorily around the island.

It was I who saw the message first, large letters scrawled on the corner nearest the park. Was it Lorna's or Carol's handwriting? It rather shocked me, for it looked semi-literate. But she must have had to use a stone as a pencil, which couldn't have helped; indeed, some letters had had to be dug out of the moss which coated stretches of the pavement. MARK SEE YOU AT SHELTER, the message said.

I felt him withdraw a little. "Which shelter?" he muttered.

"I expect they mean the one near the kiosk," I said, to reassure him.

We hurried along Orphan Drive. Above the lamps, patches of foliage shone harshly. Before we reached the pool we crossed the bridge, from which in daylight manna rained down to the ducks, and entered the park. The fair had gone into hibernation; the paths, and the mazes of tree trunks, were silent and very dark. Occasional dim movements made me think that we were passing the girls, but the figure that was wandering a nearby path looked far too bulky.

The shelter was at the edge of the main green, near the football pitch. Beyond the green, tower blocks loomed in glaring auras. Each of the four sides of the shelter was an alcove housing a bench. As we peered into each, jeers or curses challenged us.

"I know where they'll be," Mark said. "In the one by the bowling green. That's near where they live."

But we were closer to the shelter by the pool. Nevertheless I followed him onto the park road. As we turned toward the bowling green I glanced toward the pool, but the streetlamps dazzled me. I followed him along a narrow path between hedges to the green, and almost tripped over his ankles as he stopped short. The shelter was empty, alone with its view of the decaying Georgian houses on the far side of the bowling green.

To my surprise and annoyance, he still didn't head for the pool. Instead, we made for the disused bandstand hidden in a ring of bushes. Its only tune now was the clink of broken bricks. I was sure that the girls wouldn't have called it a shelter, and of course it was deserted. Obese dim bushes hemmed us in. "Come on," I said, "or we'll miss them. They must be by the pool."

"They won't be there," he said—stupidly, I thought.

Did I realize how nervous he suddenly was? Perhaps, but it only annoyed me. After all, how else could I meet Carol again? I didn't know her address. "Oh, all right," I scoffed, "if you want us to miss them."

I saw him stiffen. Perhaps my contempt hurt him more than Ben's had; for one thing, he was older. Before I knew what he intended he was striding toward the pool, so rapidly that I would have had to run to keep up with him—which, given the hostility that had flared between us, I refused to do. I strolled after him rather disdainfully. That was how I came to glimpse movement in one of the islands of dimness between the lamps of the park road. I glanced toward it and saw, several hundred yards away, the girls.

After a pause they responded to my waving—somewhat timidly, I thought. "There they are," I called to Mark. He must have been at the pool by now, but I had difficulty in glimpsing him beyond the glare of the lamps. I was beckoning the girls to hurry when I heard his radio blur into speech.

At first I was reminded of a sailor's parrot. "Aye, aye," it was croaking. The distorted voice sounded cracked, uneven, almost too old to speak. "You know what I mean, son?" it grated triumphantly. "Aye aye." I was growing uneasy, for my mind had begun to interpret the words as "Eye eye"—when suddenly, dreadfully, I realized Mark hadn't brought his radio.

There might be someone in the shelter with a radio. But I was terrified, I wasn't sure why. I ran toward the pool, calling, "Come on, Mark, they're here!" The lamps dazzled me; everything swayed with my running—which was why I couldn't be sure what I saw.

I know I saw Mark at the shelter. He stood just within, confronting darkness. Before I could discern whether anyone else was there, Mark staggered out blindly, hands covering his face, and collapsed into the pool.

Did he drag something with him? Certainly by the time I reached the margin of the light he appeared to be tangled in something, and to be struggling feebly. He was drifting, or being dragged, toward the center of the pool by a half-submerged heap of litter. At the end of the heap nearest Mark's face was a pale ragged patch in which gleamed two round objects— bottle caps? I could see all this because I was standing helpless, screaming at the girls, "Quick, for Christ's sake! He's drowning!" He was drowning, and I couldn't swim.

"Don't be stupid," I heard Lorna say. That enraged me so much that I turned from the pool. "What do you mean?" I cried. "What do you mean, you stupid bitch?"

"Oh, be like that," she said haughtily, and refused to say more. But Carol took pity on my hysteria, and explained, "It's only three feet deep. He'll never drown in there."

I wasn't sure that she knew what she was talking about, but that was no excuse for me not to try to rescue him. When I turned to the pool I gasped miserably, for he had vanished— sunk. I could only wade into the muddy water, which engulfed my legs and closed around my waist like ice, ponderously hindering me.

The floor of the pool was fattened with slimy litter. I slithered, terrified of losing my balance. Intuition urged me to head for the center of the pool. And it was there I found him, as my sluggish kick collided with his ribs.

When I tried to raise him, I discovered that he was pinned down. I had to grope blindly over him in the chill water, feeling how still he was. Something like a swollen cloth bag, very large, lay over his face. I couldn't bear to touch it again, for its contents felt soft and fat. Instead I seized Mark's ankles and managed at last to drag him free. Then I struggled toward the edge of the pool, heaving him by his shoulders, lifting his head above water. His weight was dismaying. Eventually the girls waded out to help me.

But we were too late. When we dumped him on the concrete, his face stayed agape with horror; water lay stagnant in his mouth. I could see nothing wrong with his eyes. Carol grew hysterical, and it was Lorna who ran to the hospital, perhaps in order to get away from the sight of him. I only made Carol worse by demanding why they hadn't waited for us at the shelter; I wanted to feel they were to blame. But she denied they had written the message, and grew more hysterical when I asked why they hadn't waited at the island. The question, or the memory, seemed to frighten her.

I never saw her again. The few newspapers that bothered to report Mark's death gave the verdict "by misadventure." The police took a dislike to me after I insisted that there might be somebody else in the pool, for the draining revealed nobody. At least, I thought, whatever was there had gone away. Perhaps I could take some credit for that, at least.

But perhaps I was too eager for reassurance. The last time I ventured near the shelter was years ago, one winter night on the way home from school. I had caught sight of a gleam in the depths of the shelter. As I went close, nervously watching both the shelter and the pool, I saw two disks glaring at me from the darkness beside the bench. They were Coca-Cola caps, not eyes at all, and it must have been a wind that set the pool slopping and sent the caps scuttling toward me. What frightened me most as I fled through the dark was that I wouldn't be able to see where I was running if, as I desperately wanted to, I put up my hands to protect my eyes.

FOLLOWING THE WAY

By
Alan Ryan

Alan Ryan is well aware that texture has as much to do with a story's ultimate success as anything else. His gift for the sardonic, and for the language, is more than evident in his novels, but seldom more expertly wielded than in his shorter works. A short story is, as any writer can tell you, infinitely more difficult to write than a novel; so when it's done right, it is a justifiable source of pride. And when others like it as well, there aren't words enough to describe the feeling of satisfaction and thanks. "Following the Way" follows an honored tradition—coming to grips, in some way, with the writer's past. To do it at this length is, believe me, far more painful, far more unsettling than taking three hundred pages or so. This is, I think, what gives this piece its texture, and its power.

TWENTY YEARS AGO, in my senior year at Regis High School—a very fine and very private Jesuit preparatory school on the upper east side of Manhattan—vocations to the priesthood were the order of the day. As I recall, twenty-five or so of the one hundred and fifty members of my graduating class entered the seminary, most of them, not surprisingly, choosing the Society of Jesus. Not all of them are priests today. (For that matter, not all of the Jesuits who taught me at Regis are priests today.) But vocations were in the air in that school, then half a century old already, and I suspect that, even today, few boys pass through their four years of study without at least considering, however briefly, the possibility of the priesthood. I did. I think we all did. We had behind us, though immediate in our thoughts, a long and impressive tradition. And before us we had some very powerful male role models: priests whom we respected as teachers and scholars, men who had devoted their lives to God, to an ideal, and to us, men who were clearly happy in their work, and who were, at the same time, interesting. The exceptions—sadly and most notably, the headmaster of the school during my four years there—only emphasized the union of humanity and spirituality in the others. For a boy with the inclination, the lure was hard to resist.

Those boys who were so inclined naturally sought and found willing advisers among the priests and scholastics on the faculty. But the rest of us—a spiritually silent majority—were not overlooked by the ever-thorough Jesuits—oh, no—and, sometime during the first half of our senior year, each of us was invited into the office of the Jesuit student counselor for a private chat. (I should stress that there was no coercion here. At Regis we were seldom "ordered" to do things; rather, we were "invited.") I remember that, in my case, the priest—a kind, charming, very learned, and often sickly man named William

Day—who will figure prominently in this chronicle of my vocation—engaged me in polite conversation for some minutes without raising the question that I knew very well was at hand. The idea was that, if I had been reluctant to acknowledge interest in the priesthood before now, this would be my golden opportunity. I said nothing, and the poor man—as he had no doubt done a hundred times in the previous two weeks—had to broach the subject himself. Had I, he wondered casually, ever considered becoming a priest? Yes, Father, I answered, I had. Ah ha, he said, nodding gently. You've thought about it? Oh, yes, I said. And what conclusion have you reached? It's not for me, I said. Oh, he said, I see, and stopped nodding. And why is that? he asked. Sex, I said. Apparently I said it with such conviction that he was thoroughly convinced of my thinking on the subject and ended the conversation there and then.

But times and people change.

I went from four years with the Jesuits at Regis High School to four years with the Jesuits at Fordham University. The Lincoln Center campus was then only in the planning stage, and I was always glad I missed it. (Leave it to the Jebbies, we joked in the cafeteria, to luck into expensive real estate and a good address.) Like my classmates who accompanied me from Regis, I was happy to exchange East 84th Street for the Rose Hill campus in the north Bronx. The Third Avenue El still rattled past the campus then and the traffic was heavy and noisy on Fordham Road and Webster Avenue, but the campus itself was an island, a green and peaceful island apart from the world outside, firmly anchored in bedrock by the pylons of handsome Keating Hall, its gray fieldstone blocks and clock tower so quintessentially representative of American college architecture that fashion photographers and TV crews filming commercials were often to be found on its steps. It was a lovely place: the green expanse of Edwards Parade, the rose-covered trellis in the square beside Dealy Hall, the musty antique air of Collins Theatre, the richly detailed chapel that sang aloud to God, all of it peaceful and lovely.

The Jesuit priests there were much the same as those at Regis—a little more worldly, perhaps, a little wittier, a little more acerbic, a little more eccentric, but, in all that mattered, essentially the same. I admired them, admired the wit and the learning and the grace with which they moved through the world, the casual self-assurance, the *flair*. My father had died when I was a child and there were no other male relatives close by, so, lacking a model at home, and primed by four years at Regis, I naturally turned toward these men and sought to emulate them. It was not a bad choice.

I spent most of my time in college—intellectually, at least, and psychologically, I suppose—as a young gentleman in a nineteenth-century novel might have spent his time at Oxford. I wrote some poetry, submitted some stories to *The New Yorker* and the *Atlantic Monthly*, and spent a great deal of time pursuing women. I read—in Greek—Plato and Aristotle and Euripides and, to lighten the mood, Sappho and the poets. (Xenophon and Homer had been amply translated at Regis.) Horace, Catullus, and Livy held sway in Latin class. Ronsard, Racine, Flaubert, Camus, Ionesco, were read in French; Dante in Italian; Chaucer in Middle English. I majored in French for three of the four years, studied linguistics and the gothic novel and early American literature and European history and "gentlemen's biology" and did some Russian on the side, in addition to the equivalent of full majors in philosophy and theology that were required of all undergraduates graduates at the time. Most of my teachers were Jesuit priests.

One afternoon in the spring of my junior year, I was coming down the steps of Keating Hall when I met that same Jesuit who had offered me my golden opportunity to confess a vocation at Regis. I had heard through the Jesuit grapevine that he'd been unwell and was now at Fordham, taking courses and regaining his strength. It was a warm day—not warm by summer standards, but warm for April after winter's chill—but the priest was buttoned up tight in a black raincoat that obviously still had its winter lining in place. I knew him to be in his early forties, but a casual observer might have guessed him ten years older than that. Looks can be deceiving.

"Hello, Father Day."

He slowed his already slow progress up the shallow steps of Keating and mumbled the half-smiled greeting teachers offer former students whom they no longer recall. But I had stopped where I was and apparently something compelled him to raise his eyes to my face, and when he did so, he halted too. Eyes momentarily alive, he scrutinized my face.

"Regis," he said.

I smiled and said yes.

"Three years ago?"

"Yes."

"Of course," he said. His eyes narrowed, and before I could remind him myself, he told me my name, as casually as if I'd last been with him yesterday.

These Jesuits, I thought.

I was about to ask him how he was, but he spoke before I could.

"Sex," he said, and we laughed together, remembering. "Most succinct answer I ever had," he said, "and a good one, a good one."

We stood on the steps, chatting easily and pleasantly. He seemed eager to know how I was doing at Fordham, what I was studying, who my teachers were, what plans I had for the future. In high school there had been much talk about "the Regis spirit," one manifestation of which was the invisible but substantial tie that links alumni whenever they encounter each other in the world in later years. It can make confidants of strangers, this common baggage of shared learning, assumptions, attitudes. Father Day, I knew, was a Regis man himself, and I was warmed by this tangible evidence of the Regis spirit in action. After a few minutes, he suggested that we go to the Campus Center for coffee—his treat—and since I had been heading there myself when we met, I readily agreed.

We sat for two hours, happily telling stories about mutual acquaintances at Regis, stories that often made us laugh as we compared quite different versions of the same events as seen from the sides of students and faculty. Then the conversation gradually drifted back to me and my life at Fordham and my future and I wasn't even surprised when Father Day inquired casually if I had ever thought again about the possibility of a priestly vocation. I had, of course. In a setting like that—spiritual, intellectual, psychological—one does. It was—and here I measure my words with extra caution—a not unattractive possibility. But, still, it was not attractive enough to win me over. My interest in that direction was based primarily on practical and pragmatic considerations, and definitely not on any "call from God to His service" that I had felt. He smiled understandingly when I told him I had thought about it but my conclusion remained the same.

"No harm in asking," he said, and maintained his slight smile.

I agreed.

"And no harm in thinking about it further," he said, the smile unchanged.

I agreed again.

"Will you?" he asked.

"Think about it further?"

"Yes."

"All right," I said, my smile matching his. "Couldn't hurt."

"Right," he said. "Couldn't hurt. Which is the punch line of an old vaudeville joke." He leaned back in his chair. "Ten minutes before he's going on stage, see, this famous comedian dies in his dressing room and the stage manager has to . . ."

We talked another twenty minutes or so before I had to leave for a late class. Even then, as I rose and gathered my books, it did not occur to me that Father Day, when we first met on the steps of Keating Hall, had been heading into the building and had changed his direction entirely to spend two and a half hours talking with me in the cafeteria.

When we parted at the front doors of the Campus Center, we assured each other how good it had been to talk and sincerely wished each other well. We both felt it, I was certain: the Regis spirit, made flesh.

It was three years later and I was twenty-four, a graduate student at UCLA, before I saw him again. Either because I had promised or because it was inevitable, I had indeed been thinking further about the priesthood.

Los Angeles, UCLA, Westwood Village, and Santa Monica (where I had a furnished apartment just off Wilshire Boulevard, about ten blocks from the beach), seem unlikely places to be thinking about withdrawing—to a degree, at least—from the world and devoting one's life to the service of God. I did, however, and although I was aware of the contrast between my own thinking and that of those around me, I continued to consider, if only in a pragmatic way, the possibility of becoming a priest.

The idea had much to recommend it. I was alone in the world now, my mother having died in an automobile accident in Switzerland during the summer following my graduation from Fordham. I went to California an orphan, lacking even brothers, sisters, aunts, uncles, cousins, to form a family. There was, in that regard, no one to take into account but myself. On the other hand, a religious community could readily fill the need for a structure and a sense of purpose and continuity in my life.

Furthermore, my mother's death had left me financially independent as well, thanks to her firm belief in large amounts of travel insurance, and my independence and self-sufficiency made me, I think it fair to say, rather more mature in my judgments than others in their early twenties, and rather more than I might have been myself in different circumstances.

As for the "sex" I had mentioned to Father Day half a dozen years earlier as an overriding factor in my negative decision, it had proved, as I grew older, less of a problem. To speak the truth, I was no virgin, and I think my needs and appetites at the time, during those years, were as normal as anyone else's, which may prove a mystery to laymen who think that priests and future priests are sometimes spared the hunger. They are not; I can vouch for it. But I did find, through necessity of time and circumstance, that the urge can be controlled, not through any secret vice, which is most often only a form of self-torture, serving merely to remind us of what we lack, but through a careful discipline of the will.

In a practical sense, my life was right for the priesthood. In a psychological sense—and a practical one—I was comfortable with the idea; I would teach in any case. In a spiritual sense, it meant nothing at all; I felt no infusion of God's spirit, no call to His service, and began truly to wonder if that last were really needed.

And then, once again, I ran into Father Day.

It was early May, the end of the academic year, the oral exams for my master's degree successfully completed, and nothing before me but a summer of travel. I had driven back to the campus to return some books and was sitting near the entrance to Royce Hall, enjoying the California sun, reading a newspaper, and listening to the noon carillon concert from the undergraduate library. I had nothing to do for the afternoon, nothing to do, in fact, for a week until my plane left for Europe.

I heard a voice speak my name and say, "Well, hello."

I raised my head and there was Father Day.

He looked much the same as he had three years before. In fact, we might almost have been back on the steps of Keating Hall at Fordham, amid the elms and the dogwood, rather than here beside the Spanish architecture of Royce Hall, amid the bird of paradise plants and the palms. He still looked older than his years—the same observation I had made at Fordham, the last time I'd seen him. And he was still somewhat overdressed. The sun was warm, with only a gentle breeze blowing across the campus, but Father Day wore black woolen slacks and a black turtleneck shirt under a battered gray tweed sport jacket. Even discarding the standard clerical garb, as Jesuits feel so free to do, he had not indulged in any great license. He looked, as he had before, like a man recovering from a long illness, which indeed he was. Thin blood, I thought, meant to thicken in the sun. I said it was good to see him and that he was looking well.

We satisfied each other's curiosity and quickly provided basic information. He told me he had been on campus the whole spring term. Nominally, he was here to take courses in comparative religion. Actually, he was in California for a rest to build up his strength. He spent part of his time helping out with light duties—mass and confession—in a parish church in North Hollywood, where he was living now. He was thinking of accepting a teaching position he'd been offered at Loyola University. I told him that, unless a decent teaching position came along for me, I planned to start work on my doctorate in the fall term and, in that case, would no doubt turn into the archetypal perennial student. He smiled a little ruefully and said that it wasn't such a bad life, and then we were laughing together.

And before I realized it, we were once again talking about me and I was, once again, admitting that thoughts of the priesthood were still in my mind. And, again before I realized it, we had strolled from the campus out to Westwood Village and had found a quiet booth in a bar near the Bruin Theatre.

"You keep turning up in my life," I said when we had beers in front of us.

"Twice," he said.

"Twice is almost a pattern."

"Almost," he agreed.

"Maybe you're haunting me."

"Maybe," he said and took a long drink from his glass. "Or maybe God is haunting you through me."

I thought of all the practical reasons I had for taking Holy Orders, and of all the spiritual reasons I lacked. "Not bloody likely," I said.

"Oh?" It's a Jesuit habit to say that; it offers nothing but elicits much.

So I told him, told him all the wide range of my thoughts on the subject, told him how, although I had not reached a definitive conclusion, the inevitable answer, born of inertia, seemed certainly negative. He listened patiently, his face without expression, until I finished.

"So, then, you feel no call to the priesthood, no compulsion. Is that right?"

I shook my head. "None."

"The call can come in any variety of ways," he said. "The path to God is not a straight one."

"And there are many doors in the castle, yes, I know, Father."

"Don't be impatient."

"Sorry."

"Maybe I'm your call."

I looked at him then and, for a long moment, and for the first time, seriously wondered if perhaps he was right, perhaps he was truly haunting me.

"The path to God is not a straight one," I said, and we both smiled and relaxed, the moment of tension gone.

"If we run into each other like this again," he said, "it will definitely be a pattern."

"Indeed," I said.

"Patterns like that must be considered."

"All right," I said, "if we run into each other like this again, I'll grant you it constitutes a pattern."

"And you'll consider it?"

"The pattern?"

"The priesthood."

"Ah," I said. And a moment later: "All right."

"Good," he said. "I think this calls for another beer."

It was not three years this time, but six weeks, before I saw him again.

I took a place in the queue for tickets to the Royal Ballet at Covent Garden and there he was just in front of me. Neither of us realized it until he'd bought his ticket and turned away from the counter. Suddenly there we were. I quickly purchased my own ticket and followed him outside into Floral Street. A minute later, we were established in the Nag's Head a few doors away, two steins of cold lager before us.

"You're following me," I said. "It's beginning to look slightly sinister."

"Is it?" Jesuits love to ask questions.

"A bit. What are you doing here? I thought you were in Los Angeles."

"I was. Actually, in a way, I still am. I took the faculty position at Loyola and then rather lucked into a university travel grant. It was none of my doing, actually."

"I'll bet," I said lightly.

"Actually," he replied.

He looked, it hardly seems necessary to mention, quite the same as before. The weather in London was cool and damp even in summer, but he was still overdressed. It seemed a permanent feature of his appearance. Apparently the California sun had not succeeded in thickening his blood. I didn't imagine the chilly air of London would accomplish much in that line, but the thought seemed not to have occurred to him.

"Did you follow me here?"

He shook his head, a gentle smile on his lips. "Impossible," he said.

That, of course, was the truth, and I knew it already. Apart from the obvious reasons, if he'd appeared just behind me in the queue, I might have doubted, but he had been there in front of me when I arrived, no question about it, and I did not.

"Then you're haunting me," I said.

"So it appears," he replied. He lifted his glass and in one

long drink finished off the beer. "I have to be on my way," he said. "Let's meet for dinner."

We agreed on seven-thirty at Romano Santi in Soho, and a moment later he was gone. I stayed longer in the Nag's Head, ordered another lager and drank it as slowly as the first. After that, I walked over to Charing Cross Road and spent the rest of the afternoon in the National Portrait Gallery. I barely saw the faces in the paintings. I could see only the face of Father Day, haunting me wherever I went.

During the meal, we limited the conversation to general topics. Afterward, he invited me back to his house for drinks. As we rode in the taxi the length of Oxford Street from Soho to Notting Hill Gate, and then pulled up in front of a lovely home in Kensington Park Road which he was renting for the summer, I wondered what sort of travel grant provided that sort of living allowance. These Jesuits, I thought. They're like some fine old family, ripe with old money.

"Shall we sit in the sitting room?" he said as he gestured me inside. "It seems only proper."

By that point, I was half expecting servants, but the house was empty. We'd had chianti with the meal and he suggested a lighter burgundy now. He poured the wine himself. When we were settled in easy chairs, he wasted no time.

"I think you have a vocation," he said. "Perhaps you feel no call, nothing of the sort you've thought all along you ought to feel, but a vocation nonetheless."

"Why?" I asked. I tried to sip my drink calmly.

"Why do you have a vocation or why do I say that?"

"Both." These Jesuits, I thought again. They never stop. It comes with long practice.

"Both," he repeated, in a tone that reminded me of the classroom. "As for the first, why you have a vocation, I couldn't begin to tell you. I almost hate to say it because it sounds entirely too pat, but it's not for us to question the ways of God."

"Just lucky, I guess." I said it as much to provoke him as for anything else.

"I guess," he said, and studied me curiously, as if wondering at the oddness of God's dealings among men. While he studied me, I had the opportunity to do the same with him, and realized that, at least for the moment, he no longer looked as sickly as he had before. He looked, rather, like a man with a definite job to do, a man with a clear purpose.

"As for the second point," he said, "why I'm telling you this, remember that Christ taught us to be fishers of men."

"The wise fisherman doesn't cast his net at random," I said.

"Nicely put."

"Why me, Father?"

"You're the type."

"*What* type?"

"Why, the priestly type, of course."

"That's a tautology."

"You'll make a splendid Jesuit," he laughed. "Here, let me top up your glass."

We sat together in silence for a while, with only the wine and our thoughts.

"Have you not noticed," he said at last, "that I seem to keep recurring in your life? Oh, never mind, of course you have." He leaned forward in his chair. "Answer a question. The Church will last forever, will it not? Until, would it be safe to say, the end of time, at least? Agreed?"

I nodded.

"Why?" he snapped. "How can that be?"

I hesitated, answers that had once seemed so clear—or at least so thoroughly assumed—now failing me.

"I've forgotten a lot of my catechism," I said to cover my hesitation.

"You haven't forgotten *this* catechism," he said. "These are answers you never knew. What is the central fact in your belief?"

"That Christ was the Son of God."

"And?"

"That He died on the cross. The sacrifice of the cross."

"The sacrifice of the cross," he repeated. "And what is the central practice, the central event, of your worship?"

"The Eucharist," I said. "The sacrifice of the mass."

"The sacrifice of the mass. Can you live forever?"

"Yes."

"How?"

"My soul is eternal. Listen, I—"

"You can live forever," he said.

I looked at him.

He said it again, more slowly. "You can live forever."

It was my turn. "How?" I said.

He raised his wine glass toward me. It reflected the light from a lamp and glowed ruby red.

"This is the cup of my blood," he said. "Take and drink of it." He was smiling.

I looked from his face to the glass of wine, held aloft as it might be held above the altar, offered to God and displayed to the faithful, with the words of consecration transforming it to blood.

Of course. At last. Here was the epiphany I'd sought, the obvious thing, long regarded but never seen till now: the realization, revelation, moment, insight, the ancient sacred secret of the Church. I was surprised only in that I felt no surprise.

I thought of all the priests I'd known, thought of all the times I'd been at mass and heard a priest murmur those words, transforming wine into the blood of Jesus Christ. Thought of the cross. Thought of the ages the Church, alone of all institutions, had lasted already. Thought of the ages ahead. And, again very practical, thought of myself standing before an altar, speaking those very same words, ordained with the power of transforming ordinary wine into sacred blood, an endless supply for an endless lifetime. I held my breath a moment, then looked back at Father Day.

"Do the others know?" I asked. "Or is it only the Jesuits?"

When he was done laughing, he caught his breath and said, "Oh, this is definitely not a perfect world. Yes, the others know." And he was off again into gales of laughter.

When he'd caught his breath a second time, he raised his glass in a silent toast. Then he set it down, rose from his chair, and came and stood beside me. He bent forward and gently— very gently—placed his lips against my neck.

This was all some years ago.

What follows is forever.

I am a priest and shall remain so. I rest eternal in the bosom of the Lord. I am following the way. I am satisfied.

THE STORM

By
David Morrell

David Morrell, a bestselling novelist, doesn't need to write short stories. They certainly don't pay any bills; they don't get reviewed in leading magazines and newspapers; and they slip away as quickly as the anthology or magazine does. Yet he persists in writing them, garnering praise and nominations for them, and putting the lie to the cliché that bestselling writers don't know how to write. Morrell has his Dark Fantasy, here and in his other work, but his foremost concern is with the people he puts through all the horror, the torture, which is as it should be. He was, until just recently, a teacher in a classroom. He will always be, until he retires, a teacher in print. One could do a lot worse than paying attention to "The Storm."

GAIL SAW IT first. She came from the Howard Johnson's toward the heat haze in the parking lot where our son Jeff and I were hefting luggage into our station wagon. Actually, Jeff supervised. He gave me his excited ten-year-old advice about the best place for this suitcase and that knapsack. Grinning at his sun-bleached hair and nut-brown freckled face, I told him I could never have done the job without him.

It was 8 A.M., Tuesday, August 2, but even that early, the thermometer outside our motel unit had risen to eighty-five. The humidity was thick and smothering. Just from my slight exertion with the luggage, I'd sweated through my shirt and jeans, wishing I'd thought to put on shorts. To the east, the sun blazed, white and swollen, the sky an oppressive, chalky blue. This'd be one day when the station wagon's costly air conditioning wouldn't be a luxury but a necessity.

My hands were sweat-slick as I shut the hatch. Jeff nodded, satisfied with my work, then grinned beyond me. Turning, I saw Gail coming toward us. When she left the brown parched grass, her brow creased as her sandals touched the heat-softened asphalt parking lot.

"All set?" she asked.

Her smooth white shorts and cool blue top emphasized her tan. She looked trim and lithe and wonderful. I'm not sure how she did it, but she seemed completely unaffected by the heat. Her hair was soft and golden. Her subtle trace of makeup made the day seem somehow cooler.

"Ready. Thanks to Jeff," I answered.

He grinned up proudly.

"Well, I paid the bill. I gave them back the key," Gail said. "Let's go." She paused. "Except—"

"What's wrong?"

"Those clouds." She pointed past my shoulder.

I turned—and frowned. In contrast with the blinding, chalky, eastern sky, I stared at numbing, pitch-black western clouds. They seethed on the far horizon, roiling, churning. Lightning flickered like a string of flashbulbs in the distance, the thunder so muted it rumbled hollowly.

"Now where the hell did *that* come from?" I said. "It wasn't there before I packed the car."

Gail squinted toward the thunderheads. "You think we should wait till it passes?"

"It isn't close." I shrugged.

"But it's coming fast." She bit her lip. "And it looks bad."

Jeff grabbed my hand. I glanced at his worried face.

"It's just a storm, son."

He surprised me, though. I'd misjudged what worried him.

"I want to go back home," he said. "I don't want to wait. I miss my friends. Please, can't we leave?"

I nodded. "I'm on your side. Two votes out of three, Gail. If you're really scared, though . . ."

"No. I . . ." Gail drew a breath and shook her head. "I'm being silly. It's just the thunder. You know how storms bother me." She ruffled Jeff's hair. "But I won't make us wait. I'm homesick, too."

We'd spent the past two weeks in Colorado, fishing, camping, touring ghost towns. The vacation had been perfect. But as eagerly as we'd gone, we were just as eager to be heading back. Last night, we'd stopped here in North Platte, a small, quiet town off Interstate 80, halfway through Nebraska. Now, today, we hoped we could reach home in Iowa by nightfall.

"Let's get moving then," I said. "It's probably a local storm. We'll drive ahead of it. We'll never see a drop of rain."

Gail tried to smile. "I hope."

Jeff hummed as we got in the station wagon. I steered toward the interstate, went up the eastbound ramp, and set the cruise control at fifty-five. Ahead, the morning sun glared through the windshield. After I tugged down the visors, I turned on the air conditioner, then the radio. The local weatherman said hot and hazy.

"Hear that?" I said. "He didn't mention a storm. No need to worry. Those are only heat clouds."

I was wrong. From time to time, I checked the rearview mirror, and the clouds loomed thicker, blacker, closer, seething toward us down the interstate. Ahead, the sun kept blazing fiercely though. Jeff wiped his sweaty face. I set the air conditioner for DESERT, but it didn't seem to help.

"Jeff, reach in the ice chest. Grab us each a Coke."

He grinned. But I suddenly felt uneasy, realizing too late he'd have to turn to open the chest in the rear compartment.

"Gosh," he murmured, staring back, awestruck.

"What's the matter?" Gail swung around before I could stop her. "Oh, my God," she said. "The clouds."

They were angry midnight chasing us. Lightning flashed. Thunder jolted.

"They still haven't reached us," I said. "If you want, I'll try outrunning them."

"Do *something*."

I switched off the cruise control and sped to sixty, then sixty-five. The strain of squinting toward the white-hot sky ahead of us gave me a piercing headache. I put on Polaroids.

But all at once, I didn't need them. Abruptly, the clouds caught up to us. The sky went totally black. We drove in roiling darkness.

"Seventy. I'm doing seventy," I said. "But the clouds are moving faster."

"Like a hurricane," Gail said. "That isn't possible. Not in Nebraska."

"I'm scared," Jeff said.

He wasn't the only one. Lightning blinded me, stabbing to the right and left of us. Thunder actually shook the car. Then the air became an eerie, dirty shade of green, and I started thinking about tornados.

"Find a place to stop!" Gail said.

But there wasn't one. The next town was Kearney, but we'd already passed the exit. I searched for a roadside park, but a sign said Rest Stop, Thirty Miles. I couldn't just pull off the highway. On the shoulder, if the rain obscured another driver's vision, we could all be hit and killed. No choice. I had to keep on driving.

"At least it isn't raining," I said.

As I did, the clouds unloaded. No preliminary sprinkle. Massive raindrops burst around us, gusting, roaring, pelting.

"I can't see!" I flicked the windshield wipers to their highest setting. They flapped in sharp, staccato, triple time. I peered through murky, undulating, windswept waves of water, struggling for a clear view of the highway.

I was going too fast. When I braked, the station wagon fishtailed. We skidded on the slippery pavement. I couldn't breathe. The tires gripped. I felt the jolt. Then the car was in control.

I slowed to forty, but the rain heaved with such force against the windshield, I still couldn't see.

"Pull your seatbelts tight," I told Gail and Jeff.

Though I never found that rest stop, I got lucky when a flash of lightning showed a sign, the exit for the next town, called Grand Island. Shaking from tension, I eased down the off-ramp. At the bottom, across from me, a Best Western motel was shrouded with rain. We left a wake through the flooded parking lot and stopped under the motel's canopy. My hands were stiff from clenching the steering wheel. My shoulders ached. My eyes felt swollen, raw.

Gail and Jeff got out, rain gusting under the canopy as they ran inside. I had to move the car to park it in the lot. I locked the doors, but though I sprinted, I was drenched and chilled when I reached the motel's entrance.

Inside, a small group stared past me toward the storm—two clerks, two waitresses, a cleaning lady. I shook.

"Mister, use this towel," the cleaning lady said. She took one from a pile on her cart.

I thanked her, wiping my dripping face and soggy hair.

"See any accidents?" a waitress asked.

With the towel around my neck I shook my head.

"A storm this sudden, there ought to be accidents," the waitress said as if doubting me.

I frowned when she said *sudden.* "You mean it's just starting here?"

A skinny clerk stepped past me to the window. "Not too long before you came. A minute maybe. I looked out this window, and the sky was bright. I knelt to tie my shoe. When I stood up, the clouds were here—as black as night. I don't know where they came from all of a sudden, but I never saw it rain so hard so fast."

"But—" I shivered, puzzled. "It hit us back near Kearney. We've been driving in it for an hour."

"You were on the edge of it, I guess," the clerk said, spellbound by the storm. "It followed you."

The second waitress laughed. "That's right. You brought it with you."

My wet clothes clung cold to me, but I felt a deeper chill.

"Looks like we've got other customers," the second clerk said, pointing out the window.

Other cars splashed through the torrent in the parking lot.

"Yeah, we'll be busy, that's for sure," the clerk said. He switched on the lobby's lights, but they didn't dispel the outside gloom.

The wind howled.

I glanced through the lobby. Gail and Jeff weren't around. "My wife and son," I said, concerned.

"They're in the restaurant," the second waitress said, smiling to reassure me. "Through that arch. They ordered coffee for you. Hot and strong."

"I need it. Thanks."

Dripping travelers stumbled in.

We waited an hour. Though the coffee was as hot as promised, it didn't warm me. In the air-conditioning, my soggy clothes stuck to the chilly chrome-and-plastic seat. A bone-deep, freezing numbness made me sneeze.

"You need dry clothes," Gail said. "You'll catch pneumonia."

I'd hoped the storm would stop before I went out for the clothes. But even in the restaurant, I felt the thunder rumble. I couldn't wait. My muscles cramped from shivering. "I'll get a suitcase," I said and stood.

"Dad, be careful." Jeff looked worried.

Smiling, I leaned down and kissed him. "Son, I promise."

Near the restaurant's exit, one waitress I'd talked to came over. "You want to hear a joke?"

I didn't, but I nodded politely.

"On the radio," she said. "The local weatherman. He claims it's hot and clear."

I shook my head, confused.

"The storm." She laughed. "He doesn't know it's raining. All his instruments, his radar and his charts, he hasn't brains enough to look outside and see what kind of day it is. If anything, the rain got worse." She laughed again. "The biggest joke—that dummy's my husband."

I remembered she'd been the waitress who joked that I'd brought the storm with me. Her sense of humor troubled me, but I laughed to be agreeable and went to the lobby.

It was crowded. More rain-drenched travelers pushed in, cursing the weather. They tugged at sour, dripping clothes and bunched before the motel's counter, wanting rooms.

I squeezed among them at the big glass door, squinting out at the wildest storm I'd ever seen. Above the exclamations of the crowd, I heard the shriek of the wind.

My hand reached for the door.

It hesitated. I really didn't want to go out.

The skinny desk clerk suddenly stood next to me. "It could be you're not interested," he said.

I frowned, surprised.

"We're renting rooms so fast we'll soon be all full up," he said. "But fair is fair. You got here first. I saved a room. In case you plan on staying."

"I appreciate it. But we're leaving soon."

"You'd better take another look."

I did. Lightning split a tree. The window shook from thunder.

A scalding bath, I thought. A sizzling steak. Warm blankets while my clothes get dry.

"I changed my mind. We'll take that room."

All night, thunder shook the building. Even with the drapes shut, I saw brilliant streaks of lightning. I slept fitfully, waking with a headache. Six A.M.; it still was raining.

On the radio the weatherman sounded puzzled. As the lightning's static garbled what he said, I learned that Grand Island was suffering the worst storm in its history. Streets were flooded, sewers blocked, basements overflowing. An emergency had been declared, the damage in the millions. But the cause of the storm seemed inexplicable. The weather pattern made no sense. The front was tiny, localized, and stationary. Half a mile outside Grand Island—north and south, east and west—the sky was cloudless.

That last statement was all I needed to know. We quickly dressed and went downstairs to eat. We checked out shortly after seven.

"Driving in this rain?" the desk clerk said. He had the tact to stop before he said, "You're crazy."

"Listen to the radio," I answered. "Half a mile away, the sky is clear."

I'd have stayed if it hadn't been for Gail. Her fear of storms —the constant lightning and thunder—made her frantic.

"Get me out of here," she said.

And so we went.

And almost didn't reach the interstate. The car was hubcap-deep in water. The distributor was damp. I nearly killed the battery before I got the engine started. The brakes were soaked. They failed as I reached the local road. Skidding, blinded, I swerved around the blur of an abandoned truck, missing the entrance to the interstate. Backing up, I barely saw the ditch in time. But finally, we headed up the ramp, rising above the flood, doing twenty down the highway.

Jeff was white-faced. I'd bought some comics for him, but he was too scared to read them.

"The odometer," I told him. "Watch the numbers. Half a mile, and we'll be out of this."

I counted tenths of a mile with him. "One, two, three . . ."

The storm grew darker, stronger.

"Four, five, six . . ."

The numbers felt like broken glass wedged in my throat.

"But Dad, we're half a mile away. The rain's not stopping."

"Just a little farther."

But instead of ending, it got worse. We had to stop in Lincoln. The next day, the storm persisted. We pressed on to Omaha. We could normally drive from Colorado to our home in Iowa City in two leisured days.

But *this* trip took us seven long, slow, agonizing days. We had to stop in Omaha and then Des Moines and towns whose names I'd never heard of. When we at last reached home, we felt so exhausted, so frightened we left our bags in the car and stumbled from the garage to bed.

The rain slashed against the windows. It drummed on the roof. I couldn't sleep. When I peered out, I saw a waterfall from the overflowing eaves trough. Lightning struck a hydro pole. I settled to my knees and recollected every prayer I'd ever learned and then invented stronger ones.

The hydro was fixed by morning. The phone still worked. Gail called a friend and asked the question. As she listened to the answer, I was startled by the way her face shrank and her eyes receded. Mumbling "Thanks," she set the phone down.

"It's been dry here," she said. "Then last night at eight the storm began."

"But that's when we arrived. My God, what's happening?"

"Coincidence." She frowned. "The storm front moved in our direction. We kept trying to escape. Instead, we only followed it."

The fridge was bare. I told Gail I'd get some food and warned Jeff not to go outside.

"But Dad, I want to see my friends."

"Watch television. Don't go out till the rain stops."

"It won't end."

I froze. "What makes you say that?"

"Not today it won't. The sky's too dark. The rain's too hard."

I nodded, relaxing. "Then call your friends. But don't go out."

When I opened the garage door, I watched the torrent. Eight days since I'd seen the sun. Damp clung on me. Gusts angled toward me.

I drove from the garage and was swallowed.

Gail looked overjoyed when I came back. "It stopped for forty minutes." She grinned with relief.

"But not where I was."

The nearest supermarket was half a mile away. Despite my umbrella and raincoat, I'd been drenched when I lurched through the hissing automatic door of the supermarket. Fighting to catch my breath, I'd fumbled with the inside-out umbrella and muttered to a clerk about the goddamn endless rain.

The clerk hadn't known what I meant. "But it started just a minute ago."

I shuddered, but not from the water dripping off me.

Gail heard me out and gaped. Her joy turned into frightened disbelief. "As soon as you came back, the storm began again."

The bottom fell out of my soggy grocery bag. I found a weather station on the radio. But the announcer's static-garbled voice sounded as bewildered as his counterparts through Nebraska.

His report was the same. The weather pattern made no sense. The front was tiny, localized, and stationary. Half a mile away, the sky was cloudless. In a small circumference, however, Iowa City was enduring its most savage storm on record. Downtown streets were . . .

I shut off the radio.

Thinking frantically, I told Gail I was going to my office at the university to see if I had mail. But my motive was quite different, and I hoped she wouldn't think of it.

She started to speak as Jeff came into the kitchen, interrupting us, his eyes bleak with cabin fever. "Drive me down to Freddie's, Dad?"

I didn't have the heart to tell him no.

At the school the parking lot was flecked with rain. There weren't any puddles, though. I live a mile away. I went into the English building and asked a secretary, though I knew what she'd tell me.

"No, Mr. Price. All morning it's been clear. The rain's just beginning."

In my office I phoned home.

"The rain stopped," Gail said. "You won't believe how beautiful the sky is, bright and sunny."

I stared from my office window toward a storm so black and ugly I barely saw the whitecaps on the angry churning river.

Fear coiled in my guts, then hissed and struck.

The pattern was always the same. No matter where I went, the storm went with me. When I left, the storm left as well. It got

worse. Nine days of it. Then ten. Eleven. Twelve. Our basement
flooded, as did all the other basements in the district. Streets
eroded. There were mudslides. Shingles blew away. Attics
leaked. Retaining walls fell over. Lightning struck the hydro
poles so often the food spoiled in our freezer. We lit candles. If
our stove hadn't used gas, we couldn't have cooked. As in Grand
Island, an emergency was declared, the damage so great it
couldn't be calculated.

What hurt the most was seeing the effect on Gail and Jeff.
The constant chilly damp gave them colds. I sneezed and snif-
fled too but didn't care about myself because Gail's spirits sank
the more it rained. Her eyes became dismal gray. She had no
energy. She put on sweaters and rubbed her listless, aching
arms.

Jeff went to bed much earlier than usual. He slept later. He
looked thin and pale.

And he had nightmares. As lightning cracked, his screams
woke us. Again the hydro wasn't working. We used flashlights as
we hurried to his room.

"Wake up, Jeff! You're only dreaming!"

"The Indian!" He moaned and rubbed his frightened eyes.
Thunder rumbled, making Gail jerk.

"What Indian?" I said.

"He warned you."

"Son, I don't know what—"

"In Colorado." Gail turned sharply, startling me with the
hollows the darkness cast on her cheeks. "The weather dancer."

"You mean that witch doctor?"

On our trip we'd stopped in a dingy desert town for gas and
seen a meager group of tourists studying a roadside Indian
display. A shack, trestles, beads and drums and belts. Skeptical,
I'd walked across. A scruffy Indian, at least a hundred, dressed in
threadbare faded vestments, had chanted gibberish while he
danced around a circle of rocks in the dust.

"What's going on?" I asked a woman aiming a camera.

"He's a medicine man. He's dancing to make it rain and end
the drought."

I scuffed the dust and glanced at the burning sky. My head
ached from the heat and the long oppressive drive. I'd seen too
many sleazy roadside stands, too many Indians ripping off tour-

ists, selling overpriced inauthentic artifacts. Imperfect tur-
quoise, shoddy silver. They'd turned their back on their heritage
and prostituted their traditions.

I didn't care how much they hated us for what we'd done to
them. What bothered me was behind their stoic faces they
laughed as they duped us.

Whiskey fumes wafted from the ancient Indian as he clumsily danced around the circle, chanting.

"Can he do it?" Jeff asked. "Can he make it rain?"

"It's a gimmick. Watch these tourists put money in that so-
called native bowl he bought at Sears."

They heard me, rapt faces suddenly suspicious.

The old man stopped performing. "Gimmick?" He glared.

"I didn't mean to speak so loud. I'm sorry if I ruined your
routine."

"I made that bowl myself."

"Of course you did."

He lurched across, the whiskey fumes stronger. "You don't
think my dance can make it rain?"

"I couldn't care less if you fool these tourists, but my son
should know the truth."

"You want convincing?"

"I said I was sorry."

"White men always say they're sorry."

Gail came over, glancing furtively around. Embarrassed,
she tugged at my sleeve. "The gas tank's full. Let's go."

I backed away.

"You'll see it rain! You'll pray it stops!" the old man
shouted.

Jeff looked terrified, and that made me angry. "Shut your
mouth! You scared my son!"

"He wonders if I can make it rain? Watch the sky! I dance for
you now! When the lightning strikes, remember me!"

We got in the car. "That crazy coot. Don't let him bother
you. The sun cooked his brain."

"All right, he threatened me. So what?" I said. "Gail, you
surely can't believe he sent this storm. By dancing? Think. It
isn't possible."

"Then tell me why it's happening."

"A hundred weather experts tried but can't explain it. How can I?"

"The storm's linked to you. It never leaves you."

"It's . . ."

I meant to say "coincidence" again, but the word had lost its meaning and smothered in my lungs. I studied Gail and Jeff, and in the glare of the flashlights I realized they blamed me. We were adversaries, both of them against me.

"The rain, Dad. Can't you make it stop?"

I cried when he whispered "Please."

Department of Meteorology. A full professor, one associate, and one assistant. But I'd met the full professor at a cocktail party several years ago. We sometimes met for tennis. On occasion, we had lunch together. I knew his office hours and braved the storm to go to see him.

Again the parking lot was speckled with increasing raindrops when I got there. I ran through raging wind and shook my raincoat in the lobby of his building. I'd phoned ahead. He was waiting.

Forty-five, freckled, almost bald. In damn fine shape though, as I knew from many tennis games I'd lost.

"The rain's back." He shook his head disgustedly.

"No explanation yet?"

"I'm supposed to be the expert. Your guess would be as good as mine. If this keeps up, I'll take to reading tea leaves."

"Maybe superstition's . . ." I wanted to say "the answer," but I couldn't force myself.

"What?" He leaned forward.

I rubbed my aching forehead. "What causes thunderstorms?"

He shrugged. "Two different fronts collide. One's hot and moist. The other's cold and dry. They bang together so hard they explode. The lightning and thunder are the blast. The rain's the fallout."

"But in *this* case?"

"That's the problem. We don't have two different fronts. Even if we did, the storm would move because of vacuums the winds create. But this storm stays right here. It only shifts a half a mile or so and then comes back. It's forcing us to reassess the rules."

"I don't know how to . . ." But I told him. Everything.

He frowned. "And you believe this?"

"I'm not sure. My wife and son do. Is it possible?"

He put some papers away. He poured two cups of coffee. He did everything but rearrange his bookshelves.

"Is it possible?" I said.

"If you repeat this, I'll deny it."

"How much crazier can—?"

"In the sixties, when I was in grad school, I went on a field trip to Mexico. The mountain valleys have such complicated weather patterns they're perfect for a dissertation. One place gets so much rain the villages are flooded. Ten miles away another valley gets no rain whatsoever. In one valley I studied, something had gone wrong. It normally had lots of rain. For seven years, though, it had been completely dry. The valley next to it, normally dry, was getting all the rain. No explanation. God knows, I worked hard to find one. People were forced to leave their homes and go where the rain was. In this seventh summer they stopped hoping the weather would behave the way it used to. They wanted to return to their valley, so they sent for special help. A weather dancer. He claimed to be a descendent of the Mayans. He arrived one day and paced the valley, praying to all the compass points. Where they intersected in the valley's middle, he arranged a wheel of stones. He put on vestments. He danced around the wheel. One day later it was raining, and the weather pattern went back to the way it used to be. I told myself he'd been lucky, that he'd somehow read the signs of nature and danced when he was positive it would rain, no matter if he danced or not. But I saw those clouds rush in, and they were strange. They didn't move till the streams were flowing and the wells were full. Coincidence? Special knowledge? Who can say? But it scares me when I think about what happened in that valley."

"Then the Indian I met could cause this storm?"

"Who knows? Look, I'm a scientist. I trust in facts. But sometimes 'superstition' is a word we use for science we don't understand."

"What happens if the storm continues, if it doesn't stop?"

"Whoever lives beneath it will have to move, or else they'll die."

"But what if it follows someone?"

"You really believe it would?"

"It does!"

He studied me. "You ever hear of a superstorm?"

Dismayed, I shook my head.

"On rare occasions, several storms will climb on top of each other. They can tower as high as seven miles."

I gaped.

"But this storm's already climbed that high. It's heading up to ten now. It'll soon tear houses from foundations. It'll level everything. A stationary half-mile-wide tornado."

"If I'm right, though, if the old man wants to punish me, I can't escape. Unless my wife and son are separate from me, they'll die, too."

"Assuming you're right. But I have to emphasize—there's no scientific reason to believe you are."

"I think I'm crazy."

Eliminate the probable, then the possible. What's left must be the explanation. Either Gail and Jeff would die, or they'd have to leave me. But I couldn't bear losing them.

I knew what I had to do. I struggled through the storm to get back home. Jeff was feverish. Gail kept coughing, glaring at me in accusation.

They argued when I told them, but in desperation they agreed.

"If what we think is true," I said, "once I'm gone, the storm'll stop. You'll see the sun again."

"But what about you? What'll happen?"

"I wish I knew. Pray for me."

We kissed and wept.

I packed the car. I left.

The interstate again, heading west. The storm, of course, went with me.

Iowa. Nebraska. I spent three insane, disastrous weeks getting to Colorado. Driving through rain-swept mountains was a nightmare. But I finally reached that dingy desert town. I found that sleazy roadside stand.

No trinkets, no beads. As the storm raged, turning dust to mud, I searched the town, begging for information. "That old Indian. The weather dancer."

"He took sick."

"Where is he?"

"How should I know? Try the reservation."

It was fifteen miles away. The road wound narrow, mucky. I passed rocks so hot they steamed from rain. The car slid, crashing in a ditch, resting on its drive shaft. I ran through lightning and thunder, drenched and moaning when I stumbled to the largest building on the reservation. It was low and wide, made from stone. I pounded on the door. A man in uniform opened it, the agent for the government.

I told him.

He stared suspiciously. Turning, he spoke a different language to some Indians in the office. They answered.

He nodded. "You must want him bad," he said, "if you came out here in this storm. You're almost out of time. The old man's dying."

In the reservation's hospital, the old man lay motionless under sheets, an I.V. in his arm. Shriveled, he looked like a dry, empty cornhusk. He slowly opened his eyes. They gleamed with recognition.

"I believe you now," I said. "Please, make the rain stop."

He breathed in pain.

"My wife and son believe. It isn't fair to make them suffer. Please." My voice rose. "I shouldn't have said what I did. I'm sorry. Make it stop."

The old man squirmed.

I sank to my knees, kissed his hand, and sobbed. "I know I don't deserve it. But I'm begging. I've learned my lesson. Stop the rain."

The old man studied me and slowly nodded. The doctor tried to restrain him, but the old man's strength was more than human. He crawled from bed. He chanted and danced.

The lightning and thunder worsened. Rain slashed the windows. The old man danced harder. The frenzy of the storm increased. Its strident fury soared. It reached a crescendo, hung there—and stopped.

The old man fell. Gasping, I ran to him and helped the doctor lift him in bed.

The doctor glared. "You almost killed him."

"He isn't dead?"

"No thanks to you."

But I said, "Thanks"—to the old man and the powers in the sky.

I left the hospital. The sun, a common sight I used to take for granted, overwhelmed me.

Four days later, back in Iowa, I got the call. The agent from the government. He thought I'd want to know. That morning, the old man had died.

I turned to Gail and Jeff. Their colds were gone. From warm sunny weeks while I was away, their skin was brown again. They seemed to have forgotten how the nightmare had nearly destroyed us, more than just our lives, our love. Indeed, they now were skeptical about the Indian and told me the rain would have stopped, no matter what I did.

But they hadn't been in the hospital to see him dance. They didn't understand.

I set the phone down and swallowed, sad. Stepping from our house—it rests on a hill—I peered in admiration toward the sky.

I turned and faltered.

To the west, a massive cloudbank approached, dark and thick and roiling. Wind began, bringing a chill.

September 12. The temperature was seventy-eight. It dropped to fifty, then thirty-two.

The rain had stopped. The old man did what I asked. But I hadn't counted on his sense of humor.

He stopped the rain, all right.

But I knew the snow would never end.

THE
SILENT CRADLE

By

Leigh Kennedy

Leigh Kennedy is, like Lisa Tuttle, a writer who exercises her talent well in more than one field. Her recent collection of eclectic stories drew praise from all over the country, and not a single review that I saw failed to mention "The Silent Cradle." With good reason—it has taken one of the fears basic to the human condition and made it visible, made it plausible. The reactions then are quite natural, and what more natural reaction is there than fear? And a certain instinctive knowledge that what "The Silent Cradle" proposes is not necessarily fiction.

FLORIE O'BANNON FIRST suspected that she had a third child about mid-October.

The room at the end of the hall had been relegated to storage, mostly furnishings that Vanessa and Tim had grown out of. Florie opened the door, expecting disarray. The old crib that both children had used stood against one wall, a yellow blanket draped across the rail, as if to keep the bright sun off the mattress.

There was the smell of soured milk.

Florie stood for a moment, rubbing her arms. Everything had been packed away into the closet except those things an infant would need. A clean, dry bottle stood on the bedside stand, which was filled with folded diapers.

She walked to the window, trying to remember when she had last come into this room. A month . . . two months? She remembered closing the door one evening in late summer to hide the clutter from company. She opened the window to air out the strange smell.

"Now, why did I come in here?" she asked aloud. She'd completely forgotten. Coming through the window, the breeze was cool. Too cool. Instinctively, she shut the window.

She walked back to the living room, filled with a nostalgia about newborns. Vanessa was now eight; Tim five. Both had been joys to her at all ages, and yet sometimes she thought the newborn's day most magical, like the first days of a love affair. She had only wanted to stare at their wrinkled faces and fondle their toes.

She sat down cross-legged in front of the bookcase where they kept the baby albums.

There was a new one. Like the others, it had a padded white binding. Tentatively, Florie pulled it out and opened it.

Born: October 11, 7:45 A.M., 8 lbs., 4 oz., 21½ inches. George Russell O'Bannon.

No picture.

Florie reread the entry absently, trying to imagine what sort of joke her husband might be playing on her. He'd often told her that she enjoyed children more than discretion allowed, that two would certainly be enough. No, this was not the kind of thing he would do. The smell of milk, the casualness of the blanket on the crib . . . These things were apart from his senses, too subtle for his kind of joke.

Florie closed the book and put it away. Momentarily, she felt guilty. Yes, she would love to have another child, and for a moment she could pretend. When Tim came storming in from the backyard, calling, "Mom! Mom!" she thought that she might shush him. The baby was sleeping.

But she said nothing. She would wait to see who would finally break down and laugh with her about the book and the room.

Florie paused in the hallway. Vanessa stood at the crib with her face wedged between the side rails. An empty bottle lay in the crib.

"What are you doing?" Florie asked.

Vanessa looked up, embarrassed. "Just looking," Vanessa said.

"At what?" Florie realized that she sounded sterner than necessary out of a sudden flutter of nerves.

"Just looking," Vanessa said.

Children have a way of looking obviously secretive without knowing the adult ability to follow such nuances. Florie smiled at her daughter's coyness, feeling a flush of recognition for her as an individual. "Did you put the bottle in there?" Florie saw a thin white residue on one side.

"No." Vanessa pulled away from the crib and started past Florie without looking up.

"What are you thinking about, little one?" Florie asked, brushing her hand over Vanessa's silky hair.

"Ms. Harley asked me how my new little brother was," she said in a tone of confession.

Florie knelt and looked Vanessa in the eye. "We don't have a baby," she said. "Did you come in here to look?"

Vanessa nodded. "I thought maybe he was a secret."

Florie laughed. "It would be hard to keep that a secret, wouldn't it? Besides, wouldn't I want you to help me with a new baby?"

Vanessa smiled briefly, then a question appeared in her eyes again. "But what was that sound I heard the other night?"

"What sound?" Florie was chilled.

"It sounded like a baby crying."

Florie paused to pull herself together. "It may have been some cats in the yard."

Vanessa gave her a doubtful look but said nothing. After Vanessa went to the kitchen, Florie looked back at the silent crib. She pulled the door to.

Quietly.

The meat loaf is too salty, she thought, shaking the ketchup bottle over her plate.

"I can't imagine how a rumor like this got started, Florie," her husband said. "Don't they remember the picnic this summer? You were in shorts and a halter top. Don't they remember Bridget's birthday party? That was only a few months ago."

"Don't know, Bert," she said.

The children looked from their plates to the parents, fork tines down in their mouths, eyes curious. Tim had a milk mustache.

Florie had hoped her husband could clear up the whole affair. But in the last few minutes he had proved to be as puzzled as herself. "Well, whoever it is, is close to us," she said. And she rose to fetch the baby book she'd found.

There were new entries: a month-old birth weight and a note of the six-weeks checkup. "Healthy!" it said. She found an envelope stuck between the pages. Her husband took the book and leafed through it, frowning. "What *is* this?" he said.

She laughed. And then she began to giggle, self-consciously, knowing her amusement wasn't shared yet. Tears wet her lashes.

"Florie?" Bert said. "What's going on? Are you trying to tell me something?"

She handed him the paper and envelope which she'd just read. "He's a cheap kid anyway."

Bert smiled vaguely as he read the receipt from the pediatrician. Paid. They both ignored Vanessa's persistent, "What? What is it?"

"Florie, it's a funny joke," Bert said flatly.

"But it's not mine," she said, smiling.

Tim looked back and forth between his parents with reserve. "Mom, can I have more potatoes?"

At Christmas, Florie put a teddy bear under the tree tagged "Russell." Vanessa wanted it, but Florie playfully viewed it as a sacrifice to the prank. Into the crib it went.

By Easter it was worn. Florie thought that the children played with it surreptitiously.

By summer there had been other notes and receipts in the baby book. Florie discovered that Russell cut his first tooth earlier than her other children.

By fall she found pieces of zwieback on the floor. Anything at the edge of counters was likely to be pulled off.

She said little about it to Bert. In the beginning they had figured it lightly. But now, guiltily, she took pleasure in the situation. She no longer thought about who was pulling the prank or why.

Now that Tim was in school whole days, she'd begun to go shopping, visiting with her mother and a few nonworking friends.

She would pause at the door, staring inward, uneasy about leaving.

Whenever she stood in the extra room she felt a kind of warm spookiness. As if someone were thinking of her strongly and lovingly. She set up her sewing machine in the room. Then a comfortable chair for reading by the window.

More and more often she found an excuse to spend time by the crib.

"Florie," Bert called.

She thought he was in their bedroom, but she found him in the spare room. He was holding a small wooden truck. Bert looked stern, as he did when he had to do or say something he didn't relish.

"What's the matter?" she asked.

"We can't afford for you to be buying things like this for foolishness."

"What!" She looked at the truck. Like the mobile that hung over the crib—little blue ducks and yellow fish swimming midair —like the rattlers and teething rings, it had just suddenly been there. Where it had come from, she had no idea.

"Listen, Florie," Bert said patiently. "I know you would like to have another baby."

"Wait a minute," she said. "I don't have anything to do with this."

Bert sighed. "Why can't you just talk to me about it anymore? What's happened to you?"

Florie shook her head. "You've got it all wrong. I haven't done any of this. Well, I bought the teddy," she said, picking it up out of the crib. She felt a pang, wondering if somehow she really was responsible for whatever was going on. But how? She knew in her mind that soon a friend, her mother, or even Vanessa would own up to it.

"We can't afford this joke anymore," Bert said.

Florie knew that things were tight. Their car had thrown a rod a few months ago and they'd unexpectedly been forced to buy a new one. They'd had to have the plumber out a few times. School clothes were expensive this year, and Christmas was on the way. Prices were going up.

"Bert, believe me," Florie said.

He studied her for a long while. "I don't know what to say. I think we need for you to go back to work, even just half days."

"Bert . . ."

He put his arms around her, teddy and all. "I think it will be good for you. I suspect you're bored."

Stunned, Florie said nothing. Perhaps he was right.

She sat at her desk and squirmed. As if she itched, she longed to scratch, but she couldn't localize it. She simply was uncomfortable.

She pleaded illness and rushed home. In the bathroom a tub of cloudy tepid water stood, and a box of baking soda sat on the floor. Florie looked in the spare room. It was hot and stuffy, but she didn't dare open the window.

She lay on her bed, feeling safely at home, but worried.

Worried about what, she didn't know. By now she was used to finding unexplained things. She dozed.

As she slept, she seemed to be aware of her sleeping self—knowing where she was and why. And in that awareness she held close to her the shape of a toddler wrapped in a blanket. The child was restless, his fever radiated through the blanket to her.

"It's all right, Russell," she said in her sleep. She comforted him just as she had Vanessa and Tim, thanking God that she had already had chicken pox.

She was furious the day she came home and the kitchen was ravaged. Pots and pans, dishes and tin cans had been pulled out of the cupboards. A stick of butter hadn't yet melted enough to hide the teethmarks.

She yelled at Russell from the living room, to be sure that he heard her from wherever he was. But he was too young to understand yet, for the situation didn't improve until the receipts from the day-care center began arriving.

"Mom," Tim said, "Russell broke the crib."

Florie looked at Bert.

Bert stood. "Now, look, young man. That's going too far. You can't blame things on an imaginary being. What did you do?"

"I didn't do it," Tim said with the certainty of a clear conscience. "I heard a noise a while ago and now the crib's busted. Come and look."

Florie saw that Bert believed Tim's honesty but not the story. They followed him into Russell's room. The slats of the crib had been smashed outward.

"The bed's too small for him now," she said calmly.

"That's stupid," Bert said. "I think . . ." He shrugged. "This whole thing is stupid." And he stalked away.

They bought Timothy a new bed, had the crib hauled away, and sent Tim's old bed into the extra room. Florie went to a secondhand store and bought a bedspread for the old bed. She cleaned out the baby things and had a garage sale. All of Tim's old clothes went into Russell's dresser.

Sometimes she found them in the laundry hamper.

Tim spent time playing in Russell's room. Bert noticed it, explaining that Tim probably missed his old bed. (He never did see the need for the new one.) "Besides," he said, "we don't yell at him when he bounces on it anymore."

Vanessa found blood on the back porch one day. A few days later, a receipt came for nine stitches at the clinic.

Bert raged. "I've had enough of this!"

He called Dr. Thorn. After explaining the four-year-old prank to the pediatrician, whom Florie had always been reluctant to discuss it with, the doctor only said, "I don't know what to tell you. According to our records, Russell has always been seen by my partner, who only works on Wednesday afternoons."

"What the *hell* is going on around here?"

"I don't know, Mr. O'Bannon. Maybe you should hold a séance."

Florie heard Bert say something she thought improper and impolite. Embarrassed, she took her children to another pediatrician the next time.

One day the kitchen window was shattered by a baseball. Vanessa and Tim were not home. Florie saw no one in the yard.

Everyone disavowed responsibility for the leftovers being set out for a persistent stray dog. Eventually the dog won his way into the family. He never answered to the name they gave him and always slept on Russell's bed. Much later he got a silver tag and they found out that his name was Claude. Claude was a quiet dog; he always seemed to be waiting and listening.

Vanessa told Florie matter-of-factly that Russell would sometimes come into her room at night and hold her hand. In fact, Vanessa seemed to be his favorite. She found unexplained treats in her room—sometimes candy, sometimes a new comic book. On her sixteenth birthday she received a record. It was Vanessa who'd started long ago having a birthday celebration every October for her youngest brother.

When Russell started school, Tim tried dutifully (at Florie's instruction) to check on Russell in class. Tim was too bashful to speak to the teachers. He peeked in the windows, but saw no one he could positively identify as his brother. So Florie tried herself. He was always either on a field trip or out of the room working on a special project.

Florie found report cards in his room, along with the base-balls, comic books, jars of grasshoppers, magnifying glasses, bits of junk picked up along the walk from school to home. He was a good student, though "Shy and hard to communicate with ver-bally," as his second-grade teacher put it.

He left his parents cards on the dinner table every holiday.

Russell was treated like a fact by the children. What to them had been a bit of amusement their parents had thought up turned into a person that was always not quite there yet, or had just left. Russell's doings were reported at the dinner table.

Florie had forgotten that it was a joke. When people asked her about her children, she would say, "I have three . . ." and hesitate, or she would say she had two and be just as uncertain.

Bert didn't see it their way. The evening before Russell's eighth birthday, Bert stopped Vanessa midsentence as she talked about the cake she was going to bake.

"Enough!" he shouted.

Florie, Vanessa, and Tim stared, each shaken.

"There is no Russell, there never has been a Russell, and there never will be," Bert said, leaning toward Vanessa. "You," he said to Florie, "have two children. *Two*, Florie. This one"—he pointed to Vanessa, then to Tim—"and this one. I have no son named Russell."

"Aw, Dad," Tim said, as if this were an old argument.

"Show me," Bert said, pounding his fist on the table. "Show me!"

"Vanessa, why don't you and Tim clean up the kitchen," Florie said. She stood and held out her hand to Bert. "Let's take a walk."

Bert sat at the table until Florie brought him his jacket. He put it on and walked out of the house ahead of her. They strolled silently for a time. Florie took his hand.

Bert kicked at some leaves. "You take it for granted. I just can't. Eight years, Florie. I just can't handle it anymore. It's not funny, and yet I can't take it seriously. You can't really believe all this, can you?"

Florie shrugged. "You remember what I told you about my family? When we were growing up—the door would blow open and we would say, 'It's our ghost.'' And we said our ghost took things, broke things, did this or that. It just got to be something we said. I don't know, love. Maybe it's the same one, only now he's got a name and a place."

Bert looked at her. "Well, is he real or not?"

Florie paused.

"Is he real?" Bert insisted.

"I . . . don't know."

He shrugged.

After a silence, he said, "You know, I've been thinking about something old Dr. Thorn said years ago. Something we should have done sooner."

"What's that?"

Bert laughed a little. He hesitated long enough to let Florie know that he was embarrassed. "Maybe we should have a sé-ance."

They both laughed. Florie took his arm and felt good that they were laughing together. "Are you serious?" she asked, still giggling.

"Oh, I don't know, love. It couldn't hurt."

They heard a rustle of dried leaves in the yard they passed. Both looked, but neither saw anything. Bert frowned as he swung Florie back toward the house.

Then they laughed again as they ran.

If there could be a medium with respectability, references, and an honest, no hocus-pocus air, it was Barbara. She was young, slim, blond, and matter-of-fact. Florie had found her through a psychiatrist's reference and checked her out thoroughly.

First she listened with a pen and notepad to the whole story. She looked at Russell's room, handled some of his possessions, looked at his handwriting carefully. Florie felt odd watching those long fingers touching his things, as if that made Russell more real. Quietly, Barbara asked what kind of person they thought he was, and everyone agreed that he was a good kind of kid—no one had ever complained. He'd only done things that any boy would do. Florie chuckled about the worms in the kitchen sink (in retrospect.)

Barbara sat and explained to all of them that séances didn't often work. Rarely, in fact. But there seemed to be a strong possibility of a ghost. Why, she didn't know, unless there was a strong desire for this addition to the family that had attracted Russell.

Florie looked at her hands, guiltily avoiding Bert's face. She shivered. She realized that she'd never thought of Russell as a *ghost*, really. More a *spirit*.

"Well, do you think this is a good idea?" Barbara asked. "Suppose we do contact him?"

Florie and Bert looked at one another. Florie tried to figure her feelings about it; Bert seemed to be watching her face for the answer.

"Shall we go ahead?" Barbara asked patiently.

Florie gave Bert an "I-don't-see-why-not" look, and he nodded.

"I don't see why not," he said.

Barbara joked with Tim about his cold hands as they sat down at the dining room table. Tim's bashfulness was apparent even in the dim light. Barbara talked calmly to Russell, asking him to appear. She spoke to him as if he were shy. Then she turned to Vanessa. "You talk to him."

Vanessa stared at the table. "It won't work."

Barbara raised her eyebrows just a little. "Why?"

"Because . . ." She looked at Barbara in that quiet way that adolescent girls look at young women. "Séances are for *dead* people."

The hairs on the back of Florie's neck rose.

The family looked at Barbara for the answer. Barbara half-smiled as she considered. "Maybe you're right."

Florie glanced at Bert, who sighed. He looked worn and just a bit depressed. Barbara let go of Tim and Vanessa's hands. "Why don't we rest up. And if you decide you want to try again, we'll get together another night." She stood.

They were quiet as they watched her gather her notes almost absently. "Keep in touch," she said as she left.

Florie woke and reached out into the space beside her in the bed. She listened for a while to the early morning sounds, trying to discover the movement of her husband in the house somewhere. She slid out of the warm covers and padded through the room into the hallway. Softly, she called Bert's name.

The door to Russell's room was slightly open. Quietly, she

pushed it open. Bert sat in a chair by the bed. He lifted his sleepy chin from his chest and looked at her bleary-eyed. He put his finger to his lips.

They returned to their room. "What is it?" she whispered, climbing back into bed.

"I'm not sure. I think he had a nightmare or something."

He held her as they fell asleep again. Florie felt something had changed, but Bert never talked much about it again.

When Vanessa went to college, Russell missed her so much that he apparently spent his evenings in her room reading; his books were sometimes in a neat stack by her bed. Claude took to napping on her rug, too.

Tim became interested in computers in high school and found that his brother borrowed his magazines and books on that subject. Tim said that he figured sometimes he went to Willie's with him. Willie had a micro-computer. They sometimes found funny messages on the screen. When Florie asked what kind of messages, Tim told her that Russell suggested a computer game of hide-and-seek which they worked out and had a lot of fun with.

Florie was more embarrassed when she found the men's magazines under Russell's bed than she ever had been about Tim's. (She had been sure she was alone when she found Tim's.)

Tim went off to college.

Russell liked his schoolwork; his reports were always excellent. He won an essay award while a junior in high school, which Florie found on his dresser and framed on his wall. He left his term papers out, which Florie and Bert read with amazement. He seemed fascinated with international relations, history, and economics.

"Oh, Bert," Florie said once, "what if he goes into espionage?"

Bert assured her that he may be elusive, but he left too many clues to be a spy.

His high school yearbooks showed up on the bedroom bookshelf. Russell O'Bannon was always listed—in fact, he belonged to the computer club, Latin club, and Honor Society. He was never available for photos, however.

In the summer of his eighteenth year, the house became

uncommonly lonely. Claude wagged his tail wistfully every now and then as he sniffed through Russell's room. Florie expanded her part-time job to full-time. It wasn't easy at first to enjoy the new solitude. The holidays were the same as ever; Christmas brought a full round of presents, including gifts from Russell. He'd developed a real knack for getting something for everyone that they'd never really wished for but was a marvelous gift just the same.

Bert and Florie received the paid tuition notices from a prestigious and expensive university. Russell was apparently working several part-time jobs through the school year, including gopher work at a law firm.

He attended Vanessa's wedding but didn't make it back for summer vacation of his second year.

It was that summer, his twentieth year, when the mailgram from Italy came.

"Look," Florie said, waving it at Bert. They had been receiving postcards from England, France, and Spain for the last month. Without a close look, she tore the thin envelope open.

"What is it?" Bert said.

Florie went numb. She sat down with the letter fluttering in her hand.

Bert took the letter from her.

They wept, then called Vanessa and Tim.

Russell had been killed in a terrorist explosion at a small Italian airport. The American Embassy had written, expressing terrible regret for their loss and that the students he'd been traveling with had said only wonderful things about their brilliant young son.

Florie found Bert sitting on Russell's bed. She sat down beside him and leaned her cheek against his shoulder.

She decided then that they would keep the room just as it had been when Russell was alive.

WISH

By
Al Sarrantonio

Not all the stories that have appeared in this series are of the straightforward kind. Once in a while they get downright weird. But weird is not defined as inexplicable, or impossible, or . . . downright weird. Al Sarrantonio, in his short fiction, seems to relish the weird. And in the hands of most anyone else, such material would be difficult to take, impossible to understand, and ultimately a failure. The weird of Sarrantonio, however, somehow becomes right. Real. Which is, when all is said and done, what a good writer should be able to do. Not easily, mind you, not by a long shot. It takes skill to weave the weird with the real and come out with something that looks and reads like a story, and not like demented raving. "Wish" is weird. Sarrantonio is good.

*C*hristmas.

A baby-blanket of snow enfolded the earth, nuzzled the streets. Great lips of snow hung from gutters, caps of snow topped mailboxes and lampposts.

Christmas.

Dark green fir trees stood on corners, heavy with ornaments and blinking bulbs, dusted with silver tinsel that hung from each branch like angels' hair. Great thick round wreaths, fat red bows under their chins, hung flat against each door. Telephone poles sprouted gold stars; more lights, round fat and bright, were strung from pole to pole in parallel lines. The air, clean and cold as huffing breath, smelled of snow, was white and heavy and fat with snow.

Christmas.

Christmas was here.

It was April.

Daisy and Timothy hid tight in the cellar. Tied and dusty, April surrounded them in fly-specked seed packets, boxes of impotent tulip bulbs, rows of limp hoes and shovels. Spring was captured and caged, pushed flat into the ground and frozen over, coffined tight and dead.

Above them, out in the world, they heard the bells. A cold wind hissed past. The cellar window shadowed over as something slid past on the street.

Ching-ching-ching.

They held their breaths.

Ching-ching.

The window unshadowed; the hiss and bells moved away.

The bells faded to a distant rustle.

They breathed.

Timothy shook out a sob.

"Don't you touch me!" he bellowed when his sister put a hand on his shoulder. "It's your fault! All the rest are in that *place* because of you—don't you *touch* me!" He pushed himself farther back between two boxes marked "Beach Toys."

Outside, somewhere, a mechanical calliope began to play "Joy to the World."

Winter silence hung between them until Timothy said, "I'm sorry."

Daisy held her hand out to him, her eyes huge and lonely, haunted. He did nothing—but again when her fingers fell on his shoulder he recoiled.

"No! You wished it! It's your fault!"

Daisy hugged herself.

Timothy's face was taut with fright. "You said, 'I wish it was Christmas always! I wish this moment would last forever!'" He pointed an accusing hand at her. "I was there when you said it. By the fireplace, while we hung our stockings. I heard that voice too—*but I didn't listen to it!*" He pointed again. "*Why did you have to wish?*"

"I wish it was April! I wish it was spring!" Daisy screamed, standing up. An open carton of watermelon seeds, collected carefully by the two of them the previous summer, tilted and fell to the floor. Unborn watermelons scattered dryly everywhere. "It was just a voice, I don't know how it happened," she sobbed. "*I wish it was Spring!*"

Nothing happened.

Outside the frosted cellar window, the calliope finished "Joy to the World" and went without pause into "Silver Bells."

"You wished it and now you can't unwish it!" Timothy railed. "That voice is gone and now it will always be Christmas!"

Daisy's face changed—she ignored his squirming protest when she clamped her hand to his arm.

"Listen!" she whispered fiercely.

"I won't! It's your fault!"

"*Listen!*"

Her wild, hopeful eyes made him listen.

He heard nothing for a moment. There was only Christmas winter out there—a far-off tinkly machine playing Supermarket carols, the sound of glass ornaments pinging gently against one another on outdoor trees and, somewhere far off, the sound of bells.

But then there was something else.

Warm.

High overhead.

Blue and yellow.

A bird.

Daisy and Timothy raced for the window. Daisy got there first, but Timothy muscled her away, using the pulled cuff of his flannel shirt to rub-melt the frost from a corner of the rectangular glass. He put his eye to the hole.

Listened.

Nothing; then—

Birdsong.

He looked back at his sister, who pulled him from his peephole and glued herself to it. After a moment—

"I see it!"

Mountain-high overhead, a dark speck circled questioningly.

It was not a Christmas bird. It had nothing to do with Christmas. It was a spring bird, seeking April places—green tree branches and brown moist ground with fat red worms in it. A sun yellow and tart-sweet as lemons. Mown grass with wet odors squeezed out of each blade. Brown-orange baseball diamonds and fresh-blacktopped playfields smelling of tar.

The bird whistled.

"April!" Timothy shouted.

He pulled frantically at the latch to the window, turning it aside and pulling the glass panel back with a winter groan. Cold air bit in at them. Snow brushed at their foreheads, danced and settled in their hair.

Timothy climbed out.

High up, whirling like a ball on a string, the bird cried.

"Yes! Yes! Spring!" Timothy yelled up at it.

Daisy climbed out beside him.

"You did it!" Timothy said happily. "You undid your wish!"

The cellar window snapped shut.

Something small plummeted.

Frozen white and silver, the bird fell into a soft death-coverlet of snow.

"It was a trick!" Timothy screamed. "What are we going to do?" He turned to the locked window, tried frantically to push it in. When he opened his mouth, puffs of frosted air came out with his words.

"We've got to get away!"

Timothy and Daisy looked to the horizon. A huge red ball was there, a second sun, an ornament a hundred stories high, and from it came the faint jangle of bells, the smooth snow-brushed sound of sleigh runners.

"We'll be brought to that place—we've got to get away!"

The sleigh bells, the glassy sound of sled-packed snow, grew toward them. Before Daisy's hands could find Timothy, could pull him against the side of the house, he tore away from her. The bells rose to a hungry clang; Daisy could almost hear them sing with pleasure.

Timothy's fading voice called back:

"Why did you listen to that voice . . ."

The bells grew very loud and then very soft, and moved away.

Christmas continued. In the sky, a few hearty snowflakes pirouetted and dropped. Tinsel shimmered on tree branches. The air stayed clean and cold, newly winterized. Balsam scent tickled the nostrils. Christmas lights glowed, blinked.

From the horizon, from the giant red Christmas ball, came a sound.

Bells.

Soft silver bells.

"No!" Daisy's feet carried her from the side of the house to the white-covered sidewalk. She left tiny white feet in a path behind her.

The bells belled.

Daisy ran.

The lazy bells followed her. Like a ghost's smoky hands, they reached out at her only to melt away and re-form. Daisy passed snow-white houses, with angels in the windows and mistletoe under the eaves.

Daisy stopped.

The bells hesitated. There came a tentative *ching*, followed by silence and then another *ching-ching*.

Daisy ran, her yellow hair flying.

The houses disappeared, replaced by a row of stores with jolly front windows and Christmas-treed displays. Lights blinked. Above one store a plastic Santa drawn by plastic reindeer rose, landed, rose, landed.

Ching-ching.

The library budded into view. White-coated brick, its crystal windows were filled with cutouts of Christmas trees and holly.

At the top of the steps, the doorway stood open.

Daisy climbed, entered.

Outside, the ghoul-bells chimed.

Ching-ching.

Ching-ching.

Ching.

She heard the smooth stop of sleigh-skis in the snow.

The library door loomed wide.

Someone stepped into it.

"Daisy?" a voice called coldly. It was a voice she knew.

"Daisy?" it spoke again. Icicles formed in the corners; snow sprinkled down from the ceiling. It was the voice that had spoken to her.

Daisy pushed past the empty librarian's desk, knocked over the silver Christmas tree on the counter. She dove under the tasseled red rope into the children's section. Bright book covers glared at her. Babar the elephant walked a tightrope, the bulblike faces of Dr. Seuss characters grinned, Huckleberry Finn showed off his inviting raft to his hulking friend Jim. "I wish I could be with them," Daisy thought; but nothing happened.

Behind her, the voice, closer, called again in chilly sing-song:

"Daisy, Daisy, it's Christmas always!"

"No!" Daisy hissed to herself fiercely. She crawled under one stack of books that had been left to spill against a bookcase, making an arch. Behind it were more books—Hardy Boys and Nancy Drews, two *Treasure Islands,* one *Robinson Crusoe* tilted at an angle. Behind them a pile of *National Geographic* magazines, with color covers.

Daisy burrowed her way into the magazines, covered herself with books and periodicals, made a fort of the Hardy Boys with a fortress gate made of *The Wind in the Willows.*

Steps clacked closer against the polished oak floor.

"Where are you?" the cold voice sang.

"Christmas all the time!

"Always Christmas!

"Daisy . . ."

The footsteps ceased.

The Hardy Boys were lifted away.

"Daisy . . ."

A hard hand reached down to fall on her. She felt how death-cold he was. His suit was red ice; he wore a red cap at a jaunty angle.

His face was white, his ice-blue eyes were arctic circles filled with swirling frost.

"I wish it was spring! I wish it was April!"

"Christmas always," he said, smiling a sharp blue smile.

"I wish I could kill you!"

With her two small hands Daisy threw *The Wind in the Willows* up at him. A corner of the book hit his cold, smoky eye and he staggered back.

Miraculously, amazingly, he fell. There was a shatter like an icicle hitting the sidewalk. There was the *ching* of a million tiny bells.

He lay silent.

He lay . . . dead.

Daisy got up to see a dying blizzard blowing in his eyes. A cold blue hand lifted momentarily, reached toward her—and fell back, cracking up and down its length.

He dripped melting water.

Daisy breathed.

Outside, a bird sang.

Daisy crawled under the book arch, under the red tassel. She ran past the empty desk, the fallen silver tree, out the yawning door.

The sky was growing blue. A squirrel ran past. A blackbird dipped low, squawked and didn't fall.

It was April.

Spring.

Christmas was leaving the world.

Balsam scent grew sour and stale. The snow grew old-gray and slushy. Winter was old; the house lights, round wreaths, tinsel grew dim and left-out-too-long. In the middle of "Have Yourself a Merry—" the calliope ground to a halt.

At the horizon, the huge red ball was less shiny-bright.

His sleigh stood in front of the library. It was ice-white and red, lined with ice bells, pulled by ice reindeer. It shivered as Daisy climbed into it and snapped the reins.

"Take me to them," she said.

The sleigh shuddered into melting life.

Spring was exploding around her. They went over miles of white earth turning to green. The air was warm as hay. Fish leaped in blue-clear ponds, orange-yellow flowers burst from the ground, leaves generated spontaneously. Daisy wondered if, back in her cellar, watermelons were sprouting everywhere and hoes and shovels were dancing up the stairs to reach the loamy soil.

Beneath Daisy, the ice sleigh dripped into the ground. The soil drank it up—bells, reindeer and all. Daisy leaped from the last puddle of it, new green grass like springs pushing at her feet.

Over a short hill, touching the spring sky—and there was the red ball.

It was a blown-glass Christmas bulb halfway up the sky. Its glossy crimson was tarnishing. Winter rushed out the tiny door at the bottom, howling, eaten alive by spring. Daisy hugged herself as it blew past.

The dying snowstorm engulfed her, pulled her inside.

She sobbed at what was there.

The ball was filled with frozen Christmas. A *Nutcracker* Christmas tree, with a thousand presents underneath, filled the center of the ball. Its branches sagged. Lights were everywhere, winking out. And lining the walls all the way to the top, were frozen people keeping frozen Christmas.

A spidery white stairway wound up and around, and Daisy stepped onto it. There was the snap of melting ice. She looked in at each block, wiping warm tears of water away with her fingers. In one there was a man with a beard she knew who watered his lawn in the summer each Saturday, even if it rained. His beard was frozen now. He knelt before a Christmas tree, fitting it into its stand. There was a boy who delivered newspapers, caught removing a model airplane from its Christmas wrap. A woman was ice in her rocking chair, a mince pie cradled in her potholdered hands—the pie looked good enough to eat. A little girl made garlands out of popcorn. A mother and daughter exchanged Christmas cards.

At the end of the winding stair, at the very top, was—

Timothy.

Daisy gasped. Timothy stared out at her like wax. In his hand he held a limp, flat stocking; he bent to tack it to a rich-oiled mantel above a fireplace. A log fire burned snugly in the grate.

The ice shimmered and softened; Timothy moved.

Beside him, there was an empty space.

As Daisy reached out, the ice hardened again.

"Can't . . . unwish . . . ," Timothy said before his mouth froze closed.

Outside, she heard the bells.

Winter came rushing back. The air glinted like clear cold crystal. The tarnished ball grew metal-shiny. On the Christmas tree, limp pine boughs stiffened, grew tall. Nearby, in the walls, in the air, the calliope played "God Rest Ye Merry, Gentlemen."

Ching-ching.

The sleigh moved over the snow with a sound like *wishhhhhhh.*

Ching.

Daisy looked up, and in the red metal glass above her, someone was reflected from far below.

Someone tall and white, with red-ice coat, blue-ice eyes, black-ice boots.

"Ice is water," he explained, in his voice; "water makes ice."

"I wished you were dead!" Daisy screamed.

He put his boot on the stair.

He climbed.

He stood before her.

As he finally put his cold hand on her; as she felt Christmas brighten and stiffen around her; as she felt the red velvet stocking caress her hands, and smelled the wood smoke from the fireplace, and felt Timothy's hand on her arm, telling her not to listen; as ice filled around her and hardened and froze her forever, she heard whispered close by, in a voice she now knew

might have been any of a thousand cold or hot voices, a voice
that might become any of a thousand cold or hot things, a
laughing voice, a voice that was ancient, persistent and patient in
its longing for release, "Make a wish."

THE
SPIDER GLASS

An Edwardian Story

By
Chelsea Quinn Yarbro

It's only fitting, I think, that we end this volume with one of the series' most favorite contributors. Chelsea Quinn Yarbro was one of the first women to establish what should have been known by editors and publishers all along—that women can write "this stuff" just as well as men. Sadly, she and the other women in the field still have to prove it, it seems. That is, not to put too fine a point on it, dumb. A writer is a writer is a writer, by God, and what the hell does sex have to do with the price of apples? Nevertheless, she perseveres. She grows. She gives us some of the best writing the field has ever seen. And when Shadows *finally, inevitably comes to an end, I can only hope that it will end with something she has written.*

"THERE IS A curious tale behind this mirror, actually. I'm pleased you noticed it," their host said to the select and exclusively masculine company that had gathered in the Oak Parlor at Briarcopse after dinner. He reached for the port and rather grandly offered it around. "Surely you'll have some. It was laid down the year I was born—splendid stuff. My father was quite the expert in these matters, I assure you."

Five of his guests accepted with alacrity; the sixth declined with a polite, Continental bow, and the Earl put the decanter back onto the silver tray set out on the gleaming mahogany table. "Don't stand on ceremony, any of you," he said with a negligent wave of his long, thin hand. He then settled back in his chair, a high-backed, scallop-topped relic of the reign of Queen Anne, and propped his heels on the heavy Tudor settle before the fire. Slowly he lit his cigar, savoring the aroma and the anticipation of his guests.

"For the lord Harry, Whittenfield . . ." the rotund gentleman with the brindled mutton-chop whiskers protested, though his indignation was marred by an indulgent smirk.

Their host, Charles Whittenfield, ninth Earl of Copsehowe, blew out a cloud of fragrant, rum-scented tobacco smoke and stared at the small, dull mirror in its frame of tooled Baroque silver. "It *is* a curious tale," he said again, as much to himself as any of the company. Then, recalling his guests, he directed his gaze at his wiry, middle-aged cousin who was in the act of warming his brandy over one of the candles. "Dominick, you remember my mother's Aunt Serena, don't you?"

"I remember all the women on that side of the family," Dominick said promptly. "The most amazing passel of females. My mother refuses to mention half of them—she feels they aren't respectable. Well, of course they're not. Respectable women are boring."

"Yes, I'm always amazed by them. And why they all chose to marry such sticks-in-the-mud as they did, I will never understand. Still, they make the family lively, which is more than I can say for the males—not a privateer or adventurer among them. Nothing but solid, land-loving, rich, placid countrymen, with a yen for wild girls." He sighed. "Anyway, Dominick, Great-aunt Serena—"

Dominick nodded with vigorous distaste that concealed a curious pride. "Most misnamed female I ever encountered. That whole side of the family, as Charles says—they marry the most unlikely women. Serena came from Huguenot stock, back in the middle of the seventeenth century, I think." He added this last as if the Huguenot influence explained matters.

"Ah, yes, Great-aunt Serena was quite a handful." The host laughed quietly. "The last time I saw her—it was years ago, of course—she was careering about the Cotswolds on both sides of her horse. The whole countryside was scandalized. They barred her from the Hunt, naturally, which amused her a great deal. She could outride most of them, anyway, and said that the sport was becoming tame."

"Whittenfield . . ." the rotund man said warningly.

"Oh, yes, about the glass." He sipped his port thoughtfully. "The glass comes from Serena's family, the English side. It's an heirloom, of course. They say that the Huguenot who married into the family took the woman because no one else would have her. Scandal again." He paused to take wine, and drained his glass before continuing. "The mirror is said to be Venetian, about three hundred and forty or fifty years old. The frame was added later, and when Marsden appraised it he said he believed it to be Austrian work."

"Hungarian, actually," murmured the sixth guest, though no one heard him speak.

"Yes . . . well." Whittenfield judiciously filled his glass once more. "Really wonderful," he breathed as he savored the port.

"Charles, you should have been an actor—you're wasted on the peerage," Dominick said as he took a seat near the fire.

"Oh, very well, I'll get on with it," Whittenfield said, capitulating. "I've told you the glass is Venetian and something over three hundred years old. The latest date Marsden ventured was

1570, but that, as I say, is problematical. In any case, you may be certain that it was around in 1610, which is the critical year so far as the story is concerned. Yes, 1610." He sank back in his chair, braced his heels once more on the Tudor settle, and began, at last, in earnest.

"Doubtless you're aware that Europe was a great deal more chaotic then than it is now—"

"That's not saying much," the rotund man interjected.

"Twilford, for God's sake, don't give him an excuse to digress again," Dominick whispered furiously.

"*As* I was saying," Charles went on, "Europe was doing very badly in 1610. That was the year Henri the Fourth of France was assassinated and his nine-year-old son succeeded him, and you know how Louis the Thirteenth turned out! James was making an ass of himself by prolonging Parliament and by locking up Arabella Stuart for marrying William Seymour. One of the tsars was deposed, but I can never keep them straight, and I believe a Prussian prince was offered the job—"

"Polish," the sixth guest corrected him politely. "Vasili Shuisky was deposed in favor of Vladislav, Sigismund III's son."

"Very likely," Whittenfield agreed. "Spain and Holland were having a not-very-successful go at a truce. The German Protestant states were being harried by their neighbors. . . . That will give you some idea. Well, it happened that my Great-aunt Serena's nine times great-grandmother was living—"

"Charles," Twilford protested, "you can't be serious. Nine times great-grandmother!"

"Of course I am," Whittenfield said, astounded at being questioned. "Serena was born in 1817. Her mother, Eugenia, was born in 1792. *Her* mother, Sophia, was born in 1774. Sophia's mother, Elizabeth, was born in 1742. Her mother, Cassandra, was born in 1726. Cassandra's mother was Amelia Joanna, and she was born in 1704 or 05; there's some doubt about the actual date. There was flooding and fever that winter and they were not very careful about recording births. Amelia Joanna's mother, Margaret, was born in 1688. *Her* mother, Sophronia, was born in 1664—"

"Just in time for the Plague and the Fire," Dominick put in.

"Yes, and only three of the family survived it: Sophronia, her mother, Hannah, and one son, William. Terrible names they gave females in those days. Anyway, William had four wives and eighteen children in his lifetime and Sophronia had six children and even Hannah remarried and had three more. Hannah's mother was Lucretia and she was born in 1629. Her mother, Cesily, was born in 1607, and it was *her* mother, Sabrina, that the story concerns. So you see, nine times great-grandmother of my Great-aunt Sabrina." He gave a grin that managed to be smug and sheepish at once. "That Lucretia, now, she was a sad one— married off at thirteen to an old reprobate in his fifties who kept two mistresses in separate wings at his principal seat as well as having who knows how many doxies over the years. Lucretia turned nasty in her later life, they say, and there was an investigation over the death of her tirewoman, who apparently was beaten to death under mysterious circumstances. The judge in the case was Sir Egmont Hardie, and he—"

"Charles!" thundered his cousin.

Whittenfield coughed and turned his eyes toward the ceiling. "About Sabrina. Let me see. She was twenty in 1610, married to Captain Sir James Grossiter. Cesily was three and her boy, Herbert, was one. It is a little hard to tell about these things after so long, but apparently certain difficulties had arisen between Sabrina and her husband. Sir James had quarreled with his father when he got into trouble with his commanding general, and ran off to the Continent, which was a damned silly thing to do, considering the times. He tried a little soldiering, which was the only thing he knew, and then got caught for some petty offense and was flung into gaol, leaving his wife with two children to feed and no one to help her, and in a foreign country, to boot."

"Well, she's not the first woman to earn her bread on her back, but I shouldn't think you'd bring it up . . ." one of the guests was heard to remark.

Whittenfield shook his head. "Most men prefer whores who can speak to them, which Sabrina could not. And her children were inconvenient for such a profession. She knew some French and had been taught a few Italian songs as a child, but for the most part she was as good as mute." He drained his glass again. "She was greatly distraught, as you might suspect, and did not know which way to turn."

"That's a female for you," the same guest said, and the sixth guest turned to him.

"What makes you believe that a man, in those circumstances, would fare any better?" The sixth guest clearly did not expect an answer, and the man who had spoken glared at him.

Charles went on as if he had not heard. "She sold all that she and Sir James possessed, which was not much, and then she began to sell their clothes, so that they had only what they wore on their backs, and that quickly became rags. However, she was able to afford a few bits of food and to hire mean lodgings in a back street of Antwerp. By doing scullery work at a nearby inn she got scraps to eat and enough to buy cabbages to boil for her babes. But it was inevitable that there would come a time when she would not have enough money even for those inadequate things, and her children would have no shelter or food."

"What on earth has that to do with the glass?" Twilford asked, blustering to conceal his perplexity.

"I'm coming to that," Charles Whittenfield said with a great show of patience. "If you'll let me do it in my own way."

"Well, I don't see how we can stop you," muttered a younger man sitting in the corner, hunched over his pipe.

"Everard, please," Dominick put in imperiously.

The older man beside him gave Dominick a contemptuous glare. "No manners these days. None at all."

"Pray go on," said the sixth guest in slightly accented English. It might have been because he was the only man not drinking that his clothes were the neatest and most elegant of any man's in the room.

"I intend to," Whittenfield said to his guests. "As I've intimated, my many-times-great Aunt Sabrina was stranded in Antwerp because Sir James was in prison and she was destitute. She had been cast out by her family when she had elected to follow her husband to the Continent, so she could not turn to them for relief, not that she was the sort who would have, in any case. Of course, Sir James's family had washed their hands of him some years before and would have nothing to do with him or any of his. Sabrina could play the virginal and had a fair knowledge of botany, as many well-bred women did in those days, but those were the limits of her skills. Yet she must have had courage for all of that, because she did not despair, or if she did, she conquered it. She was determined to keep her children with her, as the alternative was giving them to the care of nuns, and being a good English churchwoman, she could not bear to surrender her unprotected babes to Roman Catholics." He recrossed his legs. "My Uncle George married a Roman Catholic, you know. There was the most frightful uproar and dire predictions, but Clara has shown herself to be a most reasonable woman and a truly excellent wife. No trouble there, I assure you. So all those warnings came to naught."

"The glass, Charles, the glass," Twilford insisted.

"I'm coming to that," the young peer protested with mock dismay. "You've no patience—positively, you haven't a jot." He held out his glass for refilling as Everard helped himself to the port. "So," he resumed after an appreciative moment, "I trust I've made her predicament clear to you. Her husband was in prison, she had no one to turn to, her children as well as herself were in real danger of starvation, she was living in the poorest part of the city in a low-ceilinged garret in a house that should have been pulled down before the Plantagenets fell. There was no reason for her to hope for anything but an early grave in Potter's Field."

"Yes, yes, yes," Dominick interrupted. "Very touching plight. But as her daughter had a daughter, we must assume that all was not lost, at least not then." He splashed a bit more port into his glass and lit another cigar.

"Well, Charles, what happened?" Everard demanded. "Did she catch the eye of an Earl traveling for pleasure, or did some other person come to her aid?"

"Not quite that," Whittenfield conceded. "Not a traveling Earl in any case, but a traveling Count."

"Same thing," Dominick scoffed.

"He was, as you perceive from the title, a foreigner," Charles persisted. "He had arrived in Antwerp from Ghent some time before and had purchased one of the buildings not far from where Sabrina lived in terrible squalor."

"And he gave her the mirror for primping," Everard finished. "There's nothing very mysterious about that."

"Now, that's the odd part of it," Whittenfield said, leaning forward as he spoke. "He gave her the glass, but not the frame; that she bought for herself." He did not wait for his listeners to exclaim at this, but went on at once. "But that comes later in the story. Let me tell it as it must be told." He puffed his cigar once and set it aside again. "She became acquainted with this foreigner through an act of theft."

"What could anyone steal from her?" Twilford asked of the air.

"You don't understand—it was Sabrina who was the thief."

The reaction ranged from guffaws to shock; the sixth guest gave a small, wry smile and said nothing.

"Yes, she had decided to steal money so that she and her children could eat that night. You must understand that she had not stolen before and she knew that the penalties for it were quite harsh, but she had come to believe that she had no other choice. It was late in the afternoon when she saw this foreigner come to his house, and she determined to wait for him and accost him as he came out. She thought that since the man was not a native of the place, he might be reluctant to complain to the authorities, and of course, since he was foreign, he was regarded with a degree of dislike throughout the neighborhood."

Everard shook his head. "Sounds like a rackety thing to do."

"It was better than starving," said the sixth guest.

The other man with the pipe coughed and made a gruff protest. "But what is the point of all this, Whittenfield? Get on with it, man."

"Lord Graveston, you are trying to rush me," Whittenfield said with the slightest hint of a slur in his pronunciation. "That won't do. You'll have to listen, the same as the rest."

"Then stop this infernal dallying about," Lord Graveston said with considerable asperity. "At this rate, it will be time for breakfast before you're half done with your story, and we'll never know what the point of it is."

Whittenfield shrugged. "I don't see the virtue in haste when one is recounting the travail of a family member, but if you insist, then I will do my humble best . . ."

"For all the saints in hell, Charles!" Dominick expostulated.

"Very well," Whittenfield sighed lavishly. "Since you insist. As I told you, Sabrina conspired to set upon this foreigner and rob him so that she would have money for food and lodging for herself and her children. She went down the street at night, filled with terror but determined now on her course. There were beggars sleeping in doorways, and a few poxy whores plied their trade in this quarter, but most of the denizens of the night left her alone. She was an Englishwoman, don't you see, and isolated from them. It was a cold, raw night and her shawl did not keep her warm. Think of her predicament, gentlemen—is it surprising that she nearly turned back half a dozen times?"

"What's surprising is that she attempted it at all," Dominick said quietly. "Not that I approve of thieving, but in this case . . ."

"Precisely my point," Whittenfield burst out, the contents of his glass sloshing dangerously. "Most women would have not been able to do a damned thing, at least not any of the women I know. Sabrina, though, was most . . . unfeminine."

"Hardly that," murmured the sixth guest.

"She reached the house of the foreigner and slipped into the doorway of the shuttered baker's shop across the street, and set herself to wait for her prey to appear."

"How do you know that?" one of the guests interrupted. "How do you know that her shawl wasn't warm, or that there was a baker's shop where she could wait for the man?"

"I know," Whittenfield said with a faintly superior air, "because she kept a diary, and I've read it. She devoted a great many pages to this unfortunate time in her life. Her description of the rooms where she lived with her children almost make me itch, so deeply does she dwell on the filth and the vermin that lived there." He shuddered as proof of his revulsion.

"Well, you've got to expect that poor housing isn't going to be pleasant," Twilford observed, appealing to the others with a wave of his hand. "Some of the tenant farmers I've visited— appalling, that's what it is."

"Now who's digressing?" Whittenfield asked.

"Charles is right," Dominick admitted. "Let it keep, Twilford."

"Well, I only wanted to let you know that I had some comprehension of what—" Twilford began but was cut off.

"We can all agree that we're shocked by the reduced circumstances of your whatever-many-times-great-aunt," Lord Graveston said portentously. "Get on with it."

Whittenfield glared around the room to be certain that all his guests had given him their attention. All but one had. His sixth guest was staring at the spider glass with a bemused smile on his attractive, foreign face. Whittenfield cleared his throat and was rewarded by the sixth guest's reluctant attention.

"Pray forgive me," he said politely. "That glass . . ."

"Precisely," Whittenfield said. "That is why it has remained intact for so long, I am convinced. In any case, I was telling you about how Sabrina Grossiter came to try to rob this foreigner in Antwerp. She took up her post outside the baker's shop, hidden in the shadows, and waited for many long hours. She had thought that the foreigner used the house for romantic assignations, but that did not seem to be the case, for no woman came to the house, or man either, for that matter. Well after midnight a middle-aged man in servant's livery left the building, but the foreigner remained. It was cold, very cold, and Sabrina's hands and feet were numb by the time she saw the lights in the upper windows go out. She hoped that the foreigner was going to leave so that she could at last try to take his purse. There was no one else on the street; even the beggars had found whatever shelter they could."

"Sounds a foolish thing to do, wait up half the night for a man to walk out of his house. Not very sensible of her." Twilford looked to the others to support him.

"All the women in our family are like that," Dominick said, at once proud and disgusted.

"She was desperate," the sixth guest said.

"In her journal," Whittenfield went on more sharply, "she remarks that it must have been an hour until dawn when the man came out. She did not remark him at first, because he was dressed all in black, and at night, in the shadow of the buildings, he was little more than another shadow."

"He was a knowing one," Lord Graveston said to the air. "Should stay away from such men, if I were her."

"But she didn't," Whittenfield put in, downing the last of his wine before going on. "She couldn't, you see. She says herself that hunger and worry had driven her slightly mad. She believed that there was no other course, but when she saw the man start away from the building, she all but failed. It was only the click of his heels on the pavement that alerted her to his departure. It may be that she dozed, though her journal insists that she did not. However it was, she did not have quite the element of surprise she wished for and took after him, stumbling in the dark so that the foreigner turned and reached out a hand to her to keep her from falling."

"Did she abandon the idea of robbing him then?" Lord Graveston asked as he filled his pipe a second time.

"No," Whittenfield said with half a smile. "She thought this might be to her advantage, so she leaned up against the man and reached out for his belt. You know how they wore them then, over the padded doublet and a trifle below the waist in front? She thought she might be able to release the buckle and pull the whole belt away. Most men carried their purses on their belts in those times, and if she got the belt she would also have the purse."

"A clever woman," said Peter Hamworthy, who had been listening in silence. "Surprising she had so much gumption."

Whittenfield glanced over at the speaker. "Gracious, Peter, I thought you were asleep," he said with sarcastic sweetness.

"Not quite, merely dozing a bit," Hamworthy responded affably. "I'm finding your tale, though circuitous, interesting."

"You relieve me," Whittenfield said, then went on. "I've told you that it was a cold night, a very cold night, and that Sabrina's hands and feet were chilled. This probably accounted, at least in part, for her ineptness. She had not stolen before, and with her hands nearly blue with cold she had little control of her fingers, which fumbled on the buckle. The foreigner seized her hands in his and held her securely."

"And then he called the Watch, and she was taken along to join her husband in gaol. And that still doesn't explain about the glass," Twilford said, exasperated.

"But he didn't summon the Watch," Whittenfield said slyly. "He held her hands and stared hard at her. And though it was deepest night, Sabrina said in her journal that she had the uneasy feeling that he could see her plainly. He demanded to know what she was about, in Dutch, of course."

"Of course," Dominick said as he refilled his glass and poured more port for his cousin.

"She does mention that he had an accent she could not place, but that is to be expected, since she had no more than a few words of the language herself. She tried to explain that she had only fallen, but he did not believe her. He also realized that her native tongue was not Dutch, for he addressed her in French and German and then English, of which, Sabrina insists, he had fluent command." Whittenfield drank half of his port with the air of a man making a sacrifice.

"Go *on*, Charles!" Twilford bellowed.

"In good time; I must not abuse this wine." He drank again, less deeply, and set the glass down on the rolled arm of his chair where it balanced precariously. "So this foreigner discovered that she was English and upon learning that, asked to be told how she came to be in a back street in Antwerp. At first Sabrina refused to answer him, saying that it was her concern. He protested that since she had attempted to rob him, he was entitled to some explanation before he called in the authorities. It was that threat that caused her to tell him what had befallen her. At least that is what her journal says on the next day, though there are later entries that hint at other factors."

"What other factors?" Hamworthy spoke up. "Don't be mysterious, Charles. What factors are you talking about?"

Whittenfield lifted his wine and stared into its garnet-colored depths. His expression was slightly bemused. "Other factors . . . well, it's hard to know how much to believe, but this man was not what Sabrina had expected. She remarks, several days later, upon his kindness, which she first perceived that night. Apparently she held nothing back, and out of caprice or compassion he made a bargain with her."

"I can imagine the bargain," Twilford said, his tremendous side-whiskers bristling like the jowls of a tomcat.

"No, you can't," Whittenfield corrected him mildly. "You know what most women, and men, too, for that matter, would expect at such times. Yet that was not Sabrina's experience. She says in her journal that she wondered at first if he was one of those whose love is inverted, but it turned out otherwise. She made a bargain with this foreigner, as I say. She agreed to live in the house he had bought, to keep it for him. He did not object to her children and gave her permission to care for them as she felt best. He did not require them to serve him—"

"Well, they were what, one and three? Hardly old enough to wait upon anyone, foreigner or not," Dominick pointed out.

"There was the matter of bonds," the sixth guest said quietly.

"Precisely," Whittenfield agreed. "And this foreigner did not require that Cesily and Herbert be bonded to him, which was something of a wonder in those times. Sabrina mentions in her journal that her employer's manservant told her that he had been a bondsman, and when his master found him he refused to continue the bond."

"One of those damned humanitarian sorts." Lord Graveston sighed portentously. "The world's full of 'em."

"Doubtless an opinion shared by the children of Whitechapel," the sixth guest commented without smiling.

"Terrible state of affairs, those slums," Dominick said indignantly. "Had to drive through there once; there'd been an accident and it was the only way round. There was the most appalling stench, and the buildings looked to be held together by filth alone. The people—a complete want of conduct." Two of the other men nodded their understanding and disapproval. "One drab tried to climb into my carriage, and those who saw her make the attempt made such rude and licentious comments . . . The children were as bad as their seniors."

"This is hardly appropriate after-dinner conversation," Hamworthy opined.

"Very true," Whittenfield said smoothly. "My great-aunt's adventures with a foreigner are much more suitable." He drank down the last of his port and let the glass tip in his fingers. "Unless, of course, you're not interested in what became of her. . . ."

"Oh, get on with it," Dominick said, nudging Everard with his elbow so that he would add his support.

Obediently Everard spoke up. "Yes, by all means, Charles, let's have the rest of the story."

"I still don't see how that bedeviled glass comes into it," Twilford muttered, dropping his chin forward.

"It *is* bedeviled, if Sabrina is to be believed," Charles said rather dreamily. "How aptly you put it, Twilford."

Lord Graveston coughed twice in an awesome way.

"Yes. Of course." Charles leaned forward in his chair and filled his glass. "I'll probably regret it in the morning, but for the present, this is precisely what's wanted." After he had settled back again and once more propped his heels on the settle, he resumed his story. "Well, as I said, Sabrina agreed to be the housekeeper to this foreigner in exchange for shelter and meals for herself and her children. She was most uneasy about the arrangement at first, because there was no saying that her bene- factor might not suddenly decide to change the nature of their arrangements and make demands of her or her children. She was also very much aware that he could dismiss her at any time and she would be in the same sorry state that she was when he made his agreement with her. Yet she had no other choice. She could not return to England, she had no one she knew who would protect her in Antwerp, or indeed any European country and there seemed to be no other way to get money. The for- eigner settled a small amount of money on her to enable her to buy cloth from the mercer so that she could dress herself and her children."

"Sounds like one of those missionary types," Twilford growled. "They're always doing that kind of thing."

"There were, naturally, certain restrictions to her duties," Whittenfield continued, "and they caused her some alarm. There were rooms of the house where she was not allowed to venture, and which were locked day and night. The foreigner often received heavily wrapped parcels from many strange lands. Gradually, Sabrina began to fear that the Count was en- gaged in nefarious or criminal activities. And she became con- vinced of it some seven months after she entered his employ. There are three entries in her journal that are at once baffling and thought-provoking. She mentions first that the Count did not often go abroad in the day. At first this disturbed her, but she saw him more than once in sunlight and noted that he did cast a shadow, and so her fear that she had fallen into the hands of a malignant spirit was lessened. Oh, you may all laugh if you choose," he said in a wounded tone. "In those times there were many with such fears. It was a superstitious age."

"And this one, of course, is not," the sixth guest said, his fine brows raising in courteous disbelief.

"Oh, those uneducated and unintelligent masses, I daresay, are still in the throes of various dreads, but for those of us who have the wit to learn, well, most of us cast off the shackles of superstition before we were out of lead strings." He took a meditative sip of his port. "Still, I suppose we can understand a little how it was that Sabrina felt the dread she did."

"Well, women, you know . . ." Hamworthy said with an indulgent smile. "Wonderful creatures, all of them, but you know what their minds are. Not one in a thousand can think, and the ones who can are always distressingly masculine. That Frenchwoman, the writer with the English name . . . Sand, isn't it? That's a case in point."

"My Great-aunt Serena was another," Whittenfield said, frowning a trifle. "Wasn't a man in the county cared to trade words with her. They respected her, of course, but you couldn't say that they liked her. Nonetheless, most of us loved her when we were children."

"Will you get back to Sabrina?" Dominick asked plaintively.

"Oh, Sabrina; yes. Told you, didn't I, that she was afraid of malign spirits? Of course. And she made up her mind that it was not the case. She thought for a while that her employer must have a mistress somewhere because of the strange hours he kept and the absolute privacy he maintained. There was always the chance that he was working for the Spanish or the French, but she found no evidence of it, and after the first few months she was looking for it. She feared that if the man was working for another government and was discovered, she would suffer as well, and after enduring so much she did not wish to expose herself to such a hazard. She came to believe that the Count was not, in fact, an agent of any of the enemies of the state. And that intrigued her even more, for there did not seem to be any reasonable explanation for his behavior, if he was not keeping a mistress or doing some other questionable thing. So she set herself the task of finding out more about her employer and his locked rooms."

"Very enterprising," Hamworthy interrupted. "Dangerous, too. I wouldn't like my housekeeper prying into my activities."

"Sabrina also had to deal with the manservant, who was as private and aloof as his master and whom she suspected of watching her. She describes him as being of middle age or a trifle older, lean, sandy-haired and blue-eyed, and yet she did not think that he was from northern Europe as such characteristics might indicate. Once she heard the manservant in conversation with the Count and she thought that they spoke in Latin, though she had not heard the language much. Their accents, if it was indeed that tongue, were strange to her, quite unlike what little scholarly intercourse she had overheard in the past, and not at all like the doggerel of the Roman Church. Yet there were a few words that made her think it was Latin, and for that reason she was more curious than ever. So she set upon a series of vigils, and after many months her patience was rewarded to a degree."

"To a degree," Lord Graveston repeated derisively. "Speak plainly for once in your life, Charles."

"Of course. I am speaking plainly. This story is not easily told, and the wine is playing great hob with my thoughts. You must make allowances for the excellence of my port, Graveston."

"I'll make allowances for anything that gets on with the tale!" was the acerbic answer.

"I'm doing my poor best," Whittenfield said in a slightly truculent manner. "I'm not certain you appreciate the intricacies of Sabrina's life."

"Of course I do. She was serving as housekeeper to a mighty private foreigner in Antwerp and her circumstances were badly reduced. There's nothing incomprehensible in that." Lord Graveston emptied out his pipe and gave Whittenfield a challenging glare through the tufts of his eyebrows.

"And that is not the least of it," Whittenfield insisted.

"Probably not, but you have yet to tell us that part," Dominick put in.

"Which I will do if only you will give me the chance," Whittenfield remonstrated. "Each of you, it seems, would rather discuss your own adventures. If that's your desire, so be it."

"Oh, Charles, you're being temperamental." Everard had dared to speak again, but he laughed a little so that his host would not think he had been reprimanded.

Whittenfield stared up at the ceiling in sublime abstraction, his eyes faintly glazed. "You know, when I first read her journal, I thought that Sabrina was indulging in fancy, but I have read a few things since then that lead me to believe she was telling the wholly accurate truth about her experiences. That disturbs me, you know. It means that a great many things I used to regard as nonsense may not be, after all."

"What are you talking about, Charles?" Dominick demanded. He had selected another cigar and paused to light it.

"You haven't read the journal, have you?" He did not
bother to look at his cousin. "Naturally not. But I have, several
times now, and it is a most—unnerving document."

"So you persist in telling us," Hamworthy sighed. "Yet you
have not particularly justified your claim."

"How little faith you have, Peter," Whittenfield said with an
assumption of piety. "If you would bear with me, you will find
out why I have said what I have about Sabrina and that glass. I
wasn't the one who brought the subject up; I have merely offered to enlighten you." He drank again, licking away the cres-
cent it left on his upper lip.

"Then be kind enough to tell us the rest," said the sixth
guest.

With this clear invitation before him, Whittenfield hesitated. "I don't know what you will make of it. I haven't sorted it
out myself yet, not since I realized she was telling the truth." He
smiled uncertainly. "Well, I'll leave it up to you. That's probably
best." He took another nervous sip of wine. "She—that is, Sabrina, of course—she continued to watch the Count. She was up
many nights, so that it was all she could do to work the next day.
During that time she took great care to do her work well. And
she made herself as useful as possible to the manservant so that
she might stay in his good graces. In her journal she related that
he never behaved in any but the most polite way, and yet she felt
the same sort of awe for the servant that she did for the master.
And she feared to face him directly, except when absolutely
necessary. When she had been the Count's housekeeper for a
few months, she had enough coins laid aside to enable her to
purchase a crucifix—she had sold her old one the year before—
and she mentions that the Count commented on it when he saw
it, saying that it was merely gold plate. She indignantly reminded him that it was the best she could afford, and that the
gold was not important, the faith it represented was. The Count
acknowledged her correction, and nothing more was said. Then,
two weeks after that, he presented her with a second crucifix of
the finest gold, finished in the Florentine style. It was in the
family for some time, I recall. Aunt Serena said that her grand-
mother used to wear it. That was a great surprise to Sabrina, and

she promptly took it off to a Roman priest, for all she did not trust him, and asked him to bless the treasure, just in case. He did as she asked, after he had satisfied himself that though Sabrina was one of the English heathen, yet she knew enough of religion to warrant his granting her request."

"And did her Count vanish in a puff of smoke next morning?" Dominick ventured sarcastically.

"No. He was unperturbed as ever. From what Sabrina says, he was a man of the utmost urbanity and self-possession. She never heard him raise his voice, never saw any evidence that he abused his manservant, never found any indication of moral excesses. I've been trying for years to puzzle out what she meant by moral excesses. Still, whatever they were he didn't do them. Finally one night, while she was keeping her vigil on the stair below one of the locked doors, being fatigued by her housekeeper's tasks during the day and having spent the better part of most nights watching, she fell asleep, in this case quite literally. She tumbled down the stairs, and in her journal she states that although she does not remember doing so, she must have cried out, for she does recall a door opening and light falling on her from one of the locked rooms."

"Was she much hurt?" Everard asked. "I fell down the stairs once, and ended up with torn ligaments in my shoulder where I'd tried to catch myself. Doctor said I was fortunate not to have broken my skull, but he is forever saying such things."

Whittenfield's brow puckered in annoyance. "She was much bruised and she had broken her arm—luckily the right one, for she was left-handed."

"Ah," Twilford said sagely. "That accounts for it."

"The left-handedness?" Whittenfield asked, momentarily diverted. "It may be. There are some odd gifts that the left-handed are supposed to have. Come to think of it, Serena was left-handed. There might be something to it."

The sixth guest smiled wryly. "And the ambidexterous?"

"I don't approve of that," Lord Graveston announced. "Isn't natural."

"You don't think so?" the sixth guest asked, but neither expected nor got an answer from the crusty old peer.

"Back to Sabrina," Dominick ordered.

"Yes, back to Sabrina," Whittenfield said, draining his glass again. "Remarkable woman that she was. Where was I?"

"She had fallen down the stairs and broken her arm," one of the guests prompted.

"Oh, yes. And her employer came out of the locked room. Yes. She swooned when she fell, or shortly after, and her next memory was of being carried, though where and by whom she could not tell, for her pain was too intense to allow her much opportunity for thought. She contented herself with closing her eyes and waiting for the worst of her feeling to pass."

"Only thing she could do, probably," Everard said grimly.

"It would seem so. This employer of hers took her into one of the rooms that had been locked, and when she came to her senses she was on a splendid couch in a small and elegant room. You may imagine her amazement at this, for until that time she had thought that the house, being in one of the poorest parts of the city, had no such finery in it. Yet there were fine paintings on the walls, and the furniture was luxuriously upholstered. And this was a time when such luxury was fairly rare, even among the wealthy. This Count was obviously a much more impressive figure than Sabrina had supposed."

"Or perhaps he was a rich tradesman, amusing himself with a pose, and that would explain the remote house and the lack of company," Dominick said cynically.

"I thought that myself, at one time," Whittenfield confessed. "I was sure that she had been hoodwinked by one of the best. But I made a few inquiries and learned that whoever this Count was, he was most certainly genuine nobility."

"How curious," the sixth guest said.

"And it became more curious still," Whittenfield went on, unaware of the sardonic note in the other man's voice. "The Count dosed her with syrup of poppies and then set her arm. She describes the whole event as unreal, and writes that she felt she was floating in a huge, warm bath though she could feel the bones grate together. There were so many questions she wanted to ask, but could not bring her thoughts to bear on any of them. Then she once again fainted, and when she woke she was in her own chamber, her arm was expertly splinted and bound with tape, and her head felt as if it were filled with enormous pillows."

"And her employer? What of him?" Twilford inquired, caught up now in spite of himself.

"He visited her the next day, very solicitous of her and anxious to do what he could to speed her recovery." Whittenfield paused for a reaction, and got one from Everard.

"Well, she was his housekeeper. She was of no use to him if she could not work."

"He never told her that," Whittenfield said, gratified that one of his guests had said what he had wanted to hear. "She made note of it in her journal. Finally, after ten days she got up sufficient courage to say something to the Count, and he reassured her at once that he would prefer she recover completely before returning to her duties. There is an entry then that hints at a more intimate exchange, but the phrases are so vague that it is impossible to tell for sure. Mind, that wasn't a mealymouthed age like this one. If something had passed between them, there would be no reason for her to hide behind metaphors, unless she feared the reproach of her husband later, which I doubt. When at last Sir James was released from gaol, he hired on as a mercenary soldier and went east into the pay of the Hapsburgs and nothing is known of his fate. On the other hand, at the end of her three years with her Count, Sabrina came back to England and set herself up in fairly good style. She never remarried but apparently had one or two lovers. Her journal is fairly explicit about them. One was named Richard and had something to do with Norfolk. The other was Henry and was some sort of relative of the Howards. She is very careful not to be too direct about their identities except in how they had to do with her. Doubtless Sir James would have gnashed his teeth to know that his wife ended up doing well for herself. Or he might have liked to live off her money."

"But surely your great-aunt did not become wealthy through the good offices of this Count, did she?" Twilford asked, eyeing his host askance.

"Probably a bequest. Those Continentals are always settling great amounts of money on their faithful servants. I read of a case not long ago where a butler in France got more than the children—" Lord Graveston stopped in the middle of his words and stared hard at the sixth guest. "No offense intended."

"Naturally not," the sixth guest said.

"You're a Count, too, they say?" Dominick inquired unnecessarily.

The sixth guest favored him with a wry smile and a slight inclination of his head. "That is one of my titles, yes."

"Smooth-spoken devil, aren't you?" Dominick challenged, his eyes growing bright.

"In the manner of my English . . . acquaintances," he replied, adding, "if I have erred, perhaps you will be kind enough to instruct me."

Everard stifled a laugh and Dominick's face reddened.

"Let it alone, Dominick, can't you?" Twilford said before Dominick could think of another insult to launch at the sixth guest.

"Get back to Sabrina, Charles, or you'll have Dominick asking to meet your foreign guest at dawn." Lord Graveston sounded both disgusted and disappointed.

"Yes, I will," Whittenfield said with alacrity. "She had broken her arm and took time to mend, during which time her employer was most solicitous of her health. He saw to it that she was well fed and that her children were cared for so that they did not impose upon their mother. Sabrina was astounded and grateful for this consideration. She had never expected such charity from a stranger. And the more she learned about the Count, the more curious she became. He was without doubt wealthy, and had chosen to live in this poor part of Antwerp so that he would not be put upon by the authorities, she suspected. Yet she doubted that he had broken the law or was engaged in espionage. Eventually she wondered if he were doing vivisections, but she never found a body or any part of one in the house, though she did once find the manservant with a large piece of raw meat. With every doubt that was quelled, another rose to take its place. She did not dare to approach him directly, for although he had never shown her anything but kindness, Sabrina reveals that she sensed a force or power in him that frightened her."

Twilford shook his head. "Women! Why *will* they endow us with godlike qualities?"

Dominick stifled a yawn.

"It was Sabrina's daughter, Cesily, who first stumbled upon the Count's secret, or one of his secrets," Whittenfield said, and

took time to top off his port. He was enjoying the sudden silence
that had fallen. Slowly he leaned back, smiling in delight with
himself.

"Charles . . ." Dominick warned.

"The secret was one that Sabrina said she should have
guessed. How it came about was—"

"You'd try the patience of half the saints in the calendar,
Whittenfield," Everard said, attempting an amused chuckle with
a distinct lack of success.

Whittenfield refused to be rushed. "Cesily came running
into her mother's chamber one afternoon with a large glass
beaker clutched in her small hands. She said she had come upon
it in the hallway near the locked door, but upon close question-
ing, she admitted that she had found the door unlocked and had
decided to explore. You may imagine how aghast Sabrina was to
hear this, and she trembled to think how the Count would react
to the news that the child had invaded his private rooms. She
thought it best to be prepared for the worst, and determined to
approach the Count before he came to her. She had a little
money set aside, and if the worst came to pass she was fairly
confident that after she had paid for the damage she would still
have enough money left to afford passage to England, though
she did not know what she would do once she got there."

"Just like a woman," Everard said, attempting to look
world-weary, though his young features did not easily lend
themselves to that expression.

"Whittenfield, have you had pipes put in, or must I seek the
necessary house in the garden?" Lord Graveston asked unexpectedly.

"You'll find what you need by the pantry door, my Lord,"
Dominick said, a malicious undertone to his good manners.

"Thanks, puppy," the old man said, getting out of his chair.
"Should be back in a little time." He walked stiff-legged to the
door and closed it sharply behind him.

"Well . . ." Whittenfield said, rather nonplussed by Lord
Graveston's departure, and uncertain now how to pick up the
threads of his narrative. "As might be expected—" he covered
his awkwardness by pouring himself yet another glass of the
excellent port "—it took her some time to convince herself that
it was appropriate to interrupt the Count at his work. She did

not want to go to that locked door and knock, for fear of his wrath. She also realized that she was not eager to be dismissed. The man was a generous master and had treated her far more kindly than she had thought he would. Yes. You can see her predicament. But if the broken beaker were not acknowledged, then it might go unpleasantly for her and her children. Sabrina was not a foolish woman—"

"What woman is not foolish where her children are concerned?" Hamworthy inquired piously. He often remarked that heaven had seen fit to visit seven daughters on him, as others were visited with plague. It was tacitly acknowledged that one of his reasons for attending this gathering was to talk with Everard about a possible alliance with his fourth daughter, Isabel.

"Be that as it may . . ." Whittenfield said more forcefully, glad that the general irritation with Hamworthy for once worked to his benefit. "Indeed, Sabrina feared for what would become of her and her children. There were several possibilities, each one more horrifying than the last. She could be dismissed. That was not desirable, but she could manage, if she acted with caution. If, however, the Count decided to take action against her or, more horribly, her daughter for her actions, then it might go very badly for them. Her thoughts were filled with tales she had heard of the fate of children in prisons, their abuses and their degradation. At the very contemplation of such a possibility, Sabrina was filled with overwhelming fright. She considered taking her children and leaving under the cover of night, and getting as far from Antwerp as she could. Lamentably, her resources would not allow her to fly a long way, or rapidly. She had to hope that she could persuade the Count that any restitution he demanded, no matter how severe, should be taken from her and not from her children. Imagine what terrors filled her as she went up the stairs—the very stairs down which she had fallen—to knock on that sinister locked door."

"Why did she not simply talk to the manservant, and ask him to explain what had happened?" Twilford suggested.

"Apparently she did consider that, but decided that if she had to face the Count, she would prefer to do it at once, rather than go through the ordeal twice. It's an understandable attitude, don't you think?"

"And this way she would have the strategic element of surprise," the sixth guest said quietly.

"Just so," Whittenfield said emphatically. "You understand
me very well, Count." He drank again, inwardly delighted at the
increased attention he had been given. "So she knocked at the
door. A gentle rap at first, and then a stronger one. You would
have thought she was far more brave than she claimed to be, so
boldly and directly did she present herself. In her journal she
says that she quaked inwardly, and there was almost nothing she
could do to keep her hands from shaking, yet she did not allow
these considerations to hold her back."

"Females, so precipitous," Twilford muttered.

"In a general, that quality would be called audacity, and
would earn glory and praise," the sixth guest pointed out.

"Not the same thing at all," Twilford said, much shocked.

"Of course not," answered the sixth guest.

"To return to Sabrina," Whittenfield said sharply, "she
knocked on the door and waited. When there was no response,
she knocked a second time, hoping all the while that the Count
would not be there or, for whatever reason, would not answer.
She had begun to worry again: what if this man were hiding men
and women in those rooms? What if he had a cache of arms or
gunpowder? What if there were other sorts of equipment, things
that would not be favored by the officials of Antwerp? Was she
required to report what she saw, assuming the Count allowed
her to leave the house at all? When she had knocked a third time,
she was convinced that the Count was away, and she turned with
relief to descend the stairs. And then the door behind her
opened and the Count asked her why she had disturbed him. He
spoke reasonably, her journal says, telling her that her errand
must be of great urgency, for she had never before gone contrary to his orders regarding that door. Sabrina gathered up her
faltering courage and told him what her daughter had done,
then stood silent, waiting for his wrath to fall on her, for it was
not rare for a master to vent his wrath with a belt or a stick on
servants who did not please him. That's not done much anymore, but in Sabrina's time she had every reason to think that
she might be beaten for her daughter's offense, and Cesily might
be beaten as well. She tried to explain to the Count, then, that
Cesily was only a child and had not intended to harm his prop-

erty, or to trespass in his private rooms. She had got halfway in
to her tangled arguments when the Count interrupted her to say
that he hoped that Cesily was not hurt. Dumbfounded, Sabrina
said that she was not. The Count expressed his relief to hear this
and assured Sabrina that he was not angry with her or her child,
but that he was upset to realize they regarded him as such an
object of terror. Sabrina demured, and tried to end this awkward
interview, but it was not the Count's intention to allow this. He
opened the door wider and asked her if she would care to see
what lay beyond. Poor Sabrina! Her curiosity was fired at this
offer, for she wanted to enter those rooms with a desire that was
close to passion, but at the same time she knew that she might be
exposing herself to danger. Had it been only herself, she wrote
in her journal, she would not have hesitated, for a moment, but
again, her consideration for her two children weighed heavily
with her and for that reason she did not at once accept his offer.
After a moment, her curiosity became the stronger force in her,
and she went back up the stairs to the open door."

"They'll do it every time. They're as bad as cats," Twilford
said, and looked to Hamworthy for support.

"Charles, you're the most infuriating of storytellers,"
Dominick said as the door opened to readmit Lord Graveston,
who made his way back to his seat without looking at any of the
others in the room.

"Doubtless," Whittenfield said, quite pleased with this en-
comium. "Let me go on. I think you'll find that most of your
doubts will be quieted. For example, I think all of you will be
gratified to learn that this mysterious Count was nothing more
ominous than an alchemist."

"Of *course!*" Everard said as the others nodded in varying
degrees of surprise.

"That was the great secret of the closed rooms. The man
had an alchemical laboratory there, as well as a library where he
kept some of his more . . . objectionable texts for perusal." He
smiled at this revelation and waited to hear what the others
might say.

"Alchemist!" Dominick scoffed. "Demented dreamer, more
like."

"Do you think so?" the sixth guest asked him.

"Base metal into gold! The Elixir of Life! Who'd believe

such trash?" Dominick got up from his chair and went to glare into the fire.

"Who indeed," murmured the sixth guest.

"You're going to tell us that all your aunt's precious Count was doing was pottering around among the retorts, trying to make his own gold?" Hamworthy demanded. "Of all the shoddy—"

"Yes, Sabrina's employer was an alchemist," Whittenfield said with completely unruffled calm.

"No wonder he bought a house in the worst part of town," Lord Graveston said. "That's not the sort of thing that you want put into a grand house. Smells, boilings, who knows what sort of flammable substances being used. He had a degree of sense, in any case, if he had such a place for his work."

"Exactly my opinion," Whittenfield said at once. "I decided, as did Sabrina, that the Count was a sensible man. He showed her his laboratory and his equipment and warned her that it was not wise for Cesily to come in because there were various substances that might harm her in the laboratory. He showed her where he made his glass vessels by blowing them himself, and the oven where many of the processes were conducted. It was called an athanor, Sabrina says, and was shaped like a very large beehive made of heavy bricks. The Count showed her, since he was not involved in any experiments at the moment, how the various vessels were placed in the athanor, and told her how long and in what manner they were heated to get the results he desired. She watched all this with great fascination and asked very few questions, though she longed to pester him with them. At last he told her he would appreciate her discretion, but if she had any doubts about remaining in his employ, she would have to tell him and he would arrange for her to have passage back to England. She was taken aback by this suggestion, for she believed that the Count wanted to be rid of her now that she had learned his secret. Apparently he discerned something of this in her countenance, and he assured her at once that he did not wish her to leave, but he was aware that there were many who did not view alchemy kindly and wished to have nothing to do with it. If that expressed her own feelings, then he wanted her to tell him at once in order to make proper arrangements for her. He had, he told her, another house in

Antwerp, and he would send her there if she felt she could not remain in good conscience so near his laboratory. Sabrina was startled by this consideration, which was a good deal rarer then than it would be now. She told the Count that she would inform him in the morning of her decision, but she wrote in her journal that she was determined to stay, and had been since she was shown the laboratory. In the morning the Count sought her out and asked to know her decision, which she told him at once. He, in turn, declared that he was very pleased to have her be willing to stay on with him. She then inquired what sorts of experiments he was making, but he did not wish to discuss that with her, not at that time. He did give her his word that he would present her with a few of the results of his labors in due time, which she, perforce, agreed to. She mentions in her journal for the next several days that she saw little of the Count because he was occupied in his secret room working on some new experiment. It isn't precisely easy to tell, but it seems she put some stock in his skill, for she states she suspects the crucifix he gave her might have been made from alchemical gold."

"Absurd!" Hamworthy declared.

"Oh, naturally," Whittenfield said. "And no doubt the Count had his own reasons behind his actions."

"Wanted to put her at her ease," Twilford ventured.

"Still, a crucifix is hardly appropriate to give an English-woman. It seems much too Roman." Lord Graveston had paused in his fiddling with his pipe to give his opinion, and having done so, went back to scraping out the burnt tobacco so that he could fill it again.

"Queen Bess herself was known to wear crucifixes," Everard mentioned, his face darkening from embarrassment. "Probably the Count, being a foreigner and a Roman Catholic—most of them were, weren't they?—wanted to make a friendly gesture. It's a more circumspect gift than any other sort of jewelry would be."

"Everard, your erudition astounds me," Dominick said with a nasty grin at the young man. "Read Classics, did you?"

"History. At Clare." His voice dropped to a mumble and he would not look at Dominick.

"Clever lad," Hamworthy said, as if to take the sting out of Dominick's remark.

"What else did your great-great *et cetera* aunt have to say for herself?" Twilford inquired with a polite nod away from Dominick.

"She said that her employer continued to treat her well, that her arm healed completely, and aside from twinges when the weather changed, it never troubled her in all her years. She did not have much opportunity to view the laboratory, but she found that the manservant, Roger, was much inclined to be helpful to her and told her once, in a moment of rare candor, that he liked her boy Herbert, and said that he had once had a son of his own, but the boy had died many years before. Sabrina was shocked to hear this, for she had not thought that he was much used to families. He offered to assist her with Cesily and Herbert when her duties made it awkward for her, and she thanked him for it but could not bring herself to trust him entirely, so aloof did he hold himself. In the end, she asked Herbert if he would like to go with Roger when he purchased certain items from the great market in the center of town. Herbert, having turned two, was developing an adventurous spirit, and he was eager to explore a greater part of the world. Roger spoke English, albeit with an accent, and told Sabrina that he would be happy to keep the boy talking in his own language, or teach him German or French. He admitted that his Dutch was not very good and his Flemish was stilted, but he would not mind being Herbert's tutor. In a moment of boldness, Sabrina said that she would rather Cesily be taught the languages for the time being, and Herbert could learn in a year or so, when he had a better grasp of speech. She did not think that the man would accept this, but he did, and inquired what languages Sabrina would like her daughter to speak. When Sabrina expressed her surprise, he reminded her that Queen Bess spoke seven languages quite fluently and it did not seem intolerable to him that other females should do likewise. So little Cesily became his student, learning French, German, Spanish and Italian. He must have been an excellent teacher, for Cesily was noted for her skill in these tongues for all her life."

"Damned silly waste," Twilford said. "If you ask me, it's a mistake to educate females. Look what happens. You start sending them to school and the next thing you know, they want to vote and who knows what else."

"Reprehensible," said the sixth guest with an ironic smile.

"It isn't fitting," Hamworthy declared. "What could your great-aunt have been thinking of, to put her daughter forward that way?" He straightened up in his chair. "Charles, you're not serious, are you? The girl didn't try to be a scholar?"

"It seems to have taken her remarkably little effort to be one," Whittenfield answered. "She took to it like a potentate takes to vice. In the next year she showed herself to be a most ready and enthusiastic pupil. She started to read then, so that by five—"

"Started to read? So young? Was Sabrina lost to all propriety?" Lord Graveston demanded.

"She must have been. Herbert soon joined his sister in her studies, but lacked her aptitude, though he did well enough. To Sabrina's surprise and, I think, disappointment, there were no further invitations to enter the labortory, though on one occasion the Count presented her with a fine silver bracelet set with amber. She says in her journal that there was nothing remarkable about the amber or the silver except that the workmanship was exceedingly good. I wish I knew what became of that bracelet," Whittenfield added in another voice. "We have the mirror, which is an object of considerable speculation, but not the bracelet, which might have had a great deal of value, both for the materials and the antiquity."

"Don't talk like a merchant, Charles. It's unbecoming," Hamworthy interjected.

"You're a fine one to talk about merchants, Peter," Dominick said to him with false good humor. "Didn't your sister marry that merchant from Leeds?"

Peter Hamworthy's face turned an amazing shade of raspberry. He stared at Dominick with such intense anger that the rest fell hopefully silent. "My sister's husband," he said at last with great care, enunciating each syllable with hard precision, "is not a merchant. His family started the rail shipping business in Leeds over eighty years ago, which hardly counts as being shop-stained."

"Naturally, naturally, and the money he brought to the family had nothing to do with it, though your father was almost ruined and your sister twenty-six years younger than her husband." Dominick strolled around the room.

"What about Sabrina and the glass?" Lord Graveston asked in awesome accents. He puffed on his pipe and waited.

"Yes, Charles, what about the glass?" Everard echoed.

"That is coming," Whittenfield said, shooting a blurred, hostile look at his cousin. "I've told you that Sabrina had been given a bracelet and that she had been in the employ of the Count well over a year. That is important to remember, because she had a fair familiarity with the man and his habits. She knew that he spent much of the night in his laboratory and a fair amount of his time otherwise in study and reading. He went out fairly often, but irregularly. If he had friends, she knew nothing of them, though she assumed he must occasionally receive them at his other house, wherever it was. She appreciated his kindness and the attention he gave to her and her children. When she had been working for him about eighteen months, her tone changes slightly. She is not more wary or more forthcoming, but she admits once or twice that he is an attractive and compelling man, and that she has had one or two vivid dreams about him. You may all guess the nature of those dreams. At first, she only mentions that she did dream that he came to her in her bed, and later her descriptions become more detailed and . . . improper. She mentions that after one such dream she met the Count in the morning room where she and her children were eating, and to her amazement she found herself blushing as she looked at him. She records in her journal that until that moment she was unaware of the penetrating strength of his eyes, which she describes as being dark and large. The Count, she says, saw her blush and smiled enigmatically, but made no comment to her. He had come to talk to Cesily in Italian, as Roger was out of the house on an errand to the docks."

"Perhaps he read her journal. M' mother always said that it was wise to read the diaries of your servants. She always kept records of what her maids said among themselves and in their diaries." Hamworthy announced with portentous confidence.

"And did she allow the maids to read *her* diary?" the sixth guest asked gently, dark eyes turned on Peter Hamworthy.

"What?" Hamworthy protested loudly.

"They probably did, you know," Dominick said bitterly. "My valet reads mine, though I've told him thousands of times that he must not."

"Sabrina doesn't seem to think that he did read it. She considered the possibility, but her attitude is one of disbelief. For more than a week she had no dreams, and then they began again. After three or four months she began to anticipate them with pleasure, and was disappointed when nights would pass without them. During the day she continued to be the sensible woman she was, looking after the house and caring for her children and overseeing their meals. Apparently her employer did his cooking in the laboratory, for he never asked Sabrina to serve him at table. She speculated that he must have his banquets and other entertainments at his other house, for never did such an event take place where Sabrina lived. She commented on it once to Roger and he told her that the Count dined in private, as it was a custom with him to take sustenance with no more than one other person. Roger himself ate alone, but he kept his meat in the cold room below the pantry."

Twilford, who had been drinking heavily, looked up with reddened eyes. "No fit place for an Englishwoman, if you ask me," he remarked. "Shouldn't have stood for it, myself."

"The children enjoyed their lives in that place, though both lacked playmates. In England there were cousins and others who would have been available to them. In that house in Antwerp there were only the poor, ragged urchins of the street nearby, and so Cesily and Herbert learned to entertain themselves. Roger became a sort of uncle to them, alternately teaching them and indulging them. Sabrina says in one of her entries that he had the remarkable knack of obtaining their obedience without beating or berating them. The Count was regarded with more awe, but neither child was afraid of him, and he often was willing to spend time with them correcting their accents in various languages and telling them tales that Sabrina commented were unusually vivid. Cesily was particularly fond of the adventures of a woman named Olivia, whom the Count cast in different roles and different times in history. Sabrina once questioned this, telling the Count that she was not sure tales of the corruption in early Rome were proper for children of such tender years. The Count told her then that he was being mild, and reminded her that there is a marked difference between ignorance and innocence, though one is often mistaken for the other."

"Sophistry!" Lord Graveston insisted.

"And patently false," Hamworthy added. "Haven't we all had cause to observe how quickly innocence departs when too much learning is present?"

"Your brother, I believe, is a don at Kebel in Oxford," the sixth guest said to Hamworthy. "A most learned man, and yet you remarked this evening that he is as naive and innocent as a babe, and it was not entirely complimentary."

Peter Hamworthy glowered at the elegant foreigner. "Not the same thing at all, Count. You're foreign . . . don't understand."

"I doubt I'm as foreign as all that," the sixth guest said mildly.

"When do we get to the glass, Charles?" Twilford asked plaintively. "You've been going on for more than an hour."

"I'm coming to that," Whittenfield said. "You have all come to understand, I trust, that this household was not a usual one, either for this country or any other in Europe. Sabrina had been with the Count for almost three years. She had put aside a fair amount of money and was beginning to hope that she would not have to return to England as a poor relation to hang upon some more resourceful relative. She writes in her journal that it was the greatest pleasure to think of her condition at that time compared to what it had been before she entered the Count's employ. Then Sir James, her husband, was released from gaol, and came searching for her."

"You said he became a mercenary, Charles," Twilford reminded him.

"He did. That was after he saw his family. He came to the house late one evening. Apparently he had been celebrating his liberation, for Sabrina says in her journal that he was half drunk when he pounded on the door, demanding admittance. She had, of course, left word with the warden of the prison where she might be found, and the warden had told Sir James. He was a pugnacious man, of hasty temper and a touchy sense of honor. A lot of men like that, then," he observed reflectively as he turned his glass of port by the stem and squinted at the reddish light passing through it. "He was most unhappy to find his wife serving as a housekeeper to a foreign Count, and in the wrong part of the city, at that. At first Sabrina was somewhat pleased to see him, and commiserated over his thinned and scarred body, but she quickly realized that the reunion was not as happy as she had intended it to be. First he berated her for her scandalous position, and then he shouted at their children, saying they were growing up among ruffians and thieves. When Sabrina tried to convince him that they were being well cared for and educated, he became irate, shouted at her, and struck her."

"As you say, a hasty temper," Twilford commented with a slow, judicious nod of his head. "Still, I can't say I'd like to see my wife in such a situation. A man can be forgiven for imagining any number of things, and if Sir James was touchy of his honor, as you say . . ."

"Probably he suspected the worst. Those three years in prison can't have been pleasant for him," Hamworthy observed.

"Poverty wasn't pleasant for Sabrina, either," the sixth guest pointed out.

"A different matter entirely," Hamworthy explained. "A woman needs the firm guidance of a man. Very sad she should have had such misfortune, but it was hardly unexpected." He reached over for a cigar and drew one out, sniffing its length with enthusiasm before reaching for a lucifer to light it.

"I see." The sixth guest sat back in his chair.

"I'm baffled," Everard confessed. "If her husband returned for her, how does it happen that she came back to England and he went into Europe? And what has the glass to do with it?"

"Yes, you keep holding that glass out as a lure, and I can't see any connection between Sabrina and it," Twilford complained.

"Have patience, have patience," Whittenfield reprimanded them gently. "Let me get on with it. You recall that I said that Sir James struck his wife? They were in the receiving hall of that house, which was quite small, about the size of a back parlor, I gather. Cesily and Herbert both cried out, for they were not in the habit of seeing their father discipline their mother. Sir James was preparing to deliver a second blow as Sabrina struggled to break free of his grasp when the inner door opened and the Count stepped into the room. Sabrina says that she is certain he knew who Sir James was, but he sharply demanded that the man desist and explain why he was assaulting his housekeeper. Sir James, astounded and enraged, turned on this new arrival and bellowed insults at him, calling him a seducer and many another dishonorable name. The Count inquired if Sabrina had said anything that led him to this conclusion, to which Sir James replied that she had in fact, denied such accusations, which made her all the more suspect. He demanded to know who the Count was, and why he had dared to take in Sabrina and her children, knowing that she was a woman in a strange country and without benefit of male protectors. The Count gave a wry answer: he would have thought that Sir James should answer that question, not himself. Sir James became more irate and demanded satisfaction. He ordered his wife and children to prepare to leave the Count's house at once, that he would not tolerate this insult to his name one night longer. In vain did the children scream their dismay. Sir James reminded them that he was their father, with rights and obligations to fulfill. The children besought their mother to refuse, but it was the Count who stayed the question."

"Impudent foreigner!" Twilford burst out, straightening up in his chair with indignation.

"How dared he?" Lord Graveston demanded.

"What did he do?" Dominick asked in a low, harsh tone.

"He said that he would not allow any man to hurt a servant in his employ. At first Sabrina was greatly shocked to hear this, for in the time she had been the Count's housekeeper he had been most respectful and rarely mentioned her subservient position in the household. But what he said again stayed Sir James's hand. Sir James was furious at the Count for making his wife a servant, and explained to him that well-born English-women were not to be hired as common servants. He insisted that he had endured unbearable insults from the Count and would demand satisfaction of him. Now, in Sabrina's journal she says that the Count laughed sadly and asked her whether or not she wanted her husband to die, but I doubt he was so audacious. Whatever it was, the Count promised to meet him at midnight, in the great hall of his other house. Sabrina, in turmoil from this, begged both men not to embark on anything so foolish, but her husband insisted and the Count told her that if this were not settled now, she would have to leave his employ and go with her husband, and in her journal Sabrina admits that that prospect was no longer a happy one. She turned to her husband and asked that he rescind the challenge, but her husband chose to interpret this request as proof of an illicit relationship between his wife and the Count, and only confirmed his belief that Sabrina was the mistress of the Count. He told her as much and asked for directions to the house the Count had mentioned and vowed he would be there. The matter of seconds was a difficult one, as Sir James, being just released from prison, had no one to act for him. The Count suggested that the matter be private and that each fight on his honor. Sir James agreed with alacrity and went off to find a sword to his liking."

"He did not insist that Sabrina accompany him?" Everard asked, quite startled.

"No, he said that if Sabrina had taken a lover, she could remain with him until he avenged her honor, not that any was left to her." Whittenfield gave a little shrug. "Sabrina says in her journal that at the moment she wished she had become the Count's mistress, for the thought of parting from him was a bitter one. Until she saw her husband, she says, she did not realize how she had come to trust and rely on her employer. At last, the night coming on and the hour of the duel approaching, she searched out the Count as he was preparing to leave the house and told him that she would pray for him, and that she hoped he would not despise her for turning against Sir James. He answered that he was grateful for her prayers and did not fault her for seeking to stay away from Sir James—if not for her own sake, then for the sake of her children, who must surely suffer at his hands. She agreed with some fear and told the Count that she wished she had not told the warden where she could be found, so that Sir James might never have found her. The Count did not chide her for this, but reminded her that she had chosen to follow her husband rather than turn to her family when his cast him out. She did not deny this, but said that part of her fears were that she would become a drudge if she appealed to her father or her uncles for maintenance. With two children to care for, she had decided it would hurt them, and when she and Sir James had come to the Continent, it was not too bad at first. The Count heard her out and offered to provide her with funds to allow her to return to England and set herself up in reasonable style. He told her that no matter what the outcome of the duel was, he feared it would be most unwise for her to continue living under his roof, for doubtless Sir James would

spend part of the time before the meeting in composing damn-
ing letters to send to various relatives. Sadly, Sabrina admitted
this was true. Shortly before the Count left, she asked him why
he had not made her his mistress. He had an equivocal answer
for her: that surely her dreams were sweeter."

"Why, that's outrageous!" Lord Graveston burst out. "And
she tolerated it? The effrontery of the fellow."

"How could he know?" Everard wondered. "If she never
told him, it may be that he was telling her that he did not fancy
her in that way."

"Any real man fancies an attractive woman in that way,"
Hamworthy said with a significant and critical glance at Everard.

"Whatever the case," Whittenfield said sharply, "the Count
left her and went to his other house. And after debating with
herself for the better part of an hour, Sabrina got her cloak and
followed him. She remembered the directions the Count had
given Sir James, and she went quickly, avoiding those streets
where taverns still did business and roistering songs rang
through the hollow night. It took her some little time to find the
house, and once she feared she was lost, but eventually she came
upon the place, a great, sprawling manor three storys high, with
an elegant façade. Most of the windows were dark, but there
were lights in the area she thought might be the kitchen, and a
few candles flickered in one of the other rooms. Now she was
faced with the problem of how to enter the building. There was a
wrought-iron gate, but she was confident she could climb it; but
the house itself puzzled her. She hitched up her skirts and
grabbed the ornamental scrollwork . . ."

"What a hoyden!" Dominick sniggered.

"I think she's jolly intrepid," Everard said, turning slightly
rosier.

"Sounds like just the bubble-headed thing she would do,
judging from the rest of your narrative," Twilford sighed.

"Well, no matter what we think, gentlemen, the fact remains
that she did it," Whittenfield said with a hint of satisfaction.

"Does she tell whether or not she stopped the duel?" the
sixth guest asked. He had been still while Whittenfield talked,
giving his host polite attention.

"She was stymied at first, she indicates in her journal. She
looked around the house and judged, from the number of rooms

she could see that were swathed in covers, that the Count was not much in attendance there. It was by the veriest chance that she found a door at the far side of the house with an improperly closed latch. With great care she opened the door and entered a small salon with elegant muraled walls she could not easily see in the dark. Realizing that if she were caught by a servant she might well be detained as a thief, she hesitated before entering the hall, but recalling what danger her husband and the Count had wished upon themselves, she got up her courage and went in search of them. It was by the veriest chance that she stumbled on the room where Sir James and the Count were met. Apparently they had already exchanged one pass of arms, and Sir James was breathing hard though the Count, according to Sabrina, seemed to be unaffected by the encounter. At the sound of the opening door, the Count reminded one whom he supposed to be a servant that he was not to be disturbed, at which admonition Sabrina revealed herself and hastened forward to confront the two men. Then, just as she neared them, Sir James reached out and took hold of her, using her as a shield as he recommenced his attack on the Count, all the while taunting him to fight back. At first the Count retreated, and then he began to fight in a style quite unknown to Sir James. Sabrina does not describe it adequately, but I gather that he would switch his sword from one hand to the other with startling rapidity, and instead of hacking and thrusting with his sword, he began to use it as if it were some sort of lash. Remember, the art of fencing was far from developed at that time, and the swords used were not the fine, flexible épée we know now, for sport, but sharp-edged lengths of steel. Yet the Count had a flexible blade that did not break, and it terrified Sir James. Finally the Count pressed a fierce attack and, while Sir James retreated, was able to wrest Sabrina from his grasp and to thrust her away from the fight. Then, in a move that Sabrina did not see clearly and does not describe well, the Count disarmed Sir James. Sabrina states that she *thinks* that the Count leaped forward and passed inside Sir James's guard, clipping his shoulder and knocking his sword from his hand. That's quite a feat, no matter how it was done, but Sabrina's impression is the only information we have, and so it is nearly impossible to guess what the man actually did. The Count held Sir James at swordpoint and politely inquired of Sabrina what she wanted done with him.''

"Dis*gust*ing!'' Twilford said.

"But the Count didn't kill Sir James, did he?'' Everard asked eagerly. He had a certain apologetic air, as if he did not entirely want to be against his countryman but liked the gallantry of the situation in spite of the Count's arrogance.

"No, he didn't kill him, though the thrust to his arm could have done so, Sabrina thought, if he had intended it to,'' Whittenfield said. "Sabrina said that she wanted Sir James out of her life, and to this the Count told Sir James that he had heard the verdict of his wronged spouse. Sir James began to curse roundly, but the Count brought his blade up and warned him that such behavior would not be tolerated. Sir James lapsed into a sullen silence and barely acknowledged his wife's presence. The Count informed him that on his honor—since Sir James was so jealous of it—he must leave within twenty-four hours and take up whatever station he wished with any noble or fighting company east of the Rhine, and he was not to seek out his wife again, either in person or by message. He required Sir James to swear to this, not only by the oaths of the Church but by his sword. Grudgingly, Sir James did this, and then the Count let him go.''

"And that's all there was to it? Charles, you disappoint me,'' Dominick remarked.

"That is not quite all. There is still the matter of the glass,'' Whittenfield pointed out.

"Ah, yes, the glass,'' the sixth guest murmured.

"The Count escorted Sabrina back to his house where she had lived for almost three years, and as they walked, he inquired why it was that she had come. She admitted that she feared for him and did not want him to come to hurt. He told her that was highly unlikely, but did not explain further until she asked if it was an alchemical secret that protected him. Again he gave her an equivocal answer, saying that it was something of the sort. Before they entered his house, she confessed to him that she would not refuse him if he wished to pass what remained of the night with her. He told her that he was much moved by this, for women did not often make that request of him, which, in her journal, Sabrina finds amazing, for according to her the Count was a pleasing man, of middle height and compact body, with attractive, slightly irregular features, who was most fastidious about his person and somber in his elegance. Once in the house, the Count led her to the laboratory and lit a branch of candles, then opened a small, red-lacquered cabinet which seemed to be of great age, and removed the glass. It was not in the frame it has now, as I believe I mentioned, but it was rimmed with silver. The Count gave this to Sabrina, telling her that when she could see the spider in the glass, he would come for her. She did not believe this, but he assured her there was the image of a jeweled spider set in the very center of the glass, and that when one stood directly in front of it, under special circumstances, it could be seen."

"Very neat," Dominick approved with a jeering toast of his glass. "I must try that myself, one day."

"Did the poor woman believe that?" Lord Graveston demanded with a shake of his head. "And you have kept that worthless piece of glass?"

"There's a bit more to it," Whittenfield remarked. "Apparently that night the Count did spend some time with Sabrina, and though she does not record what passed between them—"

"It's not difficult to guess," Hamworthy said with marked disapproval.

"I gather that it was not precisely what Sabrina expected. She mentions that the glass was put by the bed and lit with the branch of candles—"

"Really!" Twilford's expression was livid with disapproval.

"Decadent foreigner!" Hamworthy ejaculated.

"And," Whittenfield went on, giving them little attention, "Sabrina says in her journal that for one joyous, incomprehensible moment she could see the spider—that it sat in a fine diamond web, a creature of ruby and garnet and tourmaline. And she was elated at the sight, though she says in a later entry that she does not expect to see it again. She left it to Cesily with the admonition that it be kept in the family as a great treasure."

"A woman's whim for a trinket!" Dominick scoffed.

"It may be. But, as you see, it is still in the family, and no one is willing to part with it. Serena had great faith in it, and she was not given to superstition. I remember her standing here, saying that if it had brought such good fortune to Sabrina we would be fools to be rid of it. My mother wanted to put it away, but it never happened, and I admit that I'm so used to it, I would miss having it. And every now and again I stare at it, hoping to see the spider."

"Oh, Charles," Dominick sneered.

"Did you see anything?" Everard asked.

"Only my face. If there is a spider in it, only a man who cast no reflection could see it," Whittenfield leaned forward and put his glass down.

"Do you mean that after sitting here for well nigh two hours, you have the effrontery to offer us nothing more than a third-rate ghost story?" Hamworthy demanded.

"Well, that *is* the story of the glass, as it's put down in Sabrina's journal. She returned to England and set herself up well, saying that she had been given a legacy that made this possible. And you will admit that whoever her Count was, he was something of an original."

"If you look into it, you'll find he was just another charlatan," Lord Graveston said with confidence. "Generous, it seems, but nonetheless a charlatan."

"Why do you believe that?" the sixth guest asked him. There was no challenge in the question, just a certain curiosity.

"It's obvious," Lord Graveston said, rising. "Well, if that's all you're giving us, Whittenfield, I'll take myself off to bed. Excellent port and brandy." He made his way through the room and out the door.

Peter Hamworthy groaned as he got to his feet. "The hour is very late and I like to rise early. I had no idea how long this would be. It's what comes of telling stories about females." As he went to the door he made a point not to look in the direction of the Spider Glass.

"I'm for the billiard room, if anyone cares to join me," Dominick said, staring at Everard. "You may come and do your best to . . . beat me, if you like."

Everard was suddenly nervous. "I . . . in a moment, Dominick." He turned toward his host. "I thought it was a good tale. I don't understand about the mirror, but . . ." On that inconclusive note he left the room in Dominick's wake.

"Whittenfield, that was the damnedest farrago you spun us," Twilford admonished him. "Why did you begin it?"

"You asked about the glass, that's all." Whittenfield had got to his feet and stood, a little unsteadily, beside his Queen Anne chair.

"Then I was an ass to do so." He turned on his heel and stalked majestically from the room.

The sixth guest turned his dark, ironic eyes on Whittenfield. "I found your story most . . . salutary. I had no idea . . ." He got up and went toward the old mirror as if compelled to do so. He touched the glass with his small, beautiful hand, smiling faintly.

Glistening in the mirror, the spider hung in its jeweled web. The body was red as rubies or fresh blood. The eight, finely-made legs were garnet at the joints and tourmaline elsewhere. It was delicate as a dancer, and though the mirror had faded over the years, the Count could still take pride in his work. Beyond the image of the spider the muted lamps of the Oak Parlor shone like amber in the glass.

For, of course, le Comte de Saint-Germain had no reflection at all.

APPENDIX A

Shadows by Volume

SHADOWS 1

Michael Bishop	*Mory*
Robert Bloch	*Picture*
Ramsey Campbell	*Dead Letters*
Ramsey Campbell	*Little Voice, The*
John Crowley	*Where Spirits Gat Them Home*
Avram Davidson	*Naples*
Dennis Etchison	*Nighthawk, The*
Stephen King	*Nona*
R. A. Lafferty	*Splinters*
Thomas F. Monteleone	*Where All the Songs Are Sad*
Raylyn Moore	*A Certain Slant of Light*
Bill Pronzini	*Deathlove*
William Watkins	*Butcher's Thumb*

SHADOWS 2

Ruth Berman	*Dragon Sunday*
Michael Bishop	*Seasons of Belief*
Juleen Brantingham	*Holly, Don't Tell*
Ramsey Campbell	*Macintosh Willy*
Jack Dann	*Night Visions*
Alan Dean Foster	*Chair, The*
Janet Fox	*Valentine*
T. E. D. Klein	*Petey*

SHADOWS 2 (con't)

Elizabeth Lynn	*White King's Dream, The*
Richard C. Matheson	*Dead End*
William F. Nolan	*Saturday's Shadow*
Peter D. Pautz	*Closing Off of Old Doors, The*
Bill Pronzini	*Clocks*
Manley Wade Wellman	*Spring, The*
Lee Wells	*Old Man's Will, The*

SHADOWS 3

Juleen Brantingham	*Janey's Smile*
R. Chetwynd-Hayes	*Ghost Who Limped, The*
Bruce Francis	*To See You With, My Dear*
Davis Grubb	*Brown Recluse, The*
Barry Malzberg	*Opening a Vein*
Pat Murphy	*Wish Hound*
William F. Nolan	*Partnership, The*
Peter D. Pautz	*Ant*
Ray Russell	*Avenging Angel*
Alan Ryan	*Tell Mommy What Happened*
Steve Rasnic Tem	*At the Bureau*
Chelsea Q. Yarbro	*Cabin 33*

SHADOWS 4

Juleen Brantingham	*Hour of Silhouette, The*
Ramsey Campbell	*Hearing Is Believing*
Beverly Evans	*Waiting for the Knight*
William Gibson	*Belonging Kind, The*
John Keefauver	*Snow, Cobwebs, and Dust*
Tabitha King	*Blue Chair, The*
Stephen King	*Man Who Would Not Shake Hands, The*
Deirdre Kugelmeyer	*Threshold*
Tanith Lee	*Meow*
Barry Malzberg	*Calling Collect*

SHADOWS 4 (con't)

Alan Ryan	*A Visit to Brighton*
Al Sarrantonio	*Under My Bed*
Steve Rasnic Tem	*Giveaway, The*
Lisa Tuttle	*Need*
Cherie Wilkerson	*Echoes from a Darkened Shore*
Chelsea Q. Yarbro	*Spider Glass, The*
Robert F. Young	*Yours, Guy*

SHADOWS 5

Phyllis Eisenstein	*Dark Wings*
Beverly Evans	*Piano Man*
Tanith Lee	*Gorgon, The*
Terry Parkinson	*Estrella*
Marta Randall	*Singles*
Alan Ryan	*Pieta*
Alan Ryan	*Following the Way*
Al Sarrantonio	*Boxes*
Avon Swofford	*And I'll Be with You By and By*
Steve Rasnic Tem	*Stone Head*
Chelsea Q. Yarbro	*Renewal*

SHADOWS 6

Lori Allen	*We Share*
Elisabeth Burden	*Dreams*
Pat Cadigan	*Eenie, Meenie, Ipsateenie*
Jack Dann	*Reunion*
Melissa Mia Hall	*Mariana*
Leslie Horvitz	*Appearances of Georgio, The*
Leigh Kennedy	*Silent Cradle, The*
Marc Laidlaw	*Sneakers*
Joe Lansdale	*By the Hair of the Head*
David Morrell	*But at My Back I Always Hear*
Jesse Osburn	*Peppermint Kisses*
Peter D. Pautz	*Cold Heart*

SHADOWS 6 (con't)

Al Sarrantonio	*Man with Legs, The*
J. Straczynski	*A Last Testament for Nick and the Trooper*
Steve Rasnic Tem	*Crutches*
Wayne Wightnan	*Touch, The*

SHADOWS 7

Joseph P. Brennan	*Mrs. Clendon's Place*
Ramsey Campbell	*Seeing the World*
Susan Casper	*Haunting, The*
Michael Cassutt	*Stillwater, 1896*
Jere Cunningham	*Decoys*
Dennis Etchison	*Talking in the Dark*
Earl Godwin	*Daddy*
Parke Godwin	*A Matter of Taste*
Jack C. Haldeman	*Still Frame*
Melissa Mia Hall	*Rapture*
Tanith Lee	*Three Days*
David Morrell	*Storm, The*
Alan Ryan	*I Shall Not Leave England Now*
Chelsea Q. Yarbro	*Do Not Forsake Me, O My Darlin'*

SHADOWS 8

Kim Antieau	*Cycles*
Jack Dann	*By the Shores . . .*
Gene DeWeese	*Everything's Going to Be All Right*
Nancy Etchemendy	*Tuckahoe, The*
Craig S. Gardner	*Man Who Loved Water, The*
Nina Hoffman	*Shadow of the Hawk, The*
Nancy Holder	*Blood Gothic*
Terry Parkinson	*Blue Man, The*

SHADOWS 8 (con't)
Bill Pronzini   *Toy*
Alan Ryan   *Sand*
Jessica Salmonson   *Blind Man, The*
Al Sarrantonio   *Wish*
Thomas Sullivan   *A Night at the Head of the Grave*

Steve Rasnic Tem   *Battering, The*
Peter Tremayne   *Pooka, The*
Sharon Webb   *A Demon in Rosewood*
Chelsea Q. Yarbro   *Do I Dare Eat a Peach?*

SHADOWS 9

Kim Antieau   *Sanctuary*
Joseph P. Brennan   *An Ordinary Brick House*
Christopher Browne   *Lesson, The*
Galad Elflandsson   *Last Time I Saw Harris, The*
Galad Elflandsson   *Icarus*
Lou Fisher   *Overnight*
Janet Fox   *Skins You Love to Touch, The*
Leanne Frahm   *On the Turn*
Stephen Gallagher   *Jigsaw Girl, The*
Craig S. Gardner   *Walk Home Alone*
Nina Hoffman   *Ants*
Nancy Holder   *Moving Night*
Leslie Horvitz   *Fishing Village at Roebush*
Ardath Mayhar   *Nor Disregard the Humblest Voice*

Sherie Morton   *Now You See Me*
Terry Parkinson   *Father Figure*
Steve Rasnic Tem   *Bloodwolf*
Peter Tremayne   *Tavesher*

SHADOWS 10

Mona Clee	*Just Like Their Masters*
Stephen Gallagher	*Like Shadows in the Dark*
Melissa Mia Hall	*Moonflower*
Nina Higgins	*Apples*
Nancy Holder	*We Have Always Lived in the Forest*
Bob Leman	*Come Where My Love Lies Dreaming*
Cheryl Fuller Nelson	*Just a Little Souvenir*
Al Sarrantonio	*Pigs*
Thomas Sullivan	*Fence, The*
Lisa Tuttle	*Jamie's Grave*
Wendy Webb	*Law of Averages*
Douglas E. Winter	*Office Hours*
Ken Wisman	*Finder-Keeper, The*
T. W. Wright	*World Without Toys*

APPENDIX B
Shadows by Author

Lori Allen
We Share (6)

Kim Antieau
Cycles (8)
Sanctuary (9)

Ruth Berman
Dragon Sunday (2)

Michael Bishop
Mory (1)
Seasons of Belief (2)

Robert Bloch
Picture (1)

Juleen Brantingham
Holly, Don't Tell (2)
Janey's Smile (3)
Hour of Silhouette, The (4)

Joseph P. Brennan
Mrs. Clendon's Place (7)
An Ordinary Brick House (9)

Christopher Browne
Lesson, The (9)

Elisabeth Burden
Dreams (6)

Pat Cadigan
Eenie, Meenie, Ipsateenie (6)

Ramsey Campbell
Dead Letters (1)
Little Voice, The (1)

Ramsey Campbell   *Macintosh Willy* (2)
                                   Hearing Is Believing (4)
                                   Seeing the World (7)

Susan Casper   *Haunting, The* (7)

Michael Cassutt   *Stillwater, 1896* (7)

R. Chetwynd-Hayes   *Ghost Who Limped, The* (3)

Mona Clee   *Just Like Their Masters* (10)

John Crowley   *Where Spirits Gat Them
                                       Home* (1)

Jere Cunningham   *Decoys* (7)

Jack Dann   *Night Visions* (2)
                                   Reunion (6)
                                   By the Shores . . . (8)

Avram Davidson   *Naples* (1)

Gene DeWeese   *Everything's Going to Be All
                                       Right* (8)

Phyllis Eisenstein   *Dark Wings* (5)

Galad Elflandsson   *Last Time I Saw Harris,
                                       The* (9)
                                   Icarus (9)

Nancy Etchemendy   *Tuckahoe, The* (8)

Dennis Etchison   *Nighthawk, The* (1)
                                   Talking in the Dark (7)

Beverly Evans   *Waiting for the Knight* (4)
                                   Piano Man (5)

Lou Fisher   *Overnight* (9)

Alan Dean Foster   *Chair, The* (2)

Janet Fox   *Valentine* (2)
                            *Skins You Love to Touch,
                            The* (9)

Leanne Frahm   *On the Turn* (9)

Bruce Francis   *To See You With, My Dear* (3)

Stephen Gallagher   *Jigsaw Girl, The* (9)
                            Like Shadows in the Dark (10)

Craig S. Gardner   *Man Who Loved Water,
                            The* (8)
                            Walk Home Alone (9)

William Gibson   *Belonging Kind, The* (4)

Earl Godwin   *Daddy* (7)

Parke Godwin   *A Matter of Taste* (7)

Davis Grubb   *Brown Recluse, The* (3)

Jack C. Haldeman   *Still Frame* (7)

Melissa Mia Hall   *Mariana* (6)
                            Rapture (7)
                            Moonflower (10)

Nina Higgins   *Apples* (10)

Nina Hoffman   *Shadow of the Hawk, The* (8)
                            Ants (9)

Nancy Holder   *Blood Gothic* (8)
                            Moving Night (9)

Nancy Holder   *We Have Always Lived in the Forest* (10)

Leslie Horvitz   *Appearances of Georgio, The* (6)
                            Fishing Village at Roebush (9)

John Keefauver   *Snow, Cobwebs, and Dust* (4)

Leigh Kennedy   *Silent Cradle, The* (6)

Stephen King   *Nona* (1)
                            Man Who Would Not Shake Hands, The (4)

Tabitha King   *Blue Chair, The* (4)

T. E. D. Klein   *Petey* (2)

Deirdre Kugelmeyer   *Threshold* (4)

R. A. Lafferty   *Splinters* (1)

Marc Laidlaw   *Sneakers* (6)

Joe Lansdale   *By the Hair of the Head* (6)

Tanith Lee   *Meow* (4)
                            Gorgon, The (5)
                            Three Days (7)

Bob Leman   *Come Where My Love Lies Dreaming* (10)

Elizabeth Lynn   *White King's Dream, The* (2)

Barry Malzberg   *Opening a Vein* (3)
                            Calling Collect (4)

Richard C. Matheson   *Dead End* (2)

Ardath Mayhar   *Nor Disregard the Humblest*
                              Voice (9)

Thomas F. Monteleone   *Where All the Songs Are*
                              Sad (1)

Raylyn Moore   *A Certain Slant of Light* (1)

David Morrell   *But at My Back I Always*
                              Hear (6)
                              Storm, The (7)

Sherie Morton   *Now You See Me* (9)

Pat Murphy   *Wish Hound* (3)

Cheryl Fuller Nelson   *Just a Little Souvenir* (10)

William F. Nolan   *Saturday's Shadow* (2)
                              Partnership, The (3)

Jesse Osburn   *Peppermint Kisses* (6)

Terry Parkinson   *Estrella* (5)
                              Blue Man, The (8)
                              Father Figure (9)

Peter D. Pautz   *Closing Off of Old Doors,*
                              The (2)
                              Ant (3)
                              Cold Heart (6)

Bill Pronzini   *Deathlove* (1)
                              Clocks (2)
                              Toy (8)

Marta Randall   *Singles* (5)

Ray Russell   *Avenging Angel* (3)

Alan Ryan   *Tell Mommy What*
                              Happened (3)
                              A Visit to Brighton (4)
                              Pietà (5)
                              Following the Way (5)
                              I Shall Not Leave England
                              Now (7)
                              Sand (8)

Jessica Salmonson   *Blind Man, The* (8)

Al Sarrantonio   *Under My Bed* (4)
                              Boxes (5)
                              Man with Legs, The (6)
                              Wish (8)
                              Pigs (10)

J. Straczynski   *A Last Testament for Nick and*
                              the Trooper (6)

Thomas Sullivan   *A Night at the Head of the*
                              Grave (8)
                              Fence, The (10)

Avon Swofford   *And I'll Be with You By*
                              and By (5)

Steve Rasnic Tem   *At the Bureau* (3)
                              Giveaway, The (4)
                              Stone Head (5)
                              Crutches (6)
                              Battering, The (8)
                              Bloodwolf (9)

Peter Tremayne   *Pooka, The* (8)
                              Tavesher (9)

Lisa Tuttle   *Need* (4)
                              Jamie's Grave (10)

William Watkins   *Butcher's Thumb* (1)

Sharon Webb   *A Demon in Rosewood* (8)

Wendy Webb   *Law of Averages* (10)

Manley Wade Wellman   *Spring, The* (2)

Lee Wells   *Old Man's Will, The* (2)

Wayne Wightnan   *Touch, The* (6)

Cherie Wilkerson   *Echoes from a Darkened*
                                       Shore (4)

Douglas E. Winter   *Office Hours* (10)

Ken Wisman   *Finder-Keeper, The* (10)

T. W. Wright   *World Without Toys* (10)

Chelsea Q. Yarbro   *Cabin 33* (3)
                                       Spider Glass, The (4)
                                       Renewal (5)
                                       Do Not Forsake Me, O My
                                       Darlin' (7)
                                       Do I Dare Eat a Peach? (8)

Robert F. Young   *Yours, Guy* (4)

CHARLES L. GRANT is one of the most respected writers and editors in the field of horror and fantasy. He is the winner of two Nebula Awards for science fiction writing, a World Fantasy Award as the editor of the original *Shadows* anthology, and winner of the World Fantasy Award in the categories of Best Novella and Best Collection. His most recent novel is *For Fear of the Night.* In addition to the popular *Shadows* series, Mr. Grant is also the editor of the anthologies *Terrors* and *Nightmares.* He lives in New Jersey.